Rosa Aneiros
# I LOVE YOU LEO A.
ARRIVALS
TERMINAL...?

I0636489

Published in 2018 by
SMALL STATIONS PRESS
20 Dimitar Manov Street, 1408 Sofia, Bulgaria
You can order books and contact the publisher at
www.smallstations.com

This book was first published in the Galician language as *Ámote Leo A. Terminal de... chegadas?* by Edicións Xerais de Galicia (Vigo, 2014). The series GALICIAN WAVE: The Way of Fiction exists to showcase the best of Galician young adult fiction in English. More information can be found at www.smallstations.com/wave

There are quotations in this book from the following publication: Italo Calvino, *Invisible Cities*, translated by William Weaver (Vintage, 1997)

*This work received a grant from the General Secretariat of Culture of the Ministry of Culture, Education and University Planning of the Xunta de Galicia in the call for translation grants of the year 2017*

*Esta obra recibiu unha axuda da Secretaría Xeral de Cultura da Consellería de Cultura, Educación e Ordenación Universitaria da Xunta de Galicia na convocatoria de axudas para a tradución do ano 2017*

ISBN 978-954-384-092-2

# I LOVE YOU LEO A.

## Arrivals Terminal...?

### Rosa Aneiros

Translated from Galician by **Jonathan Dunne**

Small Stations Press

*for Patricia, beautiful star of Epiphany*

*for J., R. and those who will always*
*accompany them on their journey*

**I**

'Listen, Leo, you can't carry on like this,' declared Aunt Cris.

'Please, Cristina… Don't tell me off like mother, I had quite enough of that already,' protested the girl, who was fed up of so much insisting.

'But don't you see you can't just give up like that!'

'Why on earth not? I decided I would travel for six months. Six months with six thousand euros. I was relying on my bosom buddies coming with me, and it turns out those bosom buddies had other plans. OK then, so I went off on my own, but now, four months later, having travelled around most of Europe, I've decided I want to go back. Enough's enough. Lisbon, Barcelona, Granada, Marrakesh, Istanbul, Prague, Rome, Venice and now Paris… It's not bad! And I don't want to do it any more. End of story.'

'Are you going to tell me what's going on? Something serious must have happened for you to react like this from one day to the next. You were so happy just yesterday! Didn't you have a good time at the Eiffel Tower? Didn't you like the Champs-Élysées, the Arc de Triomphe? Paris has so much to offer… And besides, you still haven't used the Paris Museum Pass I got you so you could visit all the city's monuments and museums!'

'It's not that, Aunt Cris.'

'What then? Is it me? Am I overwhelming you? Do you want me to give you more space? Go on then, go somewhere else, but don't abandon your objective.'

'Oh, what nonsense! First of all, nobody wanted me to leave – you're crazy, you're all on your own, what with all the dangers there are out there, think about it twice… And now you won't stop shouting at me because I want to go home. Mother, most of all… what's got into her? There's no understanding the lot of you!'

'Your mother found it very difficult to accept your decision, but she's very proud of you. After all, you've done something she never dared to. That's why she doesn't want you to back out.'

'It's decided, Aunt Cris. Tomorrow, I'm getting a return ticket home.'

Cristina – almost forty, tiny body, extravagant air – got up off the sofa and gave a tired sigh. The two women – together with their less-than-twenty-years' difference in age – were in a small apartment in Paris' Latin Quarter, a couple of minutes away from the River Seine, Notre-Dame and the Pantheon. Outside, the pigeons were also cooing away with their bitter complaint.

'You remember what I said to you when you arrived a few days ago? I said, "I knew you wouldn't disappoint me." You're the only person in our family who's deigned to come and visit me. You know what I say to you now? I know you're not going to disappoint me. I just know it.'

It was obvious that Aunt Cris wasn't going to take this decision lying down. When she heard her, Leo felt the anger rising up her throat, but she didn't back down.

'Tomorrow morning early, I'll go to the Louvre and the

Pompidou to make use of the pass you gave me. In the afternoon, I'll endeavour to get myself a ticket. I don't know why they're so damn expensive!'

'It's the weekend of Galician Literature Day in Galicia, that's why direct flights are so prohibitive. You'll have to find another option, via Madrid or Barcelona.'

Cristina muttered this while heading downstairs and wasn't sure whether her stubborn niece had even heard her. She disappeared down the still deserted streets of the City of Light. Students were already attending lectures in the Sorbonne and visitors had yet to invade the neighbourhood, so the only activity was that of the supply vans stocking up the more touristy restaurants on this side of the Seine with cheap plonk.

The bells of Notre-Dame reminded them that time was still tick-tocking away.

And yet the city didn't seem to want to shake off the previous night's sleep. As if it were still painfully hung-over after a foolish drinking spree.

Paris, it seemed, just didn't want to stretch its legs.

# 2

When Leo was left alone, she again collapsed on the sofa and pressed the 'refresh' button in her email. Ever since she'd sent that bombshell home the previous evening, warning of her unexpected return, there had been a flood of invitations to chat on Skype, direct messages on Twitter and emails. Her promise to return home on 8 July, half a year after her departure, had been brought forward by two months and, instead of making everybody happy, this had caused a veritable uproar in her family, judging by the messages she'd received. They were all from her mother and her brother, Roi. And yet the only email she really longed for never arrived.

Andrés, the Mexican she'd been besotted with ever since Granada, or something like that, had not reappeared inside her inbox. And despite the fact his latest message, only two days earlier, was quite clear on this point, Leo hadn't lost hope that there might have been a misunderstanding.

Whose fault was it? Hers, no doubt, for having shown all her cards in that email that had come straight from the heart. The great earthquake had begun on Monday, only three days earlier. The girl looked back and felt that weeks had gone by since then. Sometimes, the most ingenuous acts provoke earth-shattering events. Because this had been a completely ingenuous act. There was no other way to describe it: ingenuous, deluded perhaps, very romantic, dumb. The fact was, in an amorous outburst possibly provoked by her visit to Montmartre and the sign on the steps of the Sacré-Cœur, Leo had written Andrés the following email:

Hello, Andrés! I know it's you who's responsible for writing '*I Love You Leo A.*' Don't pretend any more, please. The game struck me as curious to start with, but I've grown tired of all those messages painted on façades, roads and bridges that catch me by surprise wherever I go. I want to see you and know you do too, so don't hang around. You once told me, 'You say "don't come", that means "come".' So now I'm telling you, 'Come, I'm waiting for you in Paris.'

On Tuesday, after visiting the Eiffel Tower, she'd come across the boy's response, which she would have preferred not to receive:

Hello, Leo! How nice to hear from you. I don't understand anything of what you say in your email. What's this about '*I Love You Leo A.*'? Whatever it is, it has nothing to do with me, and I've no idea what game you're talking about. I wish I could see you too, but we're currently in Pula, Croatia. As you can imagine, we are not going to walk all the way to Jerusalem and have hitchhiked part of the journey. I can't make it to Paris right now, I hope you understand. We'll meet up on another occasion, just trust in the stars. Loads of kisses from all of us in Ruth & Co.

After that message and twenty-four hours of idiotic despair, she'd written a stark message home: 'Mum, I'm coming back. Now.'

It was madness, she knew, an outburst of anger because of the boy's reply. She hadn't thought too much about it, but that didn't matter. There was no backing out now! Leo had been aware that this message to her mother, a veritable time bomb, would cause widespread damage at a distance of many kilometres. No sooner said than done. It led to a huge upheaval in her family. Her mother was as mad as she'd ever been, her brother, Roi, had dispatched the Invincible Armada on the back of Twitter messages, and Aunt Cris had turned up two hours later at the door of her garret with a terrified expression it would be difficult to put out of her mind. Even her father had wanted to talk to her on Skype and had demanded she switch on the camera so he could see her!

Perhaps she'd overdone it. Or not, who knows? The fact is she wasn't sure how to back down. Her temper had caused such a furore it wasn't enough just to say it's OK now, it's over, you can forget all about it. Everybody realized behind this decision there had been a monumental upset. If they found out it was all on account of some infatuation, she would lose the little street cred she had left, so she grabbed hold of her pride as hard as she could and pushed on. As soon as she could find a last-minute plane ticket, she'd be on her way home.

Before that, she would visit the Louvre Museum and the Pompidou Centre – her heart may have been broken, but she wasn't completely insane. With the Mona Lisa on the one hand and Matisse on the other, it was certainly worth staying an extra day in Paris!

Even so, muttered the girl, what on earth could have made her complicate her life like this? What was she doing, falling for Andrés, who was just a passing encounter? She didn't even like him all that much. Tall and handsome he may be, but nothing out of this world, she attempted to console herself. And anyway he was far too much of a smooth talker, he behaved like a Casanova, there was nothing that annoyed her more than a conceited man who thinks all the girls are falling at his feet. That said, hard as she tried to notch up all his defects, she couldn't quite forget the time they'd spent together in Istanbul. And in Rome. And in Venice.

Damn fool! Why did he deny that he was the author of the graffiti that had followed her every step of the way? It must have been his hand behind the 'I Love You Leo A.' message that had first appeared at the entrance to Cádiz and had surprised her in the most unlikely parts of the cities she'd visited. Why did he refuse to meet up with her in Paris? God damn it, she needed him!

However much she thought about it, she just couldn't work it out. Or perhaps she could. What was difficult to accept was the Mexican's refusal to travel along with her.

Leo carried on pressing the 'refresh' button on her computer until it hurt. Andrés showed no signs of life. The longed-for change of heart just didn't materialize. To her surprise, however, there were other messages that turned up to create a stir in her inbox.

The first was from Sebastián, the coordinator of the book group she'd been attending for years. *Read, Read, What Are You Reading?* – that was the name of the group Leo had been a key member of and continued to participate fervently in, even at a distance.

The second was from Martiño, one of her bosom buddies – perhaps a little more than that – who'd let her down at the very last moment.

Sebastián's head was in the clouds, as always. He'd only just worked out that Leo was in Paris, thanks to her public message on Twitter, that clothes line the girl hung a remnant on from each point of the globe she set foot on, which served to give her exact position. It seemed he hadn't read any of the messages Leo had sent the club, telling them about the *bouquinistes* and the bookstore Shakespeare and Company. As soon as the coordinator found out she was in the City of Light, he started writing down the names of authors who were essential to understanding Paris. 'More than a city, it's a state of mind!' he exclaimed. 'Rimbaud, Baudelaire, Hemingway, Sartre, Katherine Pancol, Simone de Beauvoir, Muriel Barbery, Victor Hugo, María Casares, Exupéry, Anna Gavalda... Remember *Hunting and Gathering*, the book we read last year? That's a good way to see Paris,' he remarked after the mad spate of literary recommendations.

Remember? Of course Leo remembered, how could she forget *Hunting and Gathering*? She'd loved that novel. But right now she was more in the mood for romantic liaisons and happy endings. You bet! Her state of mind was rather like that of Paloma, the introspective girl in *The Elegance of the Hedgehog* who had planned to commit suicide on turning thirteen. She didn't answer, though, because she was fed up of giving explanations. She'd done nothing else for the last twenty-four hours!

Sebastián's literary recommendations would have to wait until she got home, they'd have plenty of time to discuss book choices in person. Paris, she concluded, had nothing left to offer.

As for Martiño's email, of course she didn't even open it. That was all she needed to send her state of mind plummeting to the depths of the earth! This boy hadn't lost the curious habit he had of making wounds itch. The further away they got, the more he fought to clear a space for himself in her thoughts. Together, on the other hand, they repelled each other like the poles of a magnet. Can't live with you, can't live without you, God damn it!

The girl abruptly switched off the computer and went back to bed, intending to doze for a while.

Ahhhhh… the sails of her blasted head just wouldn't stop turning!

# 3

Leo opened one eye, then the other, stuck one foot out of bed and pressed her arms against her chest. It wasn't cold, and the first rays of sun were beating against the upper window. The light filtered through into that room in an attic in Paris with more goodwill than strength and drew beams of dust and brightness all over the shaded furniture. She was thirsty, a little hungry, and needed to go to the bathroom, but her body didn't wish to leave behind the warmth of her bed. She closed her eyes again, wanting to hook back on to sleep, but couldn't manage. She was awake now and would have to confront a new day, perhaps the last not only of her stay in Paris, but also of her travels.

It was 11:17 in the morning of Friday 13 May, exactly four months and five days after she'd set out on her adventures. Suddenly the memories of her journey gathered together and barricaded her thoughts. Yes, that 8 January, it had been bucketing down at the airport when she'd left, and the downpour had welcomed her to Lisbon as well, the first destination on her trip. The days were short, it was cold, and the bad weather clung to the pores of her skin. To begin with, she hadn't liked Lisbon all that much, perhaps because of Rubén and probably because of the melancholy. Rubén had welcomed her into his gloomy apartment in the Chiado and been an attentive and responsible host, but Leo knew this wasn't what she wanted. She didn't want a tutor to guide her every step, she wanted to fly on her own, to discover the cities one by one without being permanently led along. And yet, as soon as she took off over the Tagus, she realized the city had left a deep, nostalgic mark that was far too akin to beauty.

Lisbon had been a poem by Pessoa and learning that wasn't what she longed for. That's almost as important as knowing what you do want, of course.

In Barcelona, she'd got back on the right track. No doubt meeting Ruth & Co., the group of youngsters from Latin America and their three dogs, had had a lot to do with the happiness that had caught her by surprise in that city on the Mediterranean. With them, she'd learned to sing in the street, to play the clown and that sometimes free accommodation isn't worth the runny nose and constant arguments. Also, that it's necessary to renounce some things in order to gain others. Ruth & Co. had certainly been a joy for the pocket and a heaviness for the heart! From Barcelona, she recalled the scent of the sea in Barceloneta, the lights of Park Güell and the world at her feet in Tibidabo. Also, of course, the enormous whoop Andrés had given in the newly inaugurated Sagrada Família basilica, which had led to them being kindly asked to leave.

Ow, her bladder gave her an indication that she would need to get up any moment now, but Leo ignored the stabbing pain in her stomach and stayed peacefully in bed.

Sometimes, memories can be the best travel companions.

Granada, on the other hand, had been the ripeness of a peach in the mouth, the stunning beauty of the Alhambra and beers next to the river. Seville gave her the overpowering smell of a pig truck on the road, and Cádiz, the slap of the Atlantic and Edmundo and Lía's constant bickering. Together with these, the certainty that good things must come to an end and the enormous surprise of that first sign on the wall of the quay in Cádiz that said: 'I Love You Leo A.' She'd almost died of fright. That night, she'd understood that sometimes it's necessary to take your own decisions and company can be comforting, but also overbearing. That was why she'd left the troop behind for a couple of days and breathed in the fresh air of the Sierra de Grazalema. Then, that business with Andrés and all the rest.

Abruptly this was followed by Marrakesh. The red city at the foot of the Atlas Mountains had instilled in her renewed energy and reserved feelings towards Edmundo, her only travelling companion at that time. She had finally crossed over to the African continent, just as her brother, Roi, had recommended: 'You have to get out of Europe, you have to leave this rotten, old continent, the world out there turns with energy and verve, and here we are, crying away and clinging to the old, decrepit monuments of History.' Roi was only seventeen, he surfed the Internet a lot and watched far too many films. He was probably the most inquisitive person in her family, but she was sure he'd lifted that sentence straight out of a film. Of course he had.

No sooner said than done. Leo had left for Marrakesh on a plane that was as fast as it was cheap. From the city that bordered the desert, she'd taken the colour of henna on skin, the bustle of the souks, the world's great marketplace in Jemaa el-Fna Square, which had later been shaken by a bomb, and an irresistible attraction for the Maghreb. The light and shade, the smell of spices, the veiled women, the spectacle of streets that never stopped moving. From the political upheaval, the silences and threats of Marrakesh, she'd also learned that ignorance and a lack of information about places to be visited are not good travelling companions and can give you the odd unpleasant surprise.

In spite of this, Leo had continued her stubborn refusal not to read about the social and political situation of the places she chose at random. It was enough for there to be a last-minute plane ticket for her to launch herself at any point on the planet. That was how she'd arrived in Istanbul. The penetrating smell of petrol and salt in the Bosphorus Strait was the first memory that assailed her from that city which had one foot in Europe and the other in Asia, the ancient Byzantium, the old Constantinople… Istanbul. The sunset on the Golden Horn, the reflections of the columns in the Basilica Cistern, the letters of Hagia Sophia, Iria's ironic mood, Zerdali's tears and the lights of the oil tankers that flashed from side to side of the loft in the district of Beyoğlu.

And, of course, her shaved head like a bitter lemon. The hair, stubborn as it was, just wouldn't grow, and those tangled locks served as a constant reminder of the decision that had led her to deposit her beautiful mane in the hands of a Turkish barber in Taksim Square.

A blanket of mist dampened her memory of Prague. And when she'd got lost… of course, how to forget! What a feeling of shame! She'd had a map in her hands, but been unable to find out where she was for hours. Of course, the girl remembered perfectly well the placard behind the singer on the Charles Bridge, that 'I Love You Leo A.' that had set her body on fire and pointed her towards Italy.

An awkward itching sensation settled on her tummy button and reminded her again that she needed to visit the bathroom, but she clung on to the pillow and allowed the memories to race past. So it was the most absurd images and scenes from her journey continued bumping against the quay of her head for an undefined period of time. The robbery in Barcelona. The rip-off of the taxi in Marrakesh. The tulle skirt in Prague. The apartment in Trastevere.

Mahmut's squat, or something like that. The Grand Canal in Venice and the return of Marco Polo. The decapitated bodies in the Temple of the Vestal Virgins in the Roman Forum. Her mother's complaints on Skype about how thin she was. The kebabs in Taksim Square. The argument about the dogs in El Prat Airport. The performances on the Ramblas. The Alhambra on fire during the sunset as seen from the Mirador San Nicolás. Edmundo's snoring. The cockroaches in Raval. The grilled sardines in Eminönü. Zerdali's sad look. The dryness of Cappadocia and the fairy chimneys. The Gallery of Maps in the Vatican Museums. Roi's laughter on the other side of the computer screen. The cobras in Jemaa el-Fna Square. The blue men of the desert. The cries of muezzins while the storks staggered about...

Leo recalled that quote from the book *Invisible Cities* by Italo Calvino, which had kept her company on her journey. How did it go? She grabbed hold of the book. There it was, heavily underlined:

*From the number of imaginable cities we must exclude those whose elements are assembled without a connecting thread, an inner rule, a perspective, a discourse. With cities, it is as with dreams: everything imaginable can be dreamed, but even the most unexpected dream is a rebus that conceals a desire or, its reverse, a fear.*

That was right, a fear. That everything she could recall so clearly may just have been a dream, perhaps.

Suddenly the girl glanced at her watch. One o'clock! She leaped out of bed. There was no point going to the Louvre now because she'd have to have lunch and there wasn't enough time. Instead, she'd grab a tray of sushi from a stall in the Latin Quarter and go and eat lunch on the Pont des Arts, watching the waters of the River Seine race by. Outside, spring had probably broken through the dark clouds by now, and it would be nice to warm her back. In the afternoon, that's right, in the afternoon she would visit the Pompidou Centre.

She hurried as fast as she could and bumped into all the furniture before finally making it to the bathroom.

Ooh, just about.

# 4

'How annoying…' muttered Leo.

She dried her hair with one hand while cancelling the call on the French mobile her aunt had given her to keep tabs on her during her visit to Paris with the other. She couldn't believe it. Cristina had offered to accompany her to the Pompidou Centre! Just in case she decided to throw herself into the raging waters of the Seine like a crazed romantic or someone who's been caught up in the delirium of the Commune!

'I won't get lost, Aunt Cris, there's no need to waste your time. I promise I won't do anything stupid. Don't put yourself out,' she'd replied at first, with just a hint of irony.

But Aunt Cris, who was as stubborn as her mother, had given her no choice. They would meet at five at the entrance to the Pompidou Centre and make the visit together.

Ah, sighed the girl, poor thing, she still thinks she can convince me not to go home… Nothing in the world will persuade me to change my mind. Nothing.

At that precise moment, Leo forgot all her grandmother Carmiña's favourite expressions, although they might have helped her a lot. From the one about not spitting into the wind to the one about not counting your chickens before they hatch, passing through never say never… The girl was so taken up and preoccupied with her implacable decision that she ignored the numerous, diverse options springing at her feet. Her stubborn refusal to back down made her blind, and that was all there was to it.

At five o'clock on the dot, the girl was twiddling her museum pass between her fingers on a bench by the Stravinsky Fountain, right in front of the Pompidou Centre. The yellows, reds, blues, greens and blacks of that enormous tangle of pipes witnessed her anxiety. The coloured robots spat and slapped against the water behind her back, while the large ventilation shafts seemed to stifle their laughter. In the corners of the square, the trees provided shade with their newly released buds and, behind them, the Church of Saint-Merri simply kept silence.

Leo carried on twirling the card through her fingers while glancing repeatedly at her watch. Her aunt was late, something not altogether uncommon in her, by the way. If it didn't suit her, then why had she arranged to meet? Leo could have been slowly perusing the collection of contemporary art by now! She needed as much time as possible to make a proper visit! Waiting inside were Picasso, Matisse and Miró, no less.

'Quarter past five,' muttered the girl, getting up off the bench impatiently. Her back was all wet from the splashes of the fountain's spouting figures. The sun beat down forcefully, and a child kept smacking his ball against the surface of the water, much to his grandmother's chagrin.

Suddenly somebody surprised her from behind, covering her eyes with their hands.

'Who is it?'

Aunt Cris' unmistakable voice. Leo protested with her eyes closed:

'I can't believe you're in the mood for jokes, Aunt Cris. It's so late already! We have to get a move on.'

She clamped her own hands on the hands covering her face and noticed something strange. She wasn't quite sure why, but this wasn't the touch she would have expected from her aunt's fingers. Hard, with bumps and swollen veins that were on the verge of exploding.

'Caetano? Is that you? Can we go now?'

The hands pressed against her face and wouldn't let her turn around.

'Will you stop with all this nonsense! I'm going to miss the exhibition if you keep on messing around!'

A burst of laughter and the murmur of voices reverberated in her ears. These weren't the sounds she would have expected from Aunt Cris, either. And yet they were familiar, strangely familiar. She struggled to put a face to those voices and those fingers. Perhaps, perhaps, it was Andrés. Those hands certainly belonged to a man, and some of that laughter. Her heart went racing up to her ears. Was it possible he'd appeared out of nowhere? Andrés, Andrés…

'Who is it then?' reiterated Aunt Cris' voice.

Leo didn't dare say out loud what it was she wanted, in case she scared him away.

'I give in. Let me see!'

Hey presto, the hands allowed her to see. And what she saw was her father with his still injured shoulder, her mother next to him and Roi hobbling about on a crutch so he could get in front of them. There they were, the three of them, standing right in the centre of the square, a tang of expectation in their eyes and on their lips.

'Ta-daah! Surprise!!!'

Leo almost fell over. She couldn't believe it. This had to be some kind of mirage. She rubbed her eyes and opened them wide. It couldn't be! Her family! In Paris!

Her mother looked taller and younger. She'd combed her hair and done her make-up. Normally she'd hide her hands because she said they looked more like a farmer's than a businesswoman's and yet, that day, she'd decided to show them off. She wore a blue, cotton dress and a white shirt. Her lips were painted crimson. Her father hadn't changed all that much. He was still as sad and vulnerable as when he'd seen her off at the airport the last time they'd seen each other. Nothing to do with the brave man he'd been before everything happened. And yet there was a hint of fear and a spark of happiness as well, yes, just a little happiness. Roi was the only one who couldn't stop laughing. He had grown since January and was out of his wheelchair, on a crutch, which he used to jump about and aim at the pigeons. His wavy hair flopped over his eyes, and he proudly wore a T-shirt that said: 'WHO THE HELL ARE YOU?'

Leo saw all of this on that May afternoon in the square outside the Pompidou Centre in Paris. But all she managed to say was:

'How long your hair is, Roi. Some have lots, while others have little. You look like Corto Maltese.'

At the same time, the girl passed her hand over her own head, which was still infested with impossible tufts.

'Ah, my daughter, how thin you are! Like a rake… The wind will blow you away! And what happened to your beautiful mane?' sighed her mother.

Aunt Cris viewed the scene with incredulity and then blurted out:

'Is that it? You're thin, and your hair's grown. You haven't seen each other for four months, and that's all you can say. At least give each other a hug. What a pathetic family I have!'

These words acted as a spring that broke their initial stupefaction and united them in an effusive embrace. They were still like this several minutes later, embracing the happiness of being together when they'd least expected it.

It was half past five in the afternoon of Friday 13 May in the Place Igor Stravinsky, right next to the Pompidou Centre of Paris. Inside, Picasso, Matisse and Miró carried on waiting for a girl who'd suddenly encountered the feeling of calm she hadn't realized she needed.

'Mum, you could have told me you were coming! I'd have got you to bring my green jacket and my blue trousers, the ones with the silver buckles... My clothes are completely ruined on account of the laundries!'

'It doesn't matter, woman. Now you're coming back with us, what need for more clothes? By the way, Leo, who's this Caetano?'

This is what could be heard as they walked towards the Île de la Cité.

# 5

'And so here we are...' Leo's mother concluded her rapid overview.

'Is that it? Twenty years waiting for you to take us to Paris, crazy as we were to go to Euro Disney and visit Aunt Cris, and, from one day to the next, you just catch a plane and turn up... I'm not that stupid! What is it you're planning behind my back?'

'No... We got your email and were just a little worried, to tell the truth. It's not normal for you to give up like that. Your father and I took a look at the calendar, saw it was the long weekend before Galician Literature Day and decided this was an ideal time to visit Paris. As for the rest? You know how it goes: travel agency, issuing of tickets and off we go. It wasn't that difficult. We also deserve the odd holiday, don't we? Or do you think you're the only one with a right to go travelling?'

'Boh... I'm not convinced, Mum.'

'Boh? You're here, what more do you want? Roi wouldn't stop fiddling about, he was so eager to come, and I thought I'd make the most of this opportunity to visit some shops and order in some exclusive clothes for our autumn-winter collection. Besides, they say nothing's as pretty as Paris in spring.'

'Another cow in the cornfield – your autumn-winter collection... You're out of your mind, Mum, you're clean out of your mind.'

'The worst part is she's serious,' laughed Roi. 'She's got a bee in her bonnet about having the latest fashion always in the shop window. She read something about coolhunters in a magazine and has become obsessed with merchandise, she keeps chasing the latest tendencies of the It Girls... It seems the crisis has got worse and either we adapt to the latest needs or the shop will go bust... She keeps saying this, day and night, you can't imagine how boring it gets! I wasn't so keen to come because of you, believe me, I didn't really care whether I saw you or not. After all, you were just about to come home... What I really wanted was to visit Album, the chain of shops that specialize in comics, and Un Regard Moderne, and Book-Off, and Junkudo... I'm going to spend all my Christmas money on comics in their original versions! First off, *Ordinary Victories* by Manu Larcenet, and then all the Asterix and Tintin I can lay hands on in second-hand shops.'

'I see things haven't changed too much in my absence. Look at you, Roi! What a pedant! What terrible things the Internet does in the world, little brother! I bet you've studied it all from top to bottom. Even the colours in the shop windows!'

'You can be sure of that,' affirmed her know-it-all little brother.

'Don't pay them any attention, daughter. It was nothing to do with Galician Literature Day, the autumn-winter collection, comics or anything else. We just missed you, that was all,' remarked her father, who'd been silent up until that point.

The sparks of happiness lighting up his eyes showed that he really was telling the truth.

'I love you too, papa.'

Leo gave him a resounding kiss that contained all the emotion that had been huddling around her tummy button. No sooner had she finished than she went completely red. She'd never said anything like that to her father before. Can you imagine? It needed them to meet up unexpectedly in Paris for them to say how much they loved and missed one another.

Leo still had a few questions buzzing around her mind but, whether or not she asked them, she didn't really care by now what had made them come. The important thing was that her family was there in person. And the girl was acutely aware… Oh, come on, now she was getting far too sentimental.

They headed towards the Latin Quarter in search of Aunt Cris' attic and used this opportunity to get the suitcases out of the car. They'd been in such a hurry to reach their appointment at the Pompidou Centre from the airport they hadn't had time to take them out before that. They'd agreed with Cristina that it wasn't necessary to book a room in a hotel and the four of them would get by in those forty square metres. It would only be for four nights since on Tuesday – Galician Literature Day – they had return tickets, and besides they weren't going to spend all that much time shut up in the attic. In only three full days, they had to squeeze in everything the city had to offer!

'Well, this is where I live, little sister,' declared Aunt Cris as she opened the door to her welcoming garret. 'Don't worry about me, I'll sleep in the house of a friend who doesn't live too far away.'

'Oh, Cristina, it's so small!'

Leo's mother said this after exploring the apartment's tiny dimensions, which didn't involve more than five footsteps. She then added, screwing up her nose:

'You never were very tidy, woman, to be quite honest.'

'All the good taste went with you,' Cristina quickly answered. 'OK then, finish up, and we'll go for a walk before it gets dark. You have so much to see.'

In her family, really important stuff was always the subject of irony.

They were happy days that went flying past. Leo let herself go and enjoyed Paris more than ever. Her trip had not turned her into a stupid know-it-all who wants to control everything, every footstep, every destination, every decision. Quite the opposite. The experience of these last four months living in diverse landscapes and with different people had taught her that, when it comes down to travelling, there are no fixed rules and no single way of understanding a place. Everybody has to find their own direction, their own objectives, without slavishly following what's been written down in guidebooks and on forums. On certain points, we may agree; on others, not.

Everybody is their own journey.

And so the days she shared with her family in Paris were a succession of boat trips on the Seine, meals in expensive restaurants, Nutella crêpes with Roi, visits to car showrooms with her father, late-night films, snobbish shop windows with her mother, her brother's irreverence before the Victory of Samothrace in the Louvre and surprise at the Venus de Milo. Also, the Paris skyline from the terrace of the Arab World Institute and Roi's amazement on the metro, when he emerged on to the surface in the district of Belleville.

'Crikey, Leo! It's like we're in the Maghreb! Or in China!'

This street market offered fruit, remnants of clothing, scrap metal, used electrical appliances, stalls for barbers and knife sharpeners, all kinds of junk. The tunics, beards, hijabs and languages revealed that cities also belong to the ones who build them up each day – and not just to the monuments that resist the passage of time.

Africa and the East also had their place in the City of Light.

And comics, cinema, opera, photos, accordions and their parents' sudden falling in love, since they didn't stop embracing as if, in a moment that was as dumb as it was unpredictable, they'd suddenly remembered how much they loved each other.

Everything fitted in Paris – even Leo's explosive happiness. Everything, except Caetano and Cristina's house in the spectacular Bois de Boulogne.

That had been the thing that most impressed the girl when she landed in Paris. Her aunt, always so bland and extravagant (it was some time now since she'd ceased to be the subject of gossip on her annual return to the village), had picked her up at the airport to take her home. And, put simply, her house was the prettiest apartment Leo had ever seen in one of the most expensive neighbourhoods in Paris. That wasn't all. In the apartment, she'd also met Caetano, a charming Brazilian for whom Aunt Cris had failed to supply an adjective, so Leo didn't know whether he was a boyfriend, a friend or simply a mortgage partner. A day later, apparently so she could have the freedom of the city, Aunt Cris had secretly offered her, without Caetano knowing anything about it, this alternative accommodation in a tiny garret she owned in the Latin Quarter, a stone's throw from Paris' main tourist attractions. Leo was amazed by her aunt's properties, but she didn't say a word. About the flats or about Caetano.

Cris didn't mention them either, and Leo realized her aunt had another Paris she preferred to keep to herself. There are certain silences that should always be respected.

That was one of the few things her family didn't discuss during those four days in Paris. They had plenty of time to wander, laugh, rage, listen to Leo's extraordinary adventures in the world, for Roi's jokes, her mother's playful slaps and her father's kiss of satisfaction.

It had been necessary for them to go to Paris so they could discover each other anew. But even so, what they never talked about was the accident. Or about the situation with her father's company. In the first few months, Leo hadn't even thought about that but, now she'd passed the equator of her journey, it had started to surface again.

'Leo, you're out of your mind! What did you do in the middle of the desert with a flat tyre?'

'Count stars, mother dear, count stars.'

By the time it was Tuesday 17 May, the girl had completely forgotten her reasons for wanting to return home.

# 6

'What time did you say your plane was leaving tomorrow?'

'Four o'clock!' replied the three of them in unison.

'Uh-oh… I'm not sure Leo will want to come with us! Now we've rented out her room to a Swedish Erasmus student who's an absolute stunner!' laughed Roi.

Nobody backed him up. On the contrary, there was an unusually hostile silence. It was the first time they'd talked about Leo returning home, at least in front of her.

The girl carried on surfing the net, oblivious to their remarks. The attic in the Latin Quarter, the A. family's current headquarters, received their cramps and sighs every night. Roi had collapsed on the sofa and kept sneezing on account of an allergy provoked by the carpet. Her mother was washing up some glasses in the sink, while her father was leafing through a hunting magazine. It was Monday 16 May 2011.

'Actually no, clever clogs, I've changed my mind! You've just reminded me how much you annoy me, so I'm looking for a flight, but not to go home,' replied Leo exuberantly. 'You can rent out my room to whoever you like.'

The three of them remained silent, as if listening to it rain, and didn't ask any more. There was no point banging their heads against Leo's brick wall once she started getting mysterious. It was better to let her get on with it and, when she was ready, she would talk. But this time she didn't talk, she screamed, quite loudly:

'You whaaaaaaaaaaaaaaat? What is this?'

Her face went from pale to red, then blue, and finally as white as snow again. She wouldn't stop hitting the mouse with her forefinger and staring disbelievingly at the screen.

It seemed she'd just seen the Holy Company of souls in torment, with her at the forefront, carrying the banner.

'What is it, Leo?' asked her mother in concern.

'Don't pay her any attention, mother dear! She's exaggerating. She's probably just broken a nail,' said Roi scornfully.

'Oh, dear me... I'm going to have an attack...' the girl was breathing with a certain amount of difficulty.

'Leo, you're starting to make me very nervous,' replied her mother.

All the family's eyes converged on the back of the girl's shaved neck. When she turned around to face them, she looked very red.

'I've just been informed that I can print out my boarding card, since my flight is due to leave in less than twenty-four hours...'

'Your flight?' asked her father in surprise. 'What flight?'

'That's right, what flight?' repeated Roi. 'Aren't you coming home with us? Don't tell me you've chickened out!'

'To Buenos Aires!!!!' exclaimed Leo nervously.

'Buenos Aires?'

'Buenos Aires?'

'Buenos Aires?'

# 7

'Buenos Aires?'

'Buenos Aires?'

'Buenos Aires?'

The name of this Argentinian city was repeated questioningly up to three times in that tiny attic in Paris.

'Buenos Aires!' confirmed Leo, as if this would make it easier to believe.

It took her mother less than five seconds to introduce the coordinates of her target.

'It's your aunt. Blow me down if it's not your aunt... That sister of mine is incorrigible. Incorrigible... Just when I'd managed to convince you to come home. Incorrigible... You let me see her, just let me see her, I'll tell her what for,' she complained bitterly.

Leo was so dumbstruck she couldn't open her mouth to reply.

All she could do was mutter in a low voice:

'Buenos Aires, Buenos Aires, Buenos Aires.'

That was right, perhaps if she kept on saying it, it would become easier to assimilate.

'Buenos Aires!'

# 8

Aunt Cris listened and remained silent. Remained silent and listened. After all, when her older sister behaved as such and was so repugnant, anything she said could be used against her. It was ten o'clock in the evening in this cute, cosy brasserie on the Rue de la Montagne, very close to the imposing Pantheon and a stone's throw from the Sorbonne. In the distance, the Eiffel Tower sent messages of light through the darkness, a kind of lighthouse guiding ships in the middle of a storm. The reproaches being bandied about that table indicated that the swell would be intense.

'Come now, sister, have you finished? Can we order now, or are you going to go on all night? I'm hungry,' protested Cristina in the end.

'Not until you tell me what made you buy Leo a ticket to Buenos Aires... Wasn't there anywhere further away? Couldn't it have been somewhere like Oslo, Berlin or London?'

'Not London, no way,' intervened Leo. 'There's nothing for me there.'

London was the most fascinating city in the world, according to Andrés, and Leo had sworn she wouldn't do anything that reminded her of the Mexican.

'Leo, pay me attention. Leave them alone, this is between the two sisters. When they get like this, there's no putting up with them,' affirmed her father. 'I would like some snails for starters and then some foie gras. Where is the wine menu?'

'Buenos Aires...' insisted Leo's mother. 'What are you expecting Leo to find on the other side of the ocean?'

'Don't be so stubborn,' protested Aunt Cris again. 'Listen, I had these air miles that were just about to expire, and I decided Leo could make good use of them. That's why I got the tickets.'

'The tickets? You mean there's more than one?' raged Leo's mother once more.

'That's right, woman. Tickets. One, Paris-Buenos Aires for tomorrow, the other, Buenos Aires-Santiago de Compostela for 7 July. That way, she'll be back home on the day she promised. You didn't think I was going to leave her there, did you?'

'Ah, that's better. If the little girl has a return ticket, then I don't mind so much,' sighed Leo's mother finally. 'But I still think it's a long way away.'

'It's just another place, don't be so difficult, honestly, when you get like this…'

'It's your fault. If you hadn't…'

'Would the two of you be quiet? You're talking about me, and I'm sitting right in front of you!!! Do I have something to say in all of this, or what? Have you both quite forgotten that it's my trip??? M-i-n-e.'

Leo rapped her knuckles on the table. A fork clattered to the floor, and Roi, who hadn't looked up from his copy of *Ordinary Victories* by Manu Larcenet, closed his book abruptly, taken aback by his sister's cries. Everybody stared at her in amazement since Leo was normally very calm but, when she got irate, it was better to stay out of her way.

'I think we'll have the Burgundy. A Burgundy is better than a Bordeaux,' continued her father.

And Roi, to round it all off, cried out suddenly:

'National Police, documents, please!!'

There were a few moments of confusion that went from face to face of the five diners sitting at this stubborn table that refused to place its order. Until Leo let out this enormous guffaw that startled everybody even more.

'Dumbo!' shouted the girl while giving her brother a pinch on the face.

'What is it between these two?' asked Aunt Cris shyly.

'Don't pay them any attention. They've been playing this joke for months. I think it has something to do with the book Roi's reading. Things between siblings, you should know what that means,' replied Leo's father. 'Would anyone like water, or shall we just have wine?'

There were no more arguments during the rest of dinner. Not when the snails arrived, or the meat, or the dessert cheeses and the richly brewed coffee.

Everybody, deep down, wished to savour this final night in Paris.

Leo didn't have the chance to thank Cris for that wonderful passport to another continent. A return ticket thanks to her aunt's accumulated miles! That was a present she wouldn't have imagined even in her wildest dreams! This trip certainly kept coming up with surprises.

'Buenos Aires,' she kept saying to herself. Buenos Aires... what would Buenos Aires have to show for itself?

That night, she would go on the Internet to search for information about the capital of Argentina. The light from the Eiffel Tower would be a faithful guide in the middle of this storm that just wouldn't clear.

She was sure from Buenos Aires there would be cheap flights to other points on the American continent.

Her head was spinning so fast she didn't notice the cream in the sauce was a little cold and a touch too bitter.

How exciting, Buenos Aires...

# 9

*'We'll always have Paris. We didn't have, we'd lost it, until you came to Casablanca. We got it back last night.'*

That was exactly what Leo's father said to her mother in the middle of the departures lounge at Charles de Gaulle Airport when he thought nobody was listening. It was Tuesday 17 May, and Paris was stunned by the brightness of spring. Leo's parents were beaming because of this new light that had come to alight on the apex of their eyes. The girl stared at them and remained silent, aware perhaps there are occasions that shouldn't be devoured by words. She pretended to be adjusting her boots and let melancholy swallow up the moment.

At the time of the accident, she'd thought things would never be the same.

And, in effect, they had never been the same.

They had just got better.

Yes, thought Leo, infinitely better. There was no doubt that difficult moments bring opportunities, and first the crisis, then the accident, had offered them a wonderful opportunity to start over. To go no further, they'd just been given the Paris they'd always dreamed of and never had.

'Oh! I can see here about the demonstrations in Spain. Amazing, don't you think?' Roi was fiddling about with his mobile phone connected to Wi-Fi, oblivious to the noise in the airport. He'd spent the whole journey with his fingers trapped between the keys.

'What are you talking about, my son?' said his mother, ever on the lookout for possible dangers in the world that might threaten the security of her family.

'Well, it's not very clear. They say it's a citizen movement to protest about the current economic and social climate ahead of Sunday's local and regional elections. They're calling themselves 15-M because that's the date when they first irrupted on to the streets. Hey, look at this, there's a demonstration in Santiago, in the Praza do Obradoiro!'

But nobody was listening. Stuff to do with Roi, they thought. And since there was no talk of dead people, or coups d'état, or typhoons and earthquakes, his mother wasn't so interested in all his nonsense.

They joined the queue for boarding.

Leo stayed behind, right beside the gate, saying goodbye before heading off to that part of the airport that would take her to Buenos Aires.

'Don't forget to post a tweet in every place you visit, so we know where you are! See you in two months!' was the last thing she heard them say.

Much further behind, Aunt Cris was disappearing down into the labyrinth of the Paris underground.

Her tears made it difficult to see which line would take her back to her house.

She knew that Leo wouldn't disappoint her.

She just knew it.

# 10

Leo mechanically repeated all the movements prior to take-off. She turned off her electronic devices, put her seat back and tray table in the full upright position, fastened her seat belt and listened to the air stewardess' safety announcements. It didn't matter what language it was in, it was always the same spiel, and the girl had managed to learn it off by heart. The bit about the emergency evacuation slide, the oxygen mask and life jacket. This time, she also took off her boots, put on some thick socks and took down the pillow and blanket, just as Aunt Cris had recommended.

'No jeans, loose-fitting tracksuit bottoms, on a long journey you have to be as comfortable as you can. Watch out for the air-conditioning! Keep a scarf handy to protect your throat!'

Her aunt kept relaying these instructions while helping her to pack her rucksack. So many days spent free in the attic in Paris had meant her luggage had swollen in size until it was almost impossible to get it all into her 55-litre rucksack. This wasn't helped by all the stuff her mother had insisted on contributing.

'Mother! Why on earth would I need an LED headlamp? Are you out of your mind?'

'You're going to South America! That's very different from Europe, my girl.'

'Yes, mother, I'm going to South America, but I'm not planning to go down any mines,' laughed Leo.

'Ah, Leo, don't say that, you'll remind me of those poor Chilean miners, and it'll give me a turn.'

There was no greater worrier in this world than her mother but, instead of getting angry, Leo gave her an effusive hug.

'Dear mother, I'll be back in only two months! The world isn't going to eat me up!'

'Get away from here, you'll make me cry.'

That was the closest Leo came to thanking her mother for making that surprise visit to Paris which had put her travels back on track. Leo hadn't found the right moment to thank her aunt for the ticket that would transport her to Buenos Aires, either.

'I've sent you an email with a list of the addresses of various researchers at South American universities, just in case you need to ask them for help. They've all been to stay with me in Paris, so perhaps now is the time for them to return the favour...'

'Aunt Cris...'

'Don't wait until the last moment before you call or write to them, they're normally away at other universities, and it's not always easy...'

'Aunt...'

'Listen, even if you don't want to stay in their homes, try and make contact with them. They're an interesting bunch...'

'Cris, give Aymara and Caetano a big kiss from me. Caetano struck me as a great guy. I'm just sorry I couldn't say goodbye to them in person.'

'Yes, yes, yes, I'll tell them. Listen, don't miss this opportunity and get in touch with them...'

Aunt Cris had gone stone-deaf. Leo accepted there was another Paris she preferred not to share with anybody else. As always in her family, things were either half said or completely omitted.

With a delay of twenty minutes, the plane finally took off. She had thirteen and a half hours of transatlantic flight ahead of her.

## 11

Five hours later, Leo had tried all possible positions, visited the toilet three times, eaten every last noodle on her plastic plate, read several chapters in *Invisible Cities* by Italo Calvino, leafed through various pages of general information about Buenos Aires, craned her neck in an attempt to follow the argument of the film they were showing five rows in front and had a good doze.

Aunt Cris was right. Transatlantic flights go on forever and, needless to say, her head wouldn't stop spinning around.

It's difficult to explain the immense solitude that can suddenly enter one's body at more than 30,000 feet above the sea. After dinner according to French time, the crew asked everybody to lower their blinds, and the cabin went dark. Outside, it was permanently daytime because they were travelling in the same direction as the sun. As they crossed the globe, the sun obstinately clung to their heels with no intention of being left behind. But inside the plane, everything was darkness, silence and the breathing of strange people trying to ease their sleep or panic in the adjoining seats. Leo became afraid. She'd never felt this way before. It wasn't nostalgia, melancholy, sadness or fear. It was just this immense solitude, wet and slightly cruel, that flooded her body and head. She tried to think about the last few days in Paris, the hours in Venice or Istanbul, the surprise of Marrakesh, her father's smile, and yet – she couldn't say why – it all seemed so far away and unattainable. Even Andrés. He'd simply vanished. Not even the memory of him could hurt her now. It was as if, thought Leo, despite the fact they were consuming fuel and air miles at a rapid rate, the memories had yet to abandon the luggage area in Charles de

Gaulle Airport. Strangely enough, the excitement of reaching a new destination had yet to take possession of her head. Neither the things she would see, nor the places she would visit, nor the people she would meet. None of it.

The past wouldn't die, and the future wouldn't arrive. She received isolated images, like bolts of lightning, but couldn't string together any coherent thoughts. In the interior of that plane, Leo felt for the first time in her life that she was in a non-place and a non-time, a kind of black hole in space that sucked her up mercilessly. The dizziness was getting more and more unbearable.

The dull, tugging turbulence that had been shaking the aircraft for several hours didn't help much, either.

Until suddenly she remembered.

'Leo, put that suitcase over there, it's bothering me on my knees.'

They were inside a railway carriage on the RER, the rapid train line taking them from the stop by the Luxembourg Gardens straight to the airport. Around them, dozens of African and Asian immigrants were heading back to their homes in the Paris suburbs. The carriages were old and dilapidated, their seats criss-crossed by knife scars and graffiti in every imaginable colour. The layers of spray-paint were superimposed, one on top of the other, which made it difficult to read the messages Roi had now devoted all his attention to.

'Look, Leo, this one here, I reckon it's a hip-hop song. It seems to rhyme, don't you think?'

'Roi, your level of French is not nearly enough to understand that. Leave it alone.'

'Hey, and look at that amazing cat. A crescent moon is hanging off its tail.'

'Yes, it's very nice.'

'How about this? Is that a hip-hop song as well? It says, ".AOEL UOYEVOLI." No, it has to be some kind of encoded message. Would you look at that? It's on all the seats, right on the headrest.'

'Yes, Roi, I see. Would you let me carry on reading?'

'".AOEL UOYEVOLI"... who knows what it means? What do you think?'

'Roi, do you have to keep going on about the graffiti?'

'OK, I get it, just don't forget, ".AOEL UOYEVOLI."'

At that point, they'd reached the end of their journey, and the conversation had been drowned out by the squeal of the brakes. Then had come all the business with their suitcases, their identity documents, the times and gates, and Leo hadn't thought any more about it, but now, at a height of more than 30,000 feet, the scene had come racing back into her mind. She quickly grabbed her notebook and copied out that strange message. She looked at it again and again. She couldn't believe what she was seeing.

How could she have been so stupid? How could she have been so stupid? How?

What it said was 'I LOVE YOU LEO A.' in reverse!

And that was when, at a height of more than 30,000 feet, the black hole sucked her up with unusual violence and the dizziness became really unbearable.

She didn't sleep for the rest of the journey and when, thirteen and a half hours later, they finally landed in Buenos Aires, her body was completely drained. Her head, even more so.

It was 8:50 local time, and Buenos Aires welcomed her with a lukewarm, autumnal embrace.

The temperature was 13 degrees Celsius, and the maximum forecast for that day did not exceed the barrier of 20 degrees. A thin mist cloaked the metropolitan area, and the sky was a little clouded over. Slight north-westerly winds. With storm clouds predicted for the evening-night and slight to moderate south-easterly winds.

That was what the captain said as soon as they touched down and all the passengers had applauded a landing manoeuvre that was as smooth as a swallow's wing.

# 12

After a flight lasting thirteen and a half hours, everything in Leo's body was hurting, and a thick cloud had descended on top of her head, making her feel terribly sleepy and dizzy...

'Ah, so this is the famous jet lag!' concluded the girl as she headed towards the hostel she'd found on the Internet.

Despite her aunt's insistence, Leo had decided to do without all her university colleagues. After twelve days of staying with her family in Paris, she felt like being alone and taking her own decisions. The freedom to choose what to do each minute of the day had turned into a pleasure she refused to renounce. The transatlantic flight had been an ideal opportunity to go over her accounts. There she had confirmed what she already suspected: that the stay in Paris and her family's tender loving care had meant the balance of her journey was exactly the same as when she'd landed in the city of the Seine on her way from Venice. She hadn't spent a centime! Nothing at all in twelve days! Her aunt first, then her mother, had prevented her from paying for any food, transport or services, so the accounts with which she'd set foot on the American continent were nothing short of exceptional.

She had the total sum of 1,450 euros in her pocket for travel and another 1,140 euros for living expenses. And her return ticket had already been bought! She added up, took away, multiplied and divided on the pages at the back of her notebook and reached the following conclusion: there were 51 days to go until she returned home on 8 July, just as she'd promised, which gave her an allowance of 22.35 euros per day for living expenses (accommodation, food and entrance tickets). The balance of 1,450 euros for transport was difficult to fathom, since she was ignorant of the destinations, distances and prices of the places she would visit.

South America had never been a real possibility, so it was time to modify her plans. Her preparations for the trip had involved months of trawling the Internet for contacts and places to see. She hadn't been alone. Given it was meant to be a shared experience, the lines on the maps revealed the weight of negotiations with Martiño, Aldara and Inés. Their likes, their obsessions, their whims. In the end, the lines across the globe had severed Europe down the middle and, after a great deal of debate, they had opted for North Africa as their final destination before returning home. India, perhaps. But after the treacherous withdrawal on the part of her three friends, Leo had had to rethink the whole journey. She'd scratched out the Indian Ocean and decreased the amount of travelling in Europe. The destinations would have to be fewer, since travelling on your own was a lot more expensive. No hitchhiking, group discounts or mixed accommodation, she had decided before leaving. And yet hooking up with Ruth & Co. had broken all the rules, both financial and sentimental. 'Yes, a joy for the pocket and a heaviness for the heart,' muttered Leo. The world had grown in size, become vast, since there was nowhere that made them afraid. No borders or dividing lines. The company silenced all her fears of solitude and possible dangers. Nothing could happen to that group of intrepid friends who were as jolly as they were unpredictable. That was why separating from them had been as natural as it had been strangely painful. The world had shrunk again for financial reasons and because of the overriding sense of vulnerability. But the trip had come up with a new surprise: Paris and her family. The unexpected plane ticket to Buenos Aires had disrupted each and every one of her plans and yet, instead of being cowed, Leo had risen to the challenge. South America, wow, she'd never envisaged that. There must be a whole wealth of amazing things to see! And that was when the dream of Machu Picchu became a distinct possibility.

These thoughts were racing through her mind as the taxi ate up the asphalt of the metropolitan area of Buenos Aires. She was feeling so dazed she hadn't dared to take public transport, which might have left her anywhere in the city. The experience of Prague had told her that, when the body is empty, no indications will suffice to point you in the right direction. The yellow car left her at the requested address, a small hostel described as 'wonderful' on social media, located between the Avenues Corrientes, Córdoba, Gallo and Pueyrredón, fairly close to the Plaza Almagro and apparently just a short hop on the Subte to the Argentinian capital's main attractions.

She confirmed her reservation in reception. That first night, suffering because of the time difference, she would go for a single room with shared bathroom, which cost the equivalent of 25 euros. The approximate worth of the Argentinian peso could be obtained by dividing the amount by five and a half to get the price in euros. The following day, she would consider the possibility of moving to a mixed room for six people, which would lower the cost of overnight accommodation to 11 euros. But that would be tomorrow, when she'd managed to calm the throbbing inside her head and made contact with the other guests. Leo had learned that sharing a room made good financial sense, but required a minimal amount of ocular and conversational inspection to ensure the night did not turn into an endless nightmare because of the smells, snores and uncomfortable suspicions about the strangers surrounding you.

She opened the door to her room, but barely paid any attention to the fittings. She only had eyes to make sure the sheets contained no unwanted residents and then she lay down, intending to rest for a couple of hours. After that, she would have to find out where she was on the map and plan her stay in a city that had escaped her attention in the taxi and about which she had nothing to say, except for the sense of mystery afforded by the mist that cloaked everything, giving it a ghostly appearance. She would have to inspect the street map so she could set about her discovery!

But that would come later. For now, her body had had enough.

Wretched jet lag.

# 13

It was exactly Leo's confusion about the time that made her wake up at an uncertain hour to the sound of soft music and raucous laughter. She glanced at her watch, the hands of which still displayed the time in Europe. Her watch said half past eleven, and it took her a couple of seconds to work out this meant it was only half past six, taking into account the five-hour time difference. But was that half past six in the morning or the evening? On what day? Leo had a quick shower and walked barefoot out of her room, taking the cramp from the aircraft and the bags hanging down to her lips along with her.

'Hello,' she murmured to the group of young people huddled in a small room with coloured windows, trees and birds flitting across the white sky of the walls and the unmistakable scent of maté that impregnated everything.

'How's it going?' chorused the seven individuals, eyeing her with curiosity. 'Hey, you look sleepy! Europe's far away, isn't it?'

'I'm sorry, what day is it? And what's the time?'

There was a loud, resounding laugh.

'It's half past six in the evening of 18 May in the year 2011.'

'You're kidding me! This day won't ever end!'

'That's right, you've gone back in time…'

They carried on arguing and messing around while Leo listened to the conversation far, far away, as if it were the murmur of a television switched on in another room. They were in a small space with high ceilings where flocks of painted swallows disappeared into the distance. Around them, three comfortable sofas and several coloured blankets gave the atmosphere some warmth. There were seven of them: a couple she later identified as the hostel's owners and another five guests. Three girls and two boys. Two of the girls declared they were students from Río Gallegos who were searching in Buenos Aires for a different adventure and a doorway into the world. The boys, on the other hand, defined themselves as travellers. They weren't all that easy to understand. They were Swiss or something. The third woman said she had been born in a small town in Tuscany. Adriana. Her name was Adriana.

She had long, slightly curly hair, a strong complexion, a sad, oily look, enormous feet and porcelain-white, freckly arms. She got stuck on her 'r's and had this strange accent that gave her an unusual form of speech. Some time later, Leo would reconsider everything she'd seen in her on that first day. All that she was. And although she never believed in empathy at first sight or anything similar, she had to accept that first evening in Buenos Aires the girl had given her an awkward shock, as if she'd suddenly encountered a twin soul, but this was something she wouldn't fathom out until later. At that precise moment in time, Adriana appealed to her about as much as a kick in the butt.

It must have been the fact she was sleepy, that was it. The way she kept tripping on her 'r's gave Leo this cradling sensation, as if she had become wrapped in her voice. She was so very sleepy she let herself be swayed by this unexpected restfulness on the other side of the ocean.

For four hours, she listened to them laugh and talk. She didn't want to go to sleep, but at the same time she couldn't follow the conversation at all coherently. When they all went off to bed, she gathered her battered body and went back to her own room. She picked up her notebook and sprinkled it with handfuls of insomnia plagued by tiredness.

At that precise moment, she would have liked to go online and talk to somebody, but she had to reject this crazy idea because, on the other side of the world, everybody was asleep.

The sense of loneliness the transatlantic flight had left in her took on monstrous proportions that night but, truly exhausted on account of the journey, Leo still managed to fall asleep.

Tomorrow was another day, and then she would succeed in driving away all this melancholy.

# 14

Leo woke up with a start. Again, she didn't know where she was or what time it was. A quick look at the shadows in her room revealed an unfamiliar territory.

'Ah, jet lag!' muttered Leo.

The irate merry-go-round of sleep-insomnia had trapped her in its feverish vortex – she'd been lost in Buenos Aires for twenty hours. Twenty hours! How was that possible! Her desire to discover the city made her get out of bed before it was even seven o'clock in the morning, local time.

At home, on the other side of the world, she reckoned they'd already had lunch, cleared the table, and were having a quick snooze before heading back to school, the shop, rehabilitation. And yet here, in this large urban agglomeration on the Plate River estuary, life was just stretching its limbs. Leo sighed. How lucky she was to be here! How she longed to go outside! Clinging to the omnipresent scent of maté, which reminded her of Mayra, she stole through the hostel like a cat and emerged on to the street. Before that:

> @ALeo90
> Finally I'm off to see Buenos Aires!
> 19 May 2011 at 8:00

The tail end of autumn had been collected in dry leaves because of a lively wind that had nothing to do with spring in Paris barely two days earlier. Leo didn't know whether it was the smell, density, humidity or strength, but this awkward breeze told her she was no longer in Europe and here, among the sleepy shadows on the pavements and the early-morning cars, life cruised along at a different speed.

There is no more wonderful sensation than stepping on to the streets of a city for the first time at dawn. The buildings with sleep still in their eyes, their half-open shutters, the sluggish traffic lights, the trees taking off their clothes to receive winter, the cold asphalt and sleepwalking pedestrians lazily open their eyes before a new day without being at all certain whether you are a dream or a nightmare. They wonder whether you are for real or just flotsam floating in with the tide. Cities, when they awake, veil themselves behind the steam of kettles, the first exhaust of cars and a low-lying mist that silently leaves the ground. The first shadows, waiting for the bus with their hands in their pockets and wrapped in coats; children tying their shoelaces and swinging their rucksacks against their hips to pick up speed; the ties and high heels heading off to the office; grandmothers disturbing dreams and cartoons to drum the three times table into children who only want to be Messi or Maradona; the newspaper deliverywoman and the seller of *alfajores*, sweet, crumbly biscuits; the local policeman directing the traffic with grandiloquent gestures, a real scarecrow keeping an eye on the starlings bustling along the road in fuming, preoccupied flocks; the mothers carrying the most important lists in the world in their heads (call the electrician, pay the insurance, buy milk, get the little boy's eyes tested, buy the elder girl some shoes, submit the latest report to a repellent boss); the *cartonero*, the collector of discarded waste, who sticks his nose out of a paper hole to sniff the light welcomed with a burp of bitter wine... all of these shadows ignored Leo's presence, which was as transparent as a jellyfish, while her crystal body registered the damp breath of those who dodged her so they could pull on the invisible thread of their daily routines.

That was how, in the early morning, Leo had discovered Istanbul. And a stab of nostalgia pierced her throat.

The memory of Andrés had come looking for her on the other side of the ocean! 'Well,' she said to herself, 'I'm not going to let him spoil the experience. I'm in Buenos Aires, can you believe it?'

When she'd left home four months earlier, Leo had realized there were burdens that hindered her journey: the sense of guilt after everything that had happened, as her mother had said numerous times, the last-minute withdrawal of her friends, fear, doubt… The girl had thought after a couple of weeks she would be able to offload this excess baggage and fly free like the swallows that adorned the walls of the hostel. And yet she'd had to learn that travelling brings with it other, unforeseen weights that accumulate on your back and are difficult to avoid. You have to learn to live with them, to deposit them in the dark room of your memory, where they won't bother you too much. Nostalgia is the same.

Leo gazed at the city that was just waking up in this extension of autumn and started wandering down the large avenues that gradually filled with words, faces and hurried steps. It was like coming across Mayra and Edmundo a thousand times over! Their gait, their clothes, the stilted accent that sank from the mouth into the stomach like caramelized milk. And as the buildings, blocks, people and trees grew up around her in an urban jungle she entered like a clever and curious explorer, Leo realized that winter was on its way. That was what this cold wind that licked her cheeks kept telling her. How difficult it was to think of the coming weeks of May and June as strides towards the snow!

Leo spent that first day coming to terms with the city, observing it without any specific agenda, letting herself be carried along by the wave of people who bustled about its streets. With no more direction than instinct and the fragile willpower of her feet, she walked and walked until cramp seized hold of her calves. With no words of advice and no set rules.

The first conclusion she reached was that this was the city of infinite zebra crossings.

In the afternoon, tiredness overtook her, and she decided to sit down for a coffee in a tiny café where the steam of the coffee machines intermingled with the conversations going on around her. She was just watching life stagger along on the far side of the window when she caught sight of Adriana. Dear me, in such a large city, and she would have to go and bump into one of the guests from her hotel. She didn't have time to hide behind a newspaper before the girl saw her and, without further ado, came and sat down beside her.

Leo's look of surprise and awkwardness didn't put her off for a moment.

'Oof, it's cold! What I need is a nice, hot coffee. With milk, if you don't mind.'

The girl couldn't get over her shock. She was like a magnet for strange people. The one day she wanted to be on her own and, even on the other side of the world, she couldn't achieve this!

'How's it going?'

'Fine, thanks.'

…

'Buenos Aires is amazing, don't you think?'

'Yes, it is.'

'Have you been to Caminito? Or Puerto Madero?'

'No.'

'To Recoleta? Palermo? San Telmo?'

'I've only just arrived!'

'Well, if it's not too much to ask, what are you doing here?'

It was obvious the girl felt like talking and wasn't prepared to accept monosyllables as an answer.

'It's a long story,' replied Leo with resignation, perhaps realizing she had no other option but to launch into a conversation.

'Oh, we've all the time in the world! We're in South America, time moves along at a different rhythm.'

Leo's quick glance through the window didn't dissuade her from her task of extracting further information.

'Whim? Chance? Promise? Flight? A secret mission, perhaps?'

Leo smiled in amusement.

'That's it. A secret mission.'

'Like me, then.'

The girl's face suddenly became sad. Leo couldn't understand a thing. She really didn't feel like wasting the last few hours of daylight with this stranger who'd turned up out of the blue to make her confession at a table in a Buenos Aires café. But after several sighs, making as if to get up and glancing desperately around, she decided to succumb to the talkative voraciousness of this girl who tripped on her 'r's with exquisite sweetness.

'When I was young, I lived in this small town in Tuscany – San Gimignano. You may know it because of the two towers that always appear in tourist photos. My parents had a *trattoria* and, like all children who are raised in a restaurant, I grew up on my own, doing my homework among oilskin tablecloths and orders, the shouts of drinkers and the soundtrack of the television in the background. Despite the fact I was an invisible child, everybody was quite certain about my purpose in life: I was to perpetuate the exquisite, unmistakable taste of the ravioli made by my *nonna*, first, and then by my *mamma*. Nobody thought I might want to be an astronaut, an engineer, a musician or an emigrant. That word, "emigrant", had always captivated my attention. It bustled about among the silences and complaints of my family, without anybody ever going so far as to pronounce it. But I knew what it was: "emigrant". I would caress it in secret with affection and devotion. I never told anybody, of course, but a sense of unease took hold in the pit of my stomach. Until one bitter day my father, leaning over the counter of the *trattoria* one Tuesday without many customers, exclaimed:

"'Young people don't know what they want! They need somebody to mark out their future, otherwise they'll turn out like a bunch of layabouts. Young people, green wood... Nothing but smoke!"

"'Don't spit so high, Antonio! Life has its twists and turns," suggested a woman, slowly sucking up her spaghetti with lots of oregano.

"'Sure it does! Look at my Adriana, as studious as you like. She'll make a wonderful continuation of the family's *trattoria*."

"'Do you want to be a cook, Adriana?" asked a poet of rounded sonnets like dregs of wine.

"'No way! What I want is to be an emigrant!" I announced with triumphant solemnity, proud that someone had finally given me the opportunity to share my secret.

'I don't know what came first – silence or the hefty slap across my face, or perhaps it was silence before, during and after the slap, who knows? I can only say I was so shocked I didn't shed a single tear. It was my mother who, worried about the silence that had fallen like a bucket of ice-cold water over the dining room, came running out of the kitchen, armed only with a spatula, and took me out of there with her floury hands.

'"What was it you said to your father? What was it, Adriana?"

'Silence.

'"You must have said something. Your father never lifted a hand against you before."

'Silence.

'"Well, whatever it was, don't go saying it again. Never again."

'No sooner said than done. I never repeated that word which, instead of rotting away, grew inside my head with unusual ferocity, as if that slap had acted like a kind of yeast. One night, I couldn't say how old I was, it may have been before or after the slap, the shouts at home unleashed a perfect storm. First of all, it was just intermittent reproaches, but after that flashes of lightning and rolls of thunder disturbed the clear skies of our family's cohabitation. I heard it, I heard it distinctly on the other side of the partition. In bed, in the dark, I clung to my teddy bear. On the other side, my father and mother were arguing.

'"It's your fault, you're the one who puts these ideas into her head."

'"What, me?"

'"Yes, you."

"'Well, you'd better tell me what ideas they are, unless you're talking about flour. All I do is knead the ravioli..."

"'And I serve the wine, what do you think? I'm not talking about that, I'm talking about your aunt Claudia.'"

"'Oh, goodness me, don't tell me you've heard from her!'"

"'Of course I haven't. Thirty years ago she left this house on a ship bound for Argentina, and you're still waiting for her! You know what I think? You're all crazy!'"

"'We don't know what happened. Something must have happened to her for her not to come back. Just those three postcards with passionate tangos on them. And I promised my mother one day I'd find out what had become of her... Poor Aunt Claudia...'"

"'Can't you see?'"

"'What?'"

"'That you're filling the little girl's head with all these crazy ideas! The other day she said she wanted to be an emigrant!'"

"'And?'"

"'Well, it's your aunt Claudia who's to blame. She carries it in her genes, or something like that...'"

"'Then perhaps she's the one who'll go looking for her. What do I know? Perhaps she needs to find her own path far away from this stupid *trattoria*.'"

'Mother didn't have the chance to carry on talking, nor me to carry on listening. But those shouts led me to a simple conclusion: if my mother had said "stupid *trattoria*", then perhaps it was a "stupid *trattoria*" and I had to get away from there. A year ago, after my latest boyfriend ditched me for a Russian girl with lank hair and exuberant tits, I decided to follow in my aunt Claudia's footsteps, this aunt I'd never met. If she had made up her mind to leave this "stupid *trattoria*" on her own account, then it must be worth getting in touch with her. And here I am. My secret mission is to find my great-aunt in the immensity of Argentina! I've been on the case for almost a year and haven't found a reliable lead, but I'm not giving up! I'll find her, or my name isn't Adriana!'

This was more or less what Leo understood in this language that was a mixture of Italian and River Plate Spanish, though deep down, she had to admit, she didn't understand a thing. No doubt her initial confusion made it impossible for her to interpret the rest: why on earth had she told her all of this? She barely even knew the girl! At this point, the woman must have read her thoughts, or the look of perplexity on her face.

'You'll be wondering why I'm telling you all of this. Well, I was tired of keeping it to myself and not finding somebody to talk to about it. Now someone else knows, it doesn't weigh so heavily on me. What a relief!'

It was obvious that nostalgia had dug its teeth into Adriana's leg, and the best method for easing the cramp had been to dress it with words and drive it away from her. The burden she carried on her back was so heavy she'd been forced to throw it off so she wouldn't sink. Leo was tempted to shrug off the millstone she'd been carrying around for months. She opened her mouth and, just as the 'Well, as for me...' seemed inevitable, she said instead:

'You did well.'

Be it chance or destiny, Adriana had found somebody to listen to her with the cramp of all the blocks in Buenos Aires stubbornly pinching her muscles. And Leo realized, with a mixture of astonishment and incredulity, that the city's surprise had slipped into her feverish body between the sips of a coffee that had gone cold by now.

'It's getting late, and the weather's not good. Shall we take a *remis* to get back to the hostel?' sighed Adriana, and Leo went along with it.

On the other side of the taxi window, the city of lazy lights bustled about. At that precise moment, Leo wondered whether it isn't better sometimes to travel through the lives of others.

No doubt, had she not been nattering with Adriana and looked outside, she would have come across an enormous sign hanging from the obelisk in the Plaza de la República which said:

### I Love You Leo A.

And instead of thinking it's sometimes better to travel through the lives of others, she might have thought something else.

But as with so much else, she didn't even notice the sign.

# 15

'Ushuaia?'

'That's right.'

'Ushuaia?'

'Oh, come on! What's so strange about that?'

Around bowls of soup and cans of beer, the guests handed out letters and information about their visits. Undoubtedly the most fun part of staying in a youth hostel was the warm atmosphere that, ensconced in slippers, made you feel at home.

'Ushuaia?' reiterated the woman in charge of the hostel, a painter who wasn't fond of debate, something difficult to avoid in a country of psychoanalysts and word therapists.

'Let's see now... I want to go to Ushuaia because I met this bloke, Edmundo, who was from there and I'm curious to know the lighthouse at the end of the world. There you go, it even rhymes,' smiled Leo, trying to play down the situation.

'How strange!' murmured François, one of the Swiss men. 'We all came in search of Bariloche, Puerto Madryn, the Iguazu Falls, Torres del Paine, Mendoza... but Ushuaia's so far away!'

'The most southerly city in the world,' affirmed Luis, the owner of the hostel, who until that moment hadn't opened his mouth. 'You do well, I'd love to go back there and hear the hum of the southern wind. But if you're going, you'd better go straight away.'

'Why? What's the hurry? Is it going to move or something?' laughed Leo ironically.

The hostel owner stared at her very seriously. There was something in his eyes that intimidated her.

'There is no European who doesn't think his is the centre of the world and it governs the rest of the planet. Your seasons are not universal, my girl. We're heading towards winter, and in a few weeks Ushuaia will be covered in snow with temperatures below zero. If you don't want to freeze, you'd better leave as soon as possible. If that can be tomorrow, then don't wait until Saturday. But it's up to you, obviously.'

Leo almost fell over. How could she have been so dumb? She had arrived with a head stuffed full of northern hemisphere rules and hadn't realized that on the other side of the world life followed a different calendar! Her ears burning, she hid her embarrassment at this monumental mistake as best she could and dissembled with a nervous laugh before the others.

'But I wanted to visit Palermo and Caminito before that! At least attend a tango session. I still haven't got the feel of the city… I don't want to leave right away,' protested Leo.

'The city will wait, believe me, Buenos Aires always waits,' sighed Adriana.

'Otherwise you'll die of cold, having turned into a stalactite because of the Antarctic winter!' laughed the other Swiss boy.

And that was why, as the others talked of the cold that was going to blast the city, Leo weighed up her colleagues' unanimous agreement about the need to leave at once. She suddenly walked over to the computer, went online and pressed the magic keys.

'Buenos Aires-Ushuaia 21 May 2011' (two days later).

As the virtual hourglass twisted and turned, the girl crossed her fingers. How much would the journey cost? She didn't have time to work it out.

'120 euros.'

The girl screwed up her nose. It wasn't a lot or a little, all the same... She pressed again.

'Buenos Aires-Ushuaia 20 May 2011' (the very next day).

Another twist of the hourglass, and the irrefutable truth: '100 euros'.

A few seconds to get used to the idea, and...

'Well, that's it decided,' she said out loud, 'I'm leaving for Ushuaia tomorrow at 17:00.'

The news was received with festive joy in the common area.

'A toast for the adventurous girl!' said the woman in charge of the hostel, as her husband grimaced with a dose of envy and a touch of resignation.

An hour's laughter later, Leo went back to her single room.

She couldn't believe it. She had just bought a ticket to Ushuaia for the following day and had barely had time to discover Buenos Aires! A few months earlier, this would have been an impossible decision but, as a result of overcoming unexpected surprises and obstacles, she had learned the very best awaits after you take a firm decision, having got over your initial fear. That was right, she tried to convince herself, common sense had won out over desire, and the Les Eclaireurs Lighthouse was calling to her. The cramp still clinging to her legs, sleep came over her before she would have liked. It was ten o'clock, Argentinian time, but her body still responded to the tiredness of a European early morning. Two hours later, she woke up, feeling uneasy. She was so afraid of nostalgia, doubt and fear that she rushed to the computer in the common area to dash off a few emails that would shatter the silence of night.

She sent messages to her mother, Roi, Sebastián, Aunt Cris and Mayra. In all of them, she omitted her new southerly destination and concentrated instead on the wonders of Buenos Aires she had barely glimpsed during her first incursion into the urban grid of unending parallel and perpendicular lines. Having thought a great deal about it, she finally sent an email to Edmundo as well. In it, she wrote:

> Am going to see how the wind roars about the tearful eyes of the Les Eclaireurs Lighthouse, sheltered from the storms that come from the much-feared Cape Horn.

Funny. There were only two emails she really wanted to send, and yet she didn't dare. One contained a question, the other an answer, but neither of them was acceptable to her sense of pride. She fell asleep slowly to the wonderful adrenalin of knowing, the very next day, she would close her eyes thousands of kilometres away. Mmm, how lovely...

# 16

Leo's flight was delayed by two and a half hours because of an overbooking that led to a great deal of dissension among the passengers. Then, as the plane rose majestically off the airfield, leaving the dull Plate River estuary at its feet, Leo emitted hiccups of boredom at another journey through the air. She still hadn't got over her transatlantic odyssey, and here she was, again, at a height of thousands of feet. Instinctively, as a way of overcoming the tedium, she grabbed hold of a book the hostel owner had lent her – according to him, so she could familiarize herself with her new destination. He'd insisted so much she hadn't dared to turn him down.

This copy – never again would she recall the title – told the story of Petiso Orejudo, 'Big-Eared Midget', a terrible criminal who'd spent his last days shut up in Ushuaia Penitentiary.

He could have lent her some poems by Alfonsina Storni, or a book of stories by Cortázar, or some verses by Alejandra Pizarnik, or a volume by Jorge Luis Borges, all famous writers that could have offered her a fresh vision of Buenos Aires in particular and Argentina in general. But the man had run his forefinger along the spines on the library bookshelf and rejected them all until he'd come across this worn book with its black covers and crude look. He'd then selected it with great delicacy and handed it to her like a treasure. The one about the serial killer…

He'd also given her a plastic jar with a lid so she could collect a gust of the wind that came whistling from Puerto Williams, on the long-drawn-out intestine of Navarino Island.

On her return, she would have to give it all back. All of it, he repeated.

And that was how, during the three-and-a-half-hour flight that separated the Argentinian capital from Ushuaia, Leo learned about the truculent affairs of this boy who had terrorized Buenos Aires society at the start of the twentieth century.

*Cayetano Santos Godino, it seemed, had been born on the last day of October 1896, the day before All Saints. His eyes opened just in time to celebrate All Souls, and perhaps this was the circumstance that marked the rest of his life. Mistreated, humiliated and sick, the young Godino slowly chewed his way through the hours of his childhood in what were then the suburbs of Buenos Aires beneath the implacable whip of his father, an alcoholic immigrant who wished to strip him of his rebellious nature. He failed to achieve this. He thought of him as an idiot. A wretch. A nobody. Hence, when Godino was only nine, he denounced him to the police and asked them to lock him up. To make something of him. Anything that would bring him back to the straight and narrow and avoid unpleasant scenes with the neighbours and macabre oddities.*

*'Tell me one of them,' the policeman must have said, 'tell me something your son has done, a good reason to lock him up.'*

*To which, amid burps of bitter wine while leaning on the counter so as not to collapse on account of his drunkenness, the father would have replied:*

*'It was night-time when I got home, you know how it is. In the absence of light, everything seems to change place, and I kept bumping into things that got in my way until I ended up kicking something hard and fell over. In the dark, lying on the floor, I took the object in my hand and tried to work*

*out what it was. I couldn't manage, what on earth could it be? When I finally located a candle, I saw it was one of my son's shoes with – and you're not going to believe this – birds inside whose heads had been torn off. Anger took hold of me, and I went to see if there were any more. No sooner said than done. Under his bed, I came across a box full of blood, worms, feathers and putrefying birds. I was so disgusted I threw up everything in my stomach. Devilish boy! But don't you worry, good sir, I still had it in me to give him a thorough beating.'*

*'But that's just the boy getting up to mischief, nothing to worry about,' the policeman may have affirmed.*

*'Believe me, officer, this child has the devil inside him,' insisted his father mournfully before finally falling down unconscious in a pool of alcohol and grime.*

*The drunkard didn't realize that, only a few days earlier, as he would later confess, his son had buried a two-year-old girl in a ditch in some wasteland. She was still breathing when the last shovelful of earth and cans buried her dying body.*

*The corpse was never found.*

*Perhaps this first victim heard the feeble tweeting of the beheaded birds beneath the dust that smothered her final sob.*


When they landed at Ushuaia Airport, night had fallen, and Leo was petrified. She cursed the airport tax she had to pay as soon as she arrived in all the languages she knew, took a taxi and gave out the address of a pension she'd been in contact with over the Internet. She didn't dare leave her room. She lay down in bed and waited for sleep while half a dozen decapitated robins chirped from the depths of her Eustachian tube.

Damn book!

# 17

The cold Leo had felt as a result of the previous evening's reading was multiplied on that Friday 21 May 2011 when, on waking up in a strange bed, she realized it was seven o'clock and the sun still hadn't climbed into the sky. She went online to pass the time. In her inbox, several messages from home were waiting impatiently with reminders of how little was left of her journey, trusting to her good sense overseas. Leo understood the bombardment of emails talking of her return would become incessant. So she said to herself:

'I'll write what I have to on Twitter and avoid mother and Roi's emails. I need to enjoy the present without growing bitter about the few days I have left of absolute freedom.'

As she offloaded all thoughts about home, the story of Petiso Orejudo took hold in her imagination like the uncomfortable shadow of a storm drawing closer on the horizon.

She had breakfast in the kitchen of the pension, a tiny house in the centre of the city run by a middle-aged woman who'd been a schoolteacher in Buenos Aires.

'I came because I had to get away from the capital. At the time of the *corralito*, you understand.'

No, Leo didn't know all that much about the *corralito*, but she realized it must have been quite important because there was no Argentinian who didn't refer to it in a conversation. That and Peronism, which some talked about with devotion and others with contempt.

'How about you… what are you doing here all on your own at the end of the world?' asked Dori, the needle-like woman with a large head and slim body who was her landlady.

'In Europe, I met this boy from Ushuaia and decided to come and see where he was from.'

The smile that flickered across her landlady's lips made Leo realize she was mistaken. She thought Leo had travelled to the end of the world because of a love affair! Before rectifying her mistake, however, Leo came to the conclusion this would involve a whole number of explanations she wasn't prepared to give, so she let it be.

'I see... How long are you planning to stay? And what are you going to do today?'

'Ah, if only I knew! I've been travelling for four months and I've learned not to plan more than two days ahead. You have to live in the moment!'

The girl heard herself and could barely recognize what she had become... Who would have thought it! The meticulous and organized Leo refusing to plan out each and every one of her movements.

'What would you suggest?' she asked her landlady.

'For sure, I would go sailing on the Beagle Channel. It's a sunny day, and there won't be many of those left...'

'That's the trip that takes you to the Les Eclaireurs Lighthouse, isn't it?'

'That's right. You know it's called the Lighthouse at the End of the World, but it isn't... The real Lighthouse at the End of the World is on Staten Island. But Les Eclaireurs is well worth a visit, though the trip is quite expensive. Three hundred pesos, or something like that.'

Leo wasn't going to give up visiting Les Eclaireurs for anything in the world. After all, that was the reason she'd come so far. Of course she didn't say this to the woman, who was as slender as a reed and eager for stories. At this continental end, all visitors carried essential news on their backs and in their eyes. Down here, a place for solitary adventurers seeking out the Antarctic's white horizon, at the point where the earth turns around, any story from the rest of the planet was received like a blessing to overcome the syndrome of isolation and eternal night. The kitchen clock struck eight in the morning, and still it didn't grow light.

'Is there a time difference between here and Buenos Aires?' murmured Leo into the last mouthful of hot milk.

'No.'

'I mean because it's still night…'

'Oof, you've no idea. We're heading towards the winter solstice, 21 June, in just a month's time. On that day in Tierra del Fuego, we celebrate the longest night, a night that starts at 16:30 and doesn't finish until 9:30. So listen, girl, apart from the intense cold you'll experience outside, you'll need to make the most of the few hours of light if you want to go sightseeing.'

Of course, that was the reason it was low season. That explained why the room had cost no more than twenty pesos, about four euros! Before she had time to complain about this strange inclination to visit such a remote place, Leo put on her coat and went outside.

The early-morning rays revealed to her the first images of this city of less than seventy thousand inhabitants. The nocturnal arrival of the plane had prevented her even imagining its dimensions. She suddenly found herself in a large town of shortish buildings and little houses perched between high, snowy mountains and the tongue of wild sea known as the Beagle Channel. Around her, roofs of corrugated iron with steep slopes to get rid of the weight of accumulated snow. Famished dogs howling into the wind. Strident colours on the house fronts to smother the sadness of night. Steep streets with pensions, bars and pick-up joints. The echo of wolves sliding down the moraines. An ostentatious casino that made a mockery of border tariffs. The Antarctic office. Sailors with weather-beaten skin and circumspect faces. The dry cold of the Martial Glacier. The quay where hundreds, thousands, of Maersk Sealand containers huddled together. They probably all went spinning around the world until grinding to a halt in Ushuaia! Leo wandered down the streets with frozen fingers for two hours, until she realized she'd already discovered the whole urban area. In the port, minutes before taking a sailing trip down the Beagle Channel, she decided it wouldn't be long before she left. This place, she concluded, had nothing special to offer! It was undoubtedly the strangest city she'd ever been in, but that was all. That was all.

And yet during the trip, the sea, calm to start with, bristling with runaway sheep after that, got into her body. The boat was small and comfortable. Inside, the radiators and hot coffees permitted her to store up enough heat so she could then face the elements on deck. The snowy mountains observed the boat's slow progress, and Leo discovered the grandeur of the landscape that surrounded her. Strange birds, unrecognizable sounds, unseen grasses... she felt like an ancient navigator ploughing through unexplored oceans. And also, there it was, the icy wind that whistled like nowhere else in the world. As if it had emerged from the throat of the Antarctic to wander the labyrinths of the planet and here, up close, it had the timbre of a newly born child.

Yes, Edmundo was right, the wind, the blasted wind.

A murmur at the front of the ship drew her in that direction. And then she saw it: the island of the sea lions with their rebellious moustaches and oily bodies. An unexpected hiccup shook Leo's body. She couldn't explain it, but all of a sudden those animals had told her she was there, against all expectation, it wasn't a film, she had reached the End of the World all by herself. Minutes later, enveloped in leaden light, the Les Eclaireurs Lighthouse stared at her, its one electric eye half-open, and Leo's face was covered in tears.

Perhaps it was the angry cold, or the light of the storm, or the emotion, who knows what it was, but she suddenly felt this warm sense of comfort.

She had got there, to the end of the world. All by herself. She'd done it. And nobody could ever rob her of that one second of plenitude, knowing she could do whatever she set out to do. Anything.

All by herself.

# 18

*And that was how the child Cayetano Godino began his lamentable round of reformatories where, instead of making something of him, they turned him into a cold, calculating, idiotic adolescent. Idiotic – that was what his teachers, neighbours, police officers and father thought. Perhaps it was this idiotic appearance that allowed his acts of cruelty to run riot in the suburbs of Buenos Aires, where panic took hold of society. Godino didn't mind. The defencelessness and tenderness of his victims afforded him indescribable pleasure. Feeling in his hands how they breathed their last almost without resistance made him an all-powerful god during the few seconds when they gave up their life. Most of the time, the soft bodies did not rebel against the sentence of condemnation, but faded away without a sound. He didn't feel any remorse, complaint or lament. At least they didn't make fun of him, they didn't beat him, they didn't laugh at him. Because he was dumb. Poor. Crippled. No, they didn't, poor fools, they didn't protest.*

*A dozen names were added to his terrible list, all under five years old, all attacked with the same murder weapon: either the string Godino used as a belt, or fire. And it was always the same temptation that seduced them: a handful of sweets. None of the victims, whether they were murdered or violently assaulted, succeeded in pricking his conscience.*

*And yet his head hurt so much! A monster had got inside, occupied each and every corner of his brain, forcing him to lay angrily into his victims. His head, it wasn't him, it was his head!*

*It was his head... It wasn't him... It wasn't him...*

Leo closed the coarse book on top of half a dozen blankets she had asked for to protect herself against the southerly cold. The story of Petiso Orejudo was awful and yet, she didn't know why, she felt this morbid curiosity. The seduction of horror. As if she couldn't back away from the fire because of a fascination for the flames that consume everything.

She fell asleep on top of a map where she'd learned how the American continent disintegrated into islands, bays, channels, headlands and peninsulas with the fantastic, evocative names of ancient sailors: Tekenika Bay, Cape Wilson, Cook Bay, the Strait of Magellan, Stokes Bay, Clarence Island, Desolation Island, Dumas Peninsula, the Murray Channel... hundreds of geological features that succumbed to the South Pole's glacial cold. Over there, on the so-called Isla Grande de Tierra del Fuego, which men with set squares had divided between Chile and Argentina on the basis of an imaginary line, the last bones of the spine of the Andes sank into the ocean with all the majesty of a Pleistocene dinosaur's tail. The column of America broke apart sometimes in the worn vertebrae of soft bays and gentle gulfs, others in the sharp canines of cliffs and hellish capes where winds from everywhere came together and only storms were able to nest. Their names rocked her to sleep, causing hiccups to windward: Sarmiento Island, Gable Island, the Le Maire Strait, Mitre Peninsula, Good Success Bay, Guanaco Point, Nassau Bay, Stewart Island... And there, sheltered from the blasphemies of the Atlantic and Pacific waters dizzily colliding with each other, there she was: Leo. In the southernmost city in the world: Ushuaia.

Ushuaia – its very name conjured up the ferociousness of the elements.

# 19

@ALeo90
I'm 12,251.85 km away from home,
fascinated by the never-ending night.
Ushuaia will be the furthest point on this
journey without return... Lots of love!
22 May 2011 at 8:00

Leo regretted the tweet as soon as she'd published it. God damn it, her mother would be unbearable when it came to that bit about the 'journey without return'. Metaphors had never been her strong point and, ever since she'd left home, she'd had to measure every single word so as not to upset her already vulnerable state of mind. She went offline as quickly as possible. She just didn't want, despite the time difference, the bombardment of messages to start, she muttered to herself.

So far away, it was a real pleasure to be able to gaze without commitment.

Dori, her landlady, wished her good morning by placing a bowl of boiled milk in her hands. Minutes later, Leo was on the way out, her dirty rucksack on her back, in search of a laundry and a travel agency that would make it easy to access the Tierra del Fuego National Park. Like everything else in this city, that was far more expensive than she'd envisaged. Well then, when it came to dinner, she'd just have to make do with a packet soup. Again.

By way of compensation, and against all expectations, the excursion was great fun, thanks to a group of friendly Brazilians who didn't stop laughing. They wandered through the forest for hours, in among mosses, the last mistletoe of autumn hanging from the Magellan's beeches, the shade of the lenga and Antarctic beeches, torrents created by the broken dams of beavers, icy lakes and the remains of the ancient Yaghan tribe that had once inhabited this area.

At a given moment, when no one else was looking, Leo took out the plastic jar the owner of the hostel in Buenos Aires had given her and opened it carefully. She placed the mouth of the jar in the direction of the suicidal wind howling angrily like a monster and then covered it quickly. She placed it against her ear and thought yes, something of that icy murmur had been trapped inside the jar. Like the slit in a conch shell with the sound of the roaring sea.

Further down, on the shores of Lapataia Bay, half hidden in a peat bog by the first snow of the year, Leo discovered some sea pink. That's right, sea pink, like the one she'd found in Santo André de Teixido when she'd gone there with her grandmother Carmiña. She kept a sprig in her room in case she needed to place it in someone special's pocket and so conquer their love, as required by tradition.

At this point, Leo realized it was time to start going back.

Sea pink only grows at the earth's extremities.

She had her own world's end tattooed in the pupils of her eyes.

# 20

Leo entered the pension with cramp in parts of her body she didn't even know existed. Inside her skin, there were still lots of places to explore, it seemed!

She wolfed down the packet soup and an *alfajor* next to the fireplace. The attraction of evil weighed more heavily on her instinct than the need to communicate with home, and she went back to the book she'd left on top of her bed.

That was how she found out about the eventual arrest of Cayetano Santos Godino.

*For years, first his youth, then the lack of proof and slippery excuses, had prevented the definitive confinement of the one who'd earned the nickname of 'Big-Eared Midget' – Petiso Orejudo – on account of his protruding ears. An idiot. A wretch. A nobody. But social pressure and his obsession with returning to the scene of the crime permitted the police to piece together the puzzle. They arrested him on the night of 4 December 1912 after he attended the wake of his final victim, the child Jesualdo. Apparently he wanted to make sure the nail he'd hammered into the side of his head to kill him was still embedded in his skull. In a pocket, he had the newspaper cutting that told of his recent crime and the belt he'd used to suffocate the child. Three years old, Jesualdo Giordano. His arrest led him to confess four murders and dozens of failed attempts, but he was again considered a fool. An idiot. A wretch. A nobody.*

*To calm the thirst for revenge of a society horrified by his crimes, the authorities decided to shut him up in Ushuaia Penitentiary, the prison at the end of the world. There, given the unusual nature of the first serial killer in Argentinian history, the doctors couldn't resist coming up with their own diagnosis and making a twisted attempt to bring him back to the straight and narrow.*

*'His ears. The evil must reside in those protruding ears.'*
*Without further ado, they opted for plastic surgery.*

*Inevitably, the results were not what they expected, and his anger grew as the size of his ears diminished. His little victims still failed to prick the conscience of Petiso Orejudo, who showed not the slightest sign of regret.*

*The doctors had to accept the obvious: the evil wasn't in his outer ears, it had got inside and was rattling around inside his head! It beat angrily against his skull and never, but never quietened down. His head... inside his head. What in Buenos Aires had been a high-pitched whistle in Ushuaia had turned into a deafening roar because of the air whooshing around the prison cells. It wasn't his ears, no, it was the wind that had addled his brains. But nobody ever listened to Cayetano Santos Godino.*

*Poor fool... Poor Petiso Orejudo, if only somebody would listen to you, if only somebody would listen to you...*

*My head... it's not me... it's my head. My head, and the wind beating against it... my head.*

Leo fell asleep with only a couple of pages still left to read. She couldn't take any more.

Outside, a gale shook the naked tops of the trees and beat mercilessly against the tinplate roof of the house.

# 21

Waking up for the third time in Ushuaia brought Leo a copious snowfall and a considerable drop in temperature. She had to ask her landlady for another jumper so she could go for a walk and live to tell the tale. That was what she did. The ships anchored in the bay lazed on the icy sea and, on the mountain slopes, the smoke of modern Patagonians defied the cruelty of a winter that was fast approaching. On the eaves of uralite roofs, icicles tinkled like early-morning bells. As the first rays hit them, the ice quickly dissipated, pouring down the city's steep slopes. There was a strong smell of petrol and alcohol. Before the snow had a chance to melt, turning the pure beauty of snowflakes into a dirty ice rink criss-crossed by car wheels, Leo decided to wander slowly in the direction of the old Ushuaia Penitentiary, which was now a museum.

As she passed through the sordidness of a world of muddy tracks, decrepit houses and mournful street lamps on the outskirts of the city, the shadow of Petiso Orejudo clung so closely to her it weighed on her Achilles heel.

In the distance, the prison was like a spaceship, an extraterrestrial object that had been violently set down on that slope overlooking the Beagle Channel.

'A guided tour has just left,' said a girl as she came in, 'hook up with them, it's worth the effort.'

So that was what she did. Leo joined a group of Argentinian retirees paying rapt attention to what the guide was saying. He insisted on extolling the wonders of the prison's design and the model treatment meted out to prisoners, but the walls said something else. The dampness, mould, graffitied surfaces, the ice, corridors where people's breath mingled and created a fine mist, the lack of light and crackling of coal in iron heaters crept into Leo's heart like slugs. The rest of the group didn't seem to register the mercilessness of that place. Perhaps they couldn't hear the sighs of prisoners, the creak of chains, the stench of rotten meat, the lashing of tortures, the tetanus of sawn bars.

So it was that, as the mood of the other visitors was lifted by the guide's narrative expertise, Leo's shrivelled bit by bit, especially when she heard the name of Petiso Orejudo. As soon as it was mentioned, a dull murmur attracted the audience like bees to honey. Leo understood his story was a familiar one; he was a kind of bogeyman to frighten children that already formed part of the Argentinian collective imagination. And yet the girl could not comprehend this morbid fascination. The visit to Petiso's former prison provoked bouts of nervous laughter, but all she felt was a shiver coursing uneasily down her spine.

His belongings, which were poor and miserable, remained motionless and impervious to the passage of time.

When Leo encountered his cold, hostile gaze in a photograph, the stabbing sensation in her Achilles heel gave her painful cramp. The guide was just explaining how the prisoner Santos Godino had died in 1944 in strange circumstances, having been confined there for twenty-one years.

In all that time, he hadn't received a single visit.

The wind, thought Leo, the wind visited Petiso until his final day. It was his only presence, his only companion. That was why it got inside his head. The wind that whistles around the Les Eclaireurs Lighthouse like nowhere else in the world. The wind that rises in the stomach of the Antarctic and has the timbre of a newly born child, before roaring through the labyrinths of the planet. The wind, the blasted wind.

The girl couldn't complete the visit, a knot seized hold of her throat, and she felt she couldn't breathe. She legged it outside and ran full speed until reaching the pension out of breath.

'My girl, you look like you've just seen the devil!' exclaimed Dori when she saw her turn up soaked to the skin and shivering with cold.

She'd seen the devil, she had; that was what she'd seen. Her only wish was to get the hell out of that city of corrugated iron that had filled her veins with cramp and mould. On the other side of the window, it started snowing profusely. The snowflakes enlarged the idea that had whispered to her from inside the prison and had rushed even faster than her to come alongside her suitcase and settle by the mouse of the computer. A ticket, she needed a ticket out of there before the snow confined her to that end of the world until next spring.

Ah, but she was so cold that night she couldn't concentrate and chose to leave the search for a ticket until the following day when she could finally get warm. Something told her this wouldn't be so easy after the terrible storm she'd endured that day.

Suddenly, somebody came along to disturb the freezing night even more. Edmundo had just sent her an invitation to have a conversation on Skype and, without quite knowing why, Leo accepted.

# 22

'I can't believe it, Leo!'

'Good evening, Edmundo, or whatever it is over there. I don't even know where you are,' muttered Leo.

'I can't believe you're in Ushuaia!'

'What's so strange about that? It's just another place.'

'It's not just another place, Leo. It's my home.'

'So what? Does that rule it out as a tourist destination?' snorted the girl. It was some seconds since she'd regretted accepting the Argentinian's invitation to have a conversation. For a moment, she'd forgotten how stubborn and unbearable he could be.

'No, of course not. It just seemed strange, that's all. How's it going?'

'Great. How about you?'

OK then. It was an obvious lie. Things weren't great at all. Leo wanted to get out of that place with all her strength, but she wasn't going to tell Edmundo this, especially after such a hostile welcome.

'Me too. Everything's fine.'

'Well, that's just brilliant.'

The conversation was as chilly as the snowfall outside.

'Say something, woman. Tell me what you've seen. Have you been to the National Park? The ski slopes? The prison?'

'The park and the prison, yes. I liked the former; the latter struck me as simply awful.'

'Oh, it's not so bad! Have you seen the replica of the San Juan de Salvamento lighthouse?'

'No. Where are you now? I hadn't heard from you since Pula.'

Leo was really anxious to find out about Ruth & Co. Her tone of voice abandoned its defensive coldness and became more affectionate.

'Pula? No way. I didn't get that far. Can you imagine me walking with all those lunatics as far as Jerusalem? Not for all the money in the world. I took a plane in Trieste and headed north, visited Amsterdam, Brussels, and now I'm in Gothenburg. I'm just dying to see the northern lights.'

There was suddenly a deep silence. The girl cared nothing about this conversation and just wanted to get out of there. If Edmundo was no longer with Ruth & Co., then there was nothing that interested her about his travels.

'That's hunky-dory, Edmundo. Listen, I have to go now, I've been online too long.'

'I understand, Leo. Actually I wanted to talk to you about something else.'

'What?'

'I need you to do me a favour right away.'

'Right now? It's night-time and it's snowing.'

'I know, but it won't be difficult. I'm going to give you the coordinates of this place and I want you to go there. All you have to do is say your name.'

'You what? Are you out of your mind?'

'Latitude 54° 48' 19.48". Longitude 68° 18' 3.76". Enjoy!'

And without further ado Edmundo disappeared from cyberspace. He must have been joking! How on earth was she going to go out in all that cold? What craziness...! And yet doubt was stronger than fear, and she introduced the coordinates on the Internet so they would give her the exact address. It wasn't difficult. It was a restaurant located two blocks away from her pension. Having chewed over the idea for half an hour with unhealthy curiosity, she said to herself, 'I'll just go and have a look, I don't want to stay with this uncertainty.' No sooner said than done. In the blink of an eye, Leo was dressed and ready to enter the dark night. Along the way, between the gusts of wind, she wondered what dirty business the Argentinian might be involved in now and muttered to herself, 'I'll just have a quick sniff. I'm not going to say my name to anybody.'

She put her hand on the door and simply went in. All the chill was trapped under the worn doormat. Inside, she was welcomed by this intense heat and the sweet smell of grilled meat. Leo sat down at the counter and ordered a beer. At the far end of the restaurant, a dozen guests were tucking into some roast lamb and chorizos.

'I don't suppose you're Leo?' The waiter's unexpected question almost made her fall off her stool.

'Me? Um, no!' she replied defensively.

The man looked at her disbelievingly, but didn't say anything. She carried on sipping her beer while quickly pondering Edmundo's intentions. All she could come up with were turbid affairs, so she kept quiet. Boh, she'd been stupid to listen to him and go outside. In the dining room, the satisfied voices of people savouring succulent cuts of meat roared out loud. That was funny. At the furthest table, the group of Brazilians from the day before were having dinner. They invited her to join them, but she had to turn them down. She didn't have any money and hadn't planned for such an expense in her tight budget, so she went back to her almost empty glass and drained the dregs. Yes, it had been stupid to listen to Edmundo.

'Are you sure you're not Leo?' insisted the waiter one last time.

'No, of course not. I have to go now.'

She suddenly felt something akin to fear. Would you believe it, complicating her life when she was so far away from home, just in order to humour Edmundo! Damn fool! How could she have done what he wanted? Wasn't it enough what they'd been through in Marrakesh? He was probably mixed up in drugs or smuggling or something, and this was a password to confirm a delivery or something like that.

'Well, that's a shame,' said the waiter mockingly. 'This Leo, she was invited to have dinner thanks to the generosity of my favourite nephew. He called from Europe less than an hour ago, but the girl hasn't turned up. A real shame, don't you think? Just smell the delicious fragrance coming from those chorizos and all that offal.'

'Yes, it smells wonderful, she doesn't know what she's missing.'

Of course, Leo, stubborn as she was, wasn't going to back down now and she left the restaurant with all her dignity trailing down her back. Boh! What did dignity matter at a time like that, if she'd gone and missed out on a dinner! The smell of roast meat clung to her hair and made her even more irate. On the other side of the window, the Brazilians roared with laughter and, all alone in the middle of the snow, Leo felt like crying. How could she have been so distrustful? All good, old Edmundo had wanted to do was fill her belly! When she got back to the pension, rage gave way to uncontrollable laughter.

The guy in the restaurant must have thought she was off her head! The rumbling of her famished intestines must still be echoing around the walls of the dining room. How stupid she had been... How stupid and untrusting!

Before heading to bed, she emitted a good-night tweet:

@ALeo90
Happy dreams! This will be my last night
in Ushuaia. But I'm staying in Patagonia.
It's the most fascinating place in the world.
For now, at least!
23 May 2011 at 20:17

She then went to bed, stocked up with books and with the firm intention of choosing her next destination.

Nothing would stop the night overwhelming her with nightmares and shivers. To her hunger was added a dull, thumping headache that landed almost noiselessly inside her head.

And besides, something had been bothering Leo ever since her conversation with Edmundo. There was something, something not quite right about what he'd said, and she didn't know what it was. However hard she tried, she just couldn't fathom the reason for her unease... That was it! There are no northern lights in the summer! They are visible between September and March! Why on earth did the Argentinian keep on lying to her?

Uncomfortable doubt and that stubborn throbbing behind her temples just wouldn't leave of their own free will. No, they wouldn't.

Quite the opposite, in fact.

My goodness, she was hungry!

## 23

'Oh, Dori, I thought I would die of cold last night… Do you have any paracetamol? My head… it doesn't hurt a lot, but… it's really quite unpleasant.'

'Listen, girl, you should get out of here as soon as you can. Go away while you still can. Go away.'

Something in Dori's voice told Leo it wasn't just the effects of the *corralito* keeping the brave Buenos Aires woman there. Something sickly and horrifying, which she wanted to chase away.

'Ah, Dori, don't get all sentimental, otherwise I'll take you with me!'

'Oh yes? Where are you going?'

'El Calafate!' Leo let out the words she'd been guarding on the tip of her tongue for the last two hours.

If the nocturnal cold, hunger and migraine – all together, mixed up and helped by the photographs in the books – had achieved something, it was to sweep away the doubts regarding her next destination. A look on the Internet before dawn had ended up convincing her: in exchange for two hours by plane and sixty euros, she would have the famous Perito Moreno Glacier before her!

'El Calafate… impressive,' murmured Dori nostalgically, and Leo knew she'd made the right decision.

The plane was leaving at two in the afternoon, and Leo used this time to organize her last visit to the city, even though she didn't much feel like it.

Suddenly, in the street, she realized an obstinate shadow was still clinging to her Achilles heel. Petiso Orejudo and his ball and chain were not going to abandon her until she departed from Ushuaia. Neither the prisoner, nor the feeble tweeting of the decapitated robins, nor the children buried beneath a heap of cans or strangled with shoelaces. Nor the wind. An idiot. A wretch. That was Santos Godino: a nobody.

Ah, but perhaps it wasn't him, perhaps it was just his head, his head...

Cramp seized hold of her leg, but she paid no attention. In the light of the sun, the city looked luminous, and of the mournful and macabre appearance of the night before nothing remained. Tired of constantly retracing her steps along central streets, she decided to go down paths she hadn't taken before, until she reached the port. In the distance, she glimpsed a familiar silhouette. That wasn't possible! It was a stone cross! She went over, feeling greater amusement than curiosity: a roadside cross in Ushuaia. But as she approached, she discovered the roadside cross, so typical in Galicia, wasn't the major surprise or anything like it. Before she spotted the plaque that identified the cross as a tribute to Galician emigrants, she discovered a torn sheet with unmistakable red letters. The cotton had been frayed by the rain and was covered in mud, but there could be no doubt.

No way, she wasn't prepared for this. For the snowfall, the cold, the loneliness, the hunger, the elements of that world's end, yes, but not for this:

### i love you leo a.

Leo burst into inconsolable sobs. On later reflection, which was only possible when the headache let up, she would blame the nostalgia she'd felt on account of the cross, the snowfall, the cold, the loneliness, the hunger and the elements, but the fact is she cried because of that message she hadn't been expecting.

And she'd missed so much.

Who cared right now who'd left it? The fact was she suddenly felt less alone. Less terribly alone. She noticed a warm breath on the back of her neck and could have sworn somebody was watching her but, against all rational logic, she wasn't afraid, she was comforted. This somebody, whoever it was, must have been following her all the time to keep her company. Silently and subtly, but keeping her company, all the same, and that was a wonderful gift in that icy, southerly corner.

At this point, Petiso Orejudo took a bite out of her heels, and Leo ran away.

She went back to the pension and stuffed her miserable possessions into her rucksack. Her clothes, notebook, washbag, passport, money, rustic book the owner of the hostel in Buenos Aires had lent her. And the jar stuffed full of wind, of course. She hoisted her luggage on to her back and gave an affectionate hug to Dori, that needle-like woman with the large head and slim body who kept introducing the words 'corralito' and 'Peronism' into every sentence like a litany.

'Leo, sometimes it's not good to run away eternally. Believe me. Others, there isn't much choice...'

The girl wasn't quite sure why, but she felt happy to leave that city with its frozen bars. And irascible wind sweeping across the surface of the Beagle Channel and Navarino Island to smash you against the canines of Cape Horn.

On the plane, she doodled at the front and back of her notebook.

At the back, she did her sums: on her arrival in Argentina, she had 1,450 euros in her pocket for transport costs and another 1,140 euros for daily expenses. On the flights from Buenos Aires to Ushuaia and from there to El Calafate, she had spent 160 euros, which she needed to take off the 1,450 euros for travel. So far, so good. As for her living expenses, she had spent six nights in Argentina, which had involved the payment of 50 euros for accommodation, a far cry from Europe! Entrance to the National Park, the prison, and the trip down the Beagle Channel had involved another 85 euros, even though she'd practically reduced her daily diet to hot soups and *alfajores*. So, she had 1,290 euros for travel and 1,005 euros for daily expenses. The illusion of dividing prices in Argentinian pesos by five and a half to work out the cost in euros had been a trap and given her the sensation she was spending less than she really was. There was no denying the figures. It wasn't a lot or a little, but she would have to tighten her belt if she wanted to complete her most optimistic travel plans. All the same, she hadn't gone past the psychological barrier of a thousand euros for daily expenses, and that was a relief. While there was still some money in the account, it meant her journey wasn't nearing its end.

At the front of her notebook, as the peaks of Mount Olivia and the Five Brothers disappeared on the horizon, revealing the naked ridge of the Andean dinosaur's tail, Leo wrote down that excerpt from Calvino's book that had been beating against her temples for several days.

Ah, Octavia! This city is over the void, in a precipice:

> *Suspended over the abyss, the life of Octavia's inhabitants is less uncertain than in other cities. They know the net will last only so long.*

In Ushuaia, there was nowhere to escape to.

Further on, there was only the abyss.

'I Love You Leo A.' – that was what it had said on that sheet hanging from the cross.

**I Love You Leo A.**

# 24

@ALeo90
The snowstorm doesn't let me see past
the wild snowflakes and roaring wind.
I hope it clears in time for Perito Moreno!
24 May 2011 at 18:35

The last stretch of the journey was shaken by turbulence. For a few unending minutes, they weren't sure whether they would be able to land in El Calafate or, on the contrary, the storm would force them to turn around and go back to Ushuaia. If to this we add the growing headache, Leo would have had to confess that those two hours became a real inferno of tremors inside and outside of her head. Fortunately, just as the captain had announced their decision to head back south, an unexpected let-up in the weather allowed them to land. The tense silence was followed by grateful applause, and the girl, who had always thought this custom of cheering the cockpit to be totally dumb, found herself banging her palms together in relief at being back on firm ground. Just half an hour later, she was placing her weary rucksack inside the shelter of another pension, the price of which was almost a joke in low season. She would have to pay 25 pesos per night, less than five euros!

The girl soon found out she was the only guest of a grumbling, unsympathetic old man who, instead of welcoming her, criticized her for being late. Poor Leo was running so low on energy she couldn't even reply. She took her key and sought refuge in the enormous bedroom. The room catered for at least eight people but, given there was nobody else there, she spread her belongings over all the beds. That way, at least her clothes wouldn't smell of damp. She was still arranging her things when the man in charge of the pension called to her. To her amazement, he informed her he left every night to go and sleep somewhere else, so he was giving her the front-door keys together with some instructions regarding the lights, the fridge, the microwave, the heating and the fireplace. Oh, and he also wrote down an emergency telephone number – for use only in dire necessity, he warned. That was what he said. Leo understood that fear of the dark on a Patagonian steppe did not count as 'dire necessity' and didn't protest. She heard the dull thud of the bolt being drawn and the desperate groan of the storm at one and the same time. Deep down, despite her initial unease, she didn't mind being alone and prepared to relax, even though it was only for one night. Or so she thought.

The first thing she did was fill the bathtub with boiling water and put in enough soap to make a layer of foam at least two fingers thick. When she got in the water, the world stopped roaring, and for more than an hour all she could hear was the gentle plop-plop of her skin against the swirling motion of the water. In that bathtub, the rotten sea resisted the gale blowing outside. How nice. Sometimes the most wonderful pleasures in the world are to be found where we least expect them, in those daily routines which, because they're repeated, seem insignificant, but which we only miss when they're not there. A hot bath. A cup of tea. A crackling fire. Soft music. A sofa all to yourself.

Outside, the snowstorm banged against the uralite and the fuel tank but, inside, paradise had come to enfold her in its warm embrace.

Leo fell asleep thanks to the soothing effects of paracetamol and a triple layer of blankets. She hadn't understood very well how the heating worked, and the night threatened to convert that room into an iceberg.

Luckily, the only thing she'd got wrong was the bit about the timer for the heating, and she awoke very early to the shouts of the landlord accusing her of wasting fuel.

'Damn girl! It must be twenty-three degrees in here, at least!' she heard him shouting in the distance, but she didn't care. She'd been longing for some heat for so long that any temperature struck her as insufficient to drive away the elements she'd had to endure in Ushuaia.

When she finally got up, she pushed back the shutters to discover what strange world lay outside that tinplate house. To her immense surprise, she saw nothing. Absolutely nothing. The snowstorm carried on shaking the world and, in that warm refuge, all she could do was wait for the mist to decide for her.

That was what her bad-tempered host told her.

'In this place, girl, it's the sky in charge, not men,' he muttered through rotten teeth.

The sky sent a flurry of wind and snow that kept her inside the pension all day long. It was 25 May 2011, and no doubt her brother, Roi, and the group from Barbanza would be inaugurating the bathing season on Aguieira Beach. They would know the temperature of the water and the movements of the sand that changed the beach's appearance every year... Here, however, on the other side of the globe, she couldn't see more than a handspan past the window in front of her! Having had breakfast, she sighed a couple of times, her gaze lost on the landscape hidden behind that white blanket stirred up by a devilish wind.

'You can forget about going outside. It's the sky in charge in this place, not men,' remarked the hostel owner again. As he spoke, a cloud of halitosis spread through the room with the same force as the storm beating on the other side of the walls.

Two and a half hours later, with all her clothes nicely washed and dry, having completed a fine tuning of her body that included cutting and painting her nails, sorting out the rebellious hairs sticking up on her head, waxing her legs and spreading moisturizing cream from top to toe, Leo sighed again at the window.

'There's a bit of food in the cupboard. Don't go out today. It's the sky in charge in this place, not men.'

That was all her landlord said before slamming the door and going away. Leo wouldn't see him again all day and had to accept another bunch of lonely hours awaited her. For this reason, having veered between desire and responsibility for the last few days, the girl finally gave in: she would go online and emit something more than a tweet. She was a little afraid that solitude would transform into a monster, and even more so that contact with home would increase her nostalgia, but she went ahead anyway. After all, she would have to face up to it eventually and, ever since reaching Argentina, all she'd done was hang out a few remnants on the clothes line of Twitter without having a chance to learn what was happening on the other side of the world.

She sat down in front of a computer that was newer than anything else in the pension and pressed the magic keys that would allow her to open the door to the people she missed. There, piled up inside her inbox, were the names and words of those she loved, on the one hand, and those she simply knew, on the other. Distance makes it easier to distinguish between one's emotions.

Her brother, Roi, usually so sparing with words, had sent at least a dozen messages. He was the first sender Leo permitted to tell his story. She was amazed. Really amazed. A quick perusal of his hasty lines told her no sooner had he returned to Santiago from Paris than he'd joined a protest movement camping out in Obradoiro Square. This social movement, nicknamed 15-M, set out to denounce the corruption of the political system, the perversion of the economic system, and to raise its voice in favour of a more equitable form of democracy. The demonstrations and occupation of public space had spread throughout Spain, with less than a week to go before the local and regional elections due to be celebrated on 22 May. Their objective was to make society reflect on the meaning of their vote and to arouse a greater sense of commitment among the political classes. Roi told her all about it with unbridled enthusiasm. He sent her photos, videos and dozens of mails in which he talked about his unconditional support for the movement, their mother's monumental tantrum ('If you fail a single exam at the end of the year, you'll know about it, lazybones!'), the discomfort of sleeping out on an inflatable mattress for someone in his condition, the infinite acts of kindness of a certain Patricia (in only three paragraphs, Leo came across the word 'pretty' twice, 'treasure' four times and 'clever' five) and, most surprisingly of all, how their father had spent a couple of afternoons joining the camp-out! Leo couldn't believe it. Her father? Part of a public demonstration? Roi had foreseen her surprise and hastened to add that their father hadn't actually intervened, but had been spotted among the hundreds of people filling the square.

He'd even smiled, he added, and clapped with his hands aloft, waggling his fingers.

Leo was stunned by what she read. All this had happened in less than a week! She glanced at the calendar with curiosity. It was 25 May, which meant the local and regional elections had already taken place. Who was the new mayor of Santiago? She consulted some online newspapers to discover the face of the town hall's next occupant and was further amazed. It seemed the difference in votes between those in government until then and the opposition was so small that various appeals had been lodged and the new mandate hadn't even started yet. A handful of ballots, no more, would decide the identity of the new official! Her own vote could be decisive! She lamented the indifference that had blinded her for so long, especially when she lied to her grandmother Carmiña – 'Yes, grandma, I've voted already!' Her grandmother always said universal suffrage – in particular votes for women – was a right won by the blood and toil of many and should not be despised. If she didn't like anybody, she could always express that opinion on her ballot paper or even put herself forward as a candidate!

Leo thought about all this as the storm beat about outside with unusual ferocity.

After her astonishment at Roi's news, the rest of the deluge of messages only served to increase her nostalgia. There was mother with her complaints about her brother's crazy behaviour; Aunt Cris, always so worried and affectionate; three emails from Aldara with unimportant news about the theatre group; five messages from the book group *Read, Read, What Are You Reading?* with effusive literary recommendations about the most eminent Argentinian authors; another from Edmundo, asking her about dinner in Ushuaia; and two she may have been expecting, or not. One from Andrés, and another from Martiño. From the Mexican, she learned that the rest of Ruth & Co. were in Thessaloniki on their way to Jerusalem. Apparently, in Greece, they had encountered a truly alarming situation owing to the government's cutbacks, with the economic crisis as an excuse, and had decided unanimously to join the street protests. It was a question of ethics, the boy declared.

So far away, Leo had the impression the world was falling apart in old Europe and she wasn't there to be a witness, an accomplice or a restraint during this cataclysm. And yet here, in El Calafate, reality was reduced to a thick, damp, sterile mist. The only storm blowing about in Patagonia was one of snow and wind blasting outside, causing each and every beam inside that tinplate house to shudder.

She was about to open Martiño's message when she pulled back and decided to answer the other mails, to show signs of life and respond to all that affection and solidarity. The task took her quite a while. When she'd finished, she decided the best thing would be to search for information about El Calafate so she could organize her visits over the coming days.

Evidently, any excuse would do so long as she didn't have to open Martiño's message.

She then wrapped herself up to her ears and went outside. She hadn't taken more than two steps before she fell to the ground on account of the strength of the wind and had to return to the pension. She took another paracetamol in an attempt to subdue that devilish headache that was turning into a torture. She then recalled her landlord's words:

'It's the sky in charge in this place, girl, not men.'

He was clearly right.

# 25

At dawn on 26 May 2011, Leo was so bored she didn't know what to do to overcome the sense of isolation on account of the storm. As soon as she woke up, she'd run to the window only to find out, to her horror, that the snow was still falling. Despair began to take hold of her body. She couldn't visit the city, or the glaciers, or even leave that place because the airport had been closed for two days on account of the severe weather. 'Patience,' Leo repeated to herself, 'patience. There's always sunshine after the rain.' On top of that, her landlord hadn't shown his face all morning. She couldn't believe she could even miss his stinking breath! He was the only person she could talk to!

She spent the morning reading any book she could find in the library of the hostel, whose every corner, leak, noise, smell, she was now familiar with. All these guides increased her eagerness to find out what was beyond that white, wounding mist. The photographs of the glaciers and tales of travellers who had set foot in Patagonia down through the centuries fired her imagination. So it was she learned about the famous writer Bruce Chatwin and his search for the brontosaurus. Guided by his pen, she followed in the footsteps of Butch Cassidy and the Sundance Kid, American outlaws who'd fled to the Argentinian steppes, and also of the Galician Antonio Soto, a syndicalist who'd taken the anarchist revolution into Patagonia. Thanks to Luis Sepúlveda's *Patagonia Express*, she flew over Patagonian estates in a light aircraft and wept in prison. With Leila Guerriero and her suicides at the end of the world, she learned that the wind and solitude can turn into your worst enemy and fiercest ally against hope on the petrol flats of Las

Heras in the province of Santa Cruz. The tales of expeditions by Darwin, Florence Dixie, Perito Moreno and FitzRoy increased her anxiety to discover the amazing landscapes that must surely be waiting on the other side of the glass, behind that blinding snowstorm.

Knock, knock, knock!

Some heavy blows on the door pulled her out of her literary navigation along a southern fjord. A hostile gust of wind had toppled the two masts, and the unstable craft that was her thoughts was cast adrift without rudder or sails. It was midday, the storm was whistling about the uralite, and those blows outside managed to frighten her a little bit. And yet some scared voices made her do the unthinkable and open the door. The first thing to come in was the wind. First the gale, then a smattering of snowflakes in her eyes. First the hurricane, then the snow, and finally some peals of laughter.

When the storm cleared in that warm hallway, she made out six shapes hidden beneath innumerable layers of clothing. As the scarves, caps, jackets, earflaps, boots and thermal jerseys were cast aside, there appeared the amusing faces of four young men and two young women. They must have been about her age. The warmth of the hallway permitted some words to emerge from their stalactite-like throats. They were a group of Chilean mountaineers on their way back from a risky expedition in El Chaltén who'd come to spend a few days in El Calafate and visit the famous glacier. They'd obviously mistaken her for the landlady.

'No, no, you're wrong. I'm just another guest. Mr Wolf only comes in the evenings.'

'Oh, that's a shame. We'd been told the landlord was a repellent character, and I thought it must have been a joke.'

'My name's Leo.'

'Fabián, Néstor, Carlos, Felipe, Laura and Marieta. The bathroom?'

All great conversations start with a stupid question, and this was no different. As their swollen bodies left behind the steep harshness of the vertical face of FitzRoy, a sense of joy came to melt the ice. The vapour of tea caused words and laughter to come bubbling out, and Leo learned about these crazy mountaineers' adventures.

'Andinism is pure emotion! If you've never hung off a rope in a glacial chasm, then you don't know what it is to be alive!'

'Andinism?' asked Leo in surprise.

Their laughter echoed around the sitting room.

'That's right, you don't know what it is! It's what you Europeans call Alpinism. You think you're the centre of the world. In South America, we talk about Andinism, as is only to be expected.'

They were great fun, or perhaps not, but so many hours of isolated solitude in that tinplate house made Leo appreciate the warmth of a conversation. The afternoon's emotion didn't last long. The youngsters were so exhausted they went to sleep before the landlord arrived, and silence took hold once more inside that uralite cave being shaken by a devilish wind.

Despair led Leo back first to the books with fantastical names and maps, then to the spaceship that was the Internet. She didn't much feel like writing, because she had nothing to tell, and it seemed things were the same on the other side of the world, because there were no new messages. All she could do was click on the unopened envelopes that had been there for weeks, almost all of them from Martiño.

No, she wouldn't do that. Whenever she was sad, Martiño's emails only served to heighten her nostalgia.

And yet, an hour later, overcome by uncertainty and the niggling pain behind her temples, Leo pressed the key that would take her into Martiño's world. She didn't know what to expect, she never did, but it wasn't what she read.

The boy told her he had spent five and a half months as an intern in some institution and worked all the time carrying out tasks that had nothing to do with him. There was no point complaining, however. The drop in civil servants' salaries, first, and then the budget cuts had been only the beginning in a succession of cutbacks that increased the number of tasks while reducing the available resources. Interns were next on the list, and the threat of this service being eliminated and its duties being taken over by another, higher department hung in the air. He wasn't worried – he had no hopes of staying there once his year-long internship was over, the question now was whether he could get through the first semester. And the worst thing was he didn't know where to go. The economic crisis had hit so hard it eradicated any project, any hope of finding a decent job. He'd thought of going abroad to improve his German. Apparently the German Chancellor was looking for technical staff for the companies in her country. That might not be such a bad option, and he was keen to know her opinion. 'What do you say, Leo? What should I do with my life? I can't talk to anybody here because we're all in the same boat. My mother would tell me not to emigrate, not to do the same as her, she's regretted it all her life. She went to Switzerland at the age of twenty and didn't come back until she was in her forties. When she had me, she decided they couldn't look after me and they left me in Galicia with my grandparents.

She keeps saying she's never forgiven herself for missing out on my childhood. When they did finally come back, I couldn't call them Mum and Dad and they were of no fixed abode, like migratory birds. But I'm not to blame for their mistakes, am I, Leo? It may be a good opportunity. What do you say, Leo? What should I do with my life?'

Leo didn't know what to reply, and so she didn't reply anything.

# 26

'Come dance with me.'

'What's that, Martiño? You're off your head.'

'They just said if you want to, go ahead and dance.'

'We're in the auditorium. It's not the best place in the world to do a dance routine.'

'Listen. *Dancer, dance with her, dancer, dance with her; she has such a pretty face, she's like a Magdalena; dancer, dance with her...*'

'Hey, be quiet, let me listen. You must be kidding. That's one of my favourite songs.'

'I know.'

Leo hadn't danced. They'd been at a concert of Berrogüetto, her favourite group. Outside the auditorium, it was pouring down. How to forget the music, the applause, the lights, the songs, she just loved their latest album! They were celebrating Martiño's name day, barely two months before the date set for their departure. The boy had invited her to the concert and then for drinks and she, stupid thing, had thought it was so he could tell her something. Deep down, she still had a glimmer of hope that he might change his mind. That he might say, 'Leo, I'm coming with you. I'm not going to leave you now. I also am dying to live out your journey.'

But he hadn't changed his mind.

He'd only asked her to dance with him.

That was all.

And she hadn't wanted.

No, she would never dance with him again.

The memory of that night of water and *alalás* had climbed on to the back of the storm howling outside, in the heart of

Argentinian Patagonia. Luckily, before going offline and letting nostalgia take hold of her, it had occurred to Leo to consult the weather forecast. Her heart gave a leap inside her chest. Inexplicably, the weather was set to improve in El Calafate the very next day! Finally, the storm would clear. She could visit Perito Moreno and get out of there before the weather cut them off again. Her fingers rushed over the keys to discover what possibilities there were for a tourist. She came to the conclusion there were three viable options: a visit to the walkways located opposite the glacier (80 pesos); a walk on the ice wearing cleats (500 pesos); or a trip along the northern channel of Lake Argentino on a catamaran (350 pesos). To that would have to be added the hundred pesos it cost to enter the National Park. A hundred pesos! A total ruin!

That alone almost exceeded her daily budget, but such an opportunity made Leo place reality before her plans. She would walk on the glacier. Yes. She would take one less flight on the continent if it was necessary, but she would walk on the glacier. You have to take life as it comes, and she was fed up of renouncing things because of her restricted budget. 'A day's a day, and the peso's been spent!' Grandma Carmiña would say. That was how it was. Leo decided she would relinquish two hundred euros for that wonderful craziness called Perito Moreno.

How to deny that Martiño's email had occupied her thoughts while taking this decision! Life only comes along once and, besides, when would she have the chance to come back to El Calafate, so many thousands of kilometres away from home?

The night was a journey through the storm of coughs, snorts and sighs of her new room-mates.

# 27

Leo couldn't believe it! It was snowing again! She rapped her knuckles violently against the windowsill.

'It's the sky in charge in this place, not men,' muttered the foul-breathed landlord behind her. 'The snow will leave this afternoon. I can feel it. Listen, girl, are you sure those Chilean mountaineers arrived early this morning?'

Leo was still in the grip of sleep and almost put her foot in it. A smothered cough by Fabián brought her to her senses.

'Oh yes, of course, Mr Wolf. They arrived early this morning, before it was light. Why do you ask?'

The old man snorted distrustfully, but didn't ask again. His hangover didn't permit him to be talkative.

They spent the afternoon playing cards in front of the burning fireplace. Her first impression had not been wrong – they really were a fun group, and their adventures in the mountains left her feeling stunned. The following year, they would travel to Tibet to climb the smallest of the eight-thousanders, Shishapangma, without oxygen. They planned to climb the fourteen roofs of the world in under a decade. They had to start at once so they could scale Mt Everest before they were thirty-five! It may have been an exaggeration – not to mention their tale of prehistoric remains found on a Bolivian summit near Lake Titicaca, which cast doubt on its Aymara past. A fantasy on a level with the delirious climb up the volcano Tungurahua in Ecuador just as it was erupting! But Leo decided to let them talk. While they talked, she didn't have to, and that snowstorm had stolen all her words. Would it really never stop snowing?

'Forty! I win with an ace!'

At that precise moment, her luck changed. The wind died suddenly, and the moon peered out from between the clouds.

'Come on, let's go outside! Down to the lake!'

She didn't have time to think twice about it and was already outside, every inch of her skin covered. Not before time! It took them less than an hour to cross the city, barely 12,000 inhabitants huddled together in a dozen streets. Dirty snow had been piled up on the pavements beneath the tracks of slowly-circulating vans. Stray dogs barked at the darkness, and only a few tremulous lights indicated those restaurants that were still working in low season. Almost all the hotels had hung up a sign saying 'closed' and wouldn't open again for several months, but fortunately the smell of roast lamb was starting to pervade the streets. The let-up in the storm's furious concert had brought people out of their houses. A few children were building snowmen while their mothers used this opportunity to stock up on supplies from the supermarket. Inside, ranchmen – black and red berets, tanned skin, thick hands, distrustful gaze – stuffed alcohol and cans in paper bags. Drunks, clinging to the street lamps, howled at the solitary moon. Their group was a knife of laughter that slashed open the icy city's silent stomach. And with the same softness with which they'd entered, they headed back to the suburbs, right next to the lake where pink flamingos nest in spring.

'Hey, what are you doing? Are you crazy?'

The youngsters started throwing stones and listening attentively to the sounds while focusing all their attention on the surface of the water.

'Perfect, it's perfect! It's thick enough to take our weight.'

Néstor opened a rucksack and took out some skates with sharp blades that glinted in the moonlight.

'OK, by turns. One after the other! We can't risk going all together in case the ice breaks.'

The consistency of the ice sheet was good enough and, one by one, they disappeared over the stony surface of the lake. Each silhouette danced and melancholically swayed its torch from side to side, causing flashes of electric light to bounce against the frozen mirror. When it was her turn, Leo wanted to back out, but there was something in that black mouth that drew her on irresistibly. She'd never skated before, not even on the ice rinks set up in the mall each Christmas, and she felt her feet sliding out of control on that slippery surface. It took her a couple of minutes to gain her balance and really enjoy the strange sensation of dancing between the ice and the sky.

Before going back to the pension, they decided to reward their famished stomachs with a nice roast and some bottles of Malbec, which started off being two and ended up being who knows how many.

Leo's headache flared up and, despite the paracetamol, it took her several hours to get to sleep.

When the clock finally struck seven in the morning, Leo discovered to her amazement that it still hadn't snowed that morning. She could finally visit the glacier!

> @ALeo90
> The fury has stopped, today I will see
> the famous Perito Moreno! Not in photos
> or in others' stories. With my own little eyes!
> 28 May 2011 at 7:35

She got up and dressed quickly before heading to the bus station to catch a bus to the National Park. She paid eighty pesos for the excursion and another hundred for entering the park, and waited patiently. Today, she would visit the walkways; the following day, she would pay for a walk on the ice – two extraordinary days lay in front of her! You bet they did! The sky gradually changed from black to an intense blue, having spattered itself with red blood for a few short minutes. The emotion hardly let her breathe.

After eighty kilometres of guanacos, low shrubs and gravel, they came to the Curve of Sighs.

And Leo knew the wait had been worthwhile.

When two fat tears slid down her face, she knew it had been worthwhile.

Wow!

# 28

*The Perito Moreno Glacier is located in the southern arm of Lake Argentino, at exactly latitude 50° 32' south, longitude 73° 10' west. It rises out of the immensity of the Southern Patagonian Ice Field and consists of a front that is five kilometres long and more than sixty metres high. Every year, the massive white sheet slowly advances. When it joins the land at the tip of the Península de Magallanes, it forms an icy tongue that is eroded by the pressure of the waters, forming the so-called Canal de los Témpanos. The shattering of this cave is a natural spectacle that occurs approximately every four years.*

Boh! However much Leo read the information panel, the words made very little impression compared to the wonder rising in front of her eyes!

Leo leaned on the railing and blinked a couple of times. She then glanced anxiously at her watch. She had more than three hours to go along the walkways that descended the side of the mountain opposite the glacier. Before paying for her ticket, it had seemed enough, but now she wasn't so sure. She started bounding down the steps of those zigzag ramps and yet, however hard she tried, she couldn't take her eyes off the icy beast. She couldn't explain it. Each cluster of light, each ray of sun, each cloud, each gust of fresh wind or gentle breeze changed the appearance of the irregular back with its metal edges and velvet clods. She'd never seen so many different blues and whites in all her life. She'd never imagined so many tons could dance between the colours of the sky and the deep. Its transparency allowed you to glimpse the icy tongue's different layers until you reached the most primitive strata that had turned solid thousands of years before. In front of her eyes was an open-pit mine of precious stones made of ice. There was sapphire, turquoise, opal, aquamarine, lapis lazuli made of glass that melted in the fire of her voracious gaze. Meanwhile, at her feet, the surface of Lake Argentino reminded her of delicate jade, a solid matt green that arose from the dead waters of fragments of the glacier. Leo was afraid this ephemeral Ali-Baba treasure might suddenly disappear if only she blinked. That was why she opened her eyes wide until they wept with emotion.

At this early hour of the morning, the walkways were almost deserted but, as time progressed and the sun climbed on to its perch, they began to fill with sighs and applause. Opposite her, on top of the glacier, tiny lines of people with their crampons scratched the majestic back that was covered in hillocks and chasms. Those must be members of the Big Ace excursion Leo planned to join the following day! Down below, on the lake, the catamarans looked like feeble paper boats next to the vast vertical wall.

The hours went by, as did the changes in the body of that extraordinary animal with its icicled body Leo hadn't even imagined. It was truly fantastical!

When she came to and looked at her watch, she almost fell over backwards. It was five minutes after the time arranged for their return to El Calafate. Oh, what a mess if she missed the bus and had to pay another forty pesos for the return journey! She ran as fast as she could up the walkways, but fortunately the bus hadn't left yet. Despite the cold, none of the passengers had gone on board – as if drawn by an invisible magnet, they continued to gaze at the glacier's beauty. There were hundreds of people. Perhaps the snowfall of the preceding days had kept all the tourists in their tinplate houses, and now there they were, standing motionless, savouring their prize, proud of the stoical patience that had withstood the onslaught of the storm. Every single one of them, as they turned away from the glacier, had a look of painful resignation, as of somebody losing a valued treasure they may never recover. Leo, however, was smiling. She was due to come back the following day and then she would walk on Perito Moreno.

As the bus pulled away, tears lined the travellers' nostalgic faces, and that was when Leo saw it. On the walkway, a white, docile sheet, rivalling the snow on the glacier's surface:

**I Love You Leo A.**

Leo saw it and yet didn't see it, because the emotion took her breath away.

No 'I Love You Leo A.' could compare with the beauty of that glacier reflected in the bus' rear-view mirror. This reptile of prehistoric ice seemed to be sobbing timidly behind her.

Its light blinded her all the way back.

# 29

'I can't be sure. The predicted storm is terrible, and I have to guarantee the safety of all our participants. Give me the name of your hotel, and we'll let you know if it's possible to do the Big Ace tomorrow. But don't get your hopes up. The forecast is for wind and snow for at least the next four days. They'll probably have to close the airport again.'

All the happiness that had surrounded Leo during the eighty kilometres back from the National Park to El Calafate came crashing down at her feet. Adrenalin upped her pulse and misted her powers of reasoning. She couldn't think. She had to take a decision as quickly as possible, but she wasn't prepared for this. Damn it, she had the whole thing planned out. Tomorrow she would join the group of mountaineers for a walk on the glacier and then they would have a dinner of pizza and Bariloche beer. That was what they'd agreed before saying goodbye that morning, as the others headed for the catamaran to sail across Lake Argentino. Just when she'd finally found some new friends to break the absolute solitude with which Argentina had received her! But that crude meteorological threat had gone and spoiled everything... Wasn't there a chance the forecast might be wrong?

'It's the sky in charge in this place, not men,' grunted the owner of the adventure company, and Leo had the impression everybody in that place was singing from the same hymn sheet.

For a few seconds, the girl remained sitting on a bench outside. A polar wind started beating furiously against her cheeks and shook the signs that showed the distance in kilometres from El Calafate to other points on the planet. She read: 'Madrid, 12,726 km'. It was five in the afternoon, night was on the way, and she had to reach a decision. She took a deep breath and got up with an overwhelming sense of defeat. She walked back to the pension, defying the icy weather, and went online. Ten minutes later, she gathered together all her things, stuffed them into her rucksack and left two notes on the table before rushing outside. She almost had a disaster when the jar of Ushuaia wind for the owner of the hostel in Buenos Aires slipped out of her hands. She'd almost forgotten it, and he wouldn't be pleased if she broke it now!

In one of the notes, Leo took her leave of the group of Andinists.

Beneath the other, she placed the payment for her stay.

'To the airport, please,' she said to the taxi-driver.

And with that she left.

On the final flight of the day heading to Buenos Aires, having managed to get a last-minute seat for the modest price of fifty euros, Leo gave in and took another paracetamol.

That blasted headache.

In her notebook, she did the final accounts for Patagonia. She'd landed in El Calafate four days earlier with 1,290 euros for travel and 1,005 for living expenses. She'd spent a hundred pesos on the pension and another hundred at the supermarket (toothpaste, *alfajores*, sanitary towels, soups, cold meat, bread), which was the equivalent of forty euros, more or less.

She'd set aside another two hundred euros – making a huge economic effort, aware she might have to do without some aerial destination – for the two excursions to the National Park but, in the end, she'd only spent forty, having had to cancel the walk with cleats. That meant she had 1,240 euros for transport and 925 euros for daily expenses. In front of her, another 42 days of travelling.

Never had her accounts made her feel so melancholy.

To drive away the figures – or at least her icy nostalgia for the glacier – Leo rummaged in her rucksack for Calvino's book. She was after a perfect phrase that would enable her to trap the magic of the drifting icebergs. She would write it down again and again; again and again, she would inscribe it at the front of her notebook. Only then, she pondered, will I succeed in removing this stupid nostalgia that has stuck to the walls of my heart. Her fingers came into contact with some pages and, as she pulled them out of the blackness of her bag, she saw it was the book about Petiso Orejudo the owner of the hostel in Buenos Aires had lent her. After her visit to the prison at the end of the world and the subsequent damp shivers, she'd chosen not to read the last chapter. And yet, up here, at a height of so many feet, with the storm twisting and turning with its lightning colic many metres further down, Leo felt protected from the elements and made up her mind to peruse the final pages. After all, she would have to give the book back as soon as she landed in Buenos Aires.

*It seems a lot has been written about Cayetano Santos Godino's last years in Ushuaia Penitentiary. And about his untimely death. He suffered abuse at the hands of the other prisoners and the guards. They all directed the anger consuming them in that world's end towards his sickly body. The damp. The cold. The hunger. The ticks. The scabs on their wounds. The blood. The putrefaction. The semen. The solitude. Petiso Orejudo resisted as best he could. He sided with the jailers and accused the prisoners; with the prisoners, and accused the jailers. None of them wanted him by their side, perhaps because there were always sparks of desire dancing in his eyes. Desire for the flames of fires. For the silent, smothered death of children. But in the end, it was a cat that killed him, the biggest serial killer in the history of Argentina. A dumb cat that miaowed when it shouldn't. That annoying, little miaow got into his head and deprived him of his sense of reason. That was why he had to rip off its head, to wring its neck and shove it inside a heater as he smiled with rotten teeth and his chilblain-infested ears twitched with pleasure. A miserable pet provoked the anger of the other prisoners, and they beat him, bringing Petiso Orejudo's wretched life to an end. Ah, his head... inside his head. It wasn't his ears, no, it was that intolerable whistling. He was just an idiot. A wretch. A nobody.*

*Poor fool... Poor Petiso Orejudo, if only somebody would listen to you, if only somebody would listen to you...*

*My head... not you... your my head. Your head and the wind beating against it... my head. My poor Petiso Orejudo!*

*The Ushuaia wind can turn men into monsters. Whoever has suffered its assault knows the only way of avoiding madness is to run far away from its puny claws of air. But however far we go, however hard we run, however fast we move, the eerie call of Cape Horn will follow us to wake us at night and remind us who we are: the murderers of prostitutes and children. Poor fools, they clung to life so desperately because they were as yet unacquainted with their rotten misery. Nobody understands us, Petiso, but it's best they don't know. Here, in Buenos Aires, we are safe because nobody recognizes us. Don't forget, it's not us, it's the head. Our head, your head, my head...*

*That is why, when they're least expecting it, we will kill again. All we need is to feel the chilly wind on the back of our necks. The Ushuaia wind. The wind...*

At the end of the manuscript, Leo came across a well-delineated signature: 'Luis S. G.'

The girl let out a stifled scream, dropped the book and pushed away her rucksack. The handwriting of the signature had revealed to her the unexpected: this text had been written by Luis, her Buenos Aires landlord. Now it all fit! She found it difficult to breathe. The ferocious elements had come looking for her all those thousands of feet in the air, in that silent place where the other passengers prayed to every possible god and the crew flashed their falsest smiles. The turbulence provoked by the storm battered the plane as if it was a vast field of barley, and Leo's temples wanted to explode.

That blasted jar, that was what was banging against her head, the stupid wind from Ushuaia! It was Edmundo's wind, the landlord's wind, that was ruining her head!

A bolt of lightning entered through one of the plane's wings and exited through the other. Inside, there was a black-out, and the thunderstorm's orchestra reached the high point of its performance.

# 30

'Doña Dolores Mato Ribia? Yes? Hello, this is Leo, Cristina's niece... Yes, the Sorbonne professor. Right, thank you. I'm sorry to bother you at this hour... I wanted to know... Yes, in Buenos Aires. Oh, she told you... Yes, I needed accommodation for tonight. Only for tonight... Now? At the airport. Oh, that would be great! Thank you very much! Yes, of course... I'll wait for you here then. Yes, there's no hurry, I can wait...'

Seated on a bench at Jorge Newbery Airfield, Leo thought a timely withdrawal is also a victory. After that horrifying discovery in her landlord's notebook, spurred on by the turbulence of the plane as it returned to the Argentinian capital, Leo decided there was no way she was going back to that hostel on the block turned circle that had been created by the Avenues Corrientes, Córdoba, Gallo and Pueyrredón. Now it all fit, you bet it did!

The landlord suffered from airsickness inside his head. He was completely crazy!

Leo's rucksack gazed at her ironically from an adjoining seat. On the other side, the jar with the blasted wind from the Beagle Channel displayed a certain amount of anger. Perhaps it could sense her sudden contempt. For almost two hours, the girl waited for her aunt's colleague. Passengers rushed about from one gate to another; beyond the vast window, night filled the Plate River estuary with murmurs. Outside, planes didn't stop taking off on their way to other destinations.

'Leo?'

'Dolores?'

One thought she was the spitting image of her aunt. The other thought pretty much the same.

'Leo? I was asking you how the flight was. It seems winter has reached the south in all its cruelty…'

'Yes, yes, I'm sorry. My head was in the clouds.'

'You need to rest. We'll be home in a jiffy.'

'Yes, yes.'

As the two women walked through the terminal, Leo tried to keep her eyes fixed on the horizon, but the circular movement of her index finger revealed that she was nervous. Her father had the same tic when he didn't know how to convey some bad news. Tic, tic, tic, we'll have to declare the company bankrupt. Tic, tic, tic, we had an accident. Roi and I are more or less fine. The car? A write-off… Tic, tic, tic. Leo, don't look back, you can't look back. Abandoned on the cold seat behind her, the ill-fated wind started roaring in a devilish spiral that shook everything like a tornado. But only Leo seemed able to hear it. Tic, tic, tic, you can't look back. Don't look back.

When Dolores' dilapidated old car left the airport car park, Leo heard this enormous boom and imagined the terminals being ripped off the ground, swallowed up by a weather bomb. Tic, tic, tic, I'm not looking back.

Ever again.

And she didn't.

When they reached a low, honey-coloured house with exquisite columns in the neighbourhood of Palermo Soho, Leo realized her headache had finally cleared.

Whether this was just a coincidence, she would never know.

On a parallel street, some loud music – a cross between tango and techno – showed her this might be a good place to start discovering Argentina.

All over again.

# 31

'Hello, little brother!'

'I can't believe it, Willy Fog is showing signs of life! We thought you'd got trapped inside some glacier. You know, like those polar bears that drift about on some ice sheet when it thaws.'

'Oh, Roi, you need to see a shrink!'

'You need to wash your hair. You look like a sheep! That hairstyle is abominable… aren't there any combs in Argentina?'

It was the first thing Leo did as soon as she put down her rucksack: go online to talk to her brother on Skype. Not have a pee, or unpack her rucksack, or change her clothes, or eat, or even behave like a proper guest and engage her pleasant host in conversation. No, the first thing she did was go in search of her brother's embrace.

'Wait, wait just a moment… Come closer to the camera, Roi. Is that an earring I see on your ear? Father will die of fright!'

'Don't you believe it. Papa's completely unrecognizable. The one who won't let go is mother. What with my studies and the earring, she's going to have a heart attack. But tell me, Leo, how was Patagonia?'

'Amazing, Roi. I think it's the most amazing place I've ever been.'

'Oh, you always say that!'

'No, it's true.'

'Right. You said something similar about Venice.'

'You can't compare the two. Venice is a fascinating city, but the nature at the end of the world… I've never felt so small and insignificant in all my life.'

'You didn't have to travel all that way to feel that. We also feel alone. The crisis is taking away all hope, any wish to do something or even dream. Everybody looks after themselves. It's just good that 15-M managed to raise people's spirits a little. That's already something.'

'Don't tell me you're still on about that! Are you still sleeping in Obradoiro Square? I can't believe it.'

'Listen, Leo, I hope your trip hasn't turned you into a moron. Of course we're still in the Obradoiro. And we'll carry on with public meetings and demonstrations until the politicians listen to us. This movement is unstoppable.'

'Don't get like that, Roi. I've been out of touch for a week and was only asking. There's no reason for me to know what's going on over there...'

'You don't even know what's going on where you are, all you do is escape from one place to another.'

'What is it with you?'

'I remembered you a lot these days. I've just finished reading a comic book, *The Lemming Travel Agency* by José Carlos Fernandes. It talks about a man who, when the summer arrives, goes to a travel agency to decide on the ideal destination for his holidays. The person in charge of the agency offers him a broad spectrum of possibilities: Kwinz, the cemetery-city; Manzil, the stampede-city; Prodromos, the chance-city; Nanopykos, the miniature-city; Gibil, the flame-city...'

'I don't get it, Roi...'

'It doesn't matter where you go, Leo. As the main character says, "The average citizen is completely ignorant of the history of the countries he visits. But don't consider this to be a sign of chauvinism, he knows absolutely nothing about the history of his own country. Time has been reduced to a tiny band we call the present, the future has become uncertain and threatening, while the past has been suppressed." People have become ignorant and are heading for the abyss like flocks of tame sheep.'

'You are dumb, Roi. You think you know everything from the books you read, but sometimes it's necessary to go outside and look the world in the face. You're right: I know nothing about the places I go to; my visits are so brief I can hardly get involved in the local life; I don't spend more than three or four days in a place, just enough to see the most relevant sights in the city, perhaps not even that; I don't dare take transport that isn't a plane and, it's true, there are times I don't sleep the whole night because of the breathing of others in the bunks around me in the places I stay to save myself five euros per night. Yes, I am a scaredy-cat and don't find out all that much about the places I visit, but you know something? At least I've given it a go and escaped the vicious circle of complaints about the crisis. The crisis, the crisis, the crisis... all you do is repeat that every day like a kind of litany. You complain all the time, but you wouldn't leave mother's protective wing if they poured boiling water on top of you. At least I don't blame others for my own fears... I've had enough of this feeling sorry for oneself!'

The expression on Roi's face went from one of pure irony to growing astonishment and ended up in complete perplexity. When Leo finished her incendiary discourse, the two of them stared at each other as if it were the first time they'd ever set eyes on one another. It wasn't because of the pixels on the screen, or the thousands of kilometres that separated them, or even the poor quality of the loudspeakers. No. It was because of what they'd said to one another and never felt before.

'Crikey, Leo!'

That was all Roi the clever clogs could say. A few seconds later, they went back to the habitual stream of nonsense, jokes, daily affairs, all the stuff that's particularly relevant to the lives of the people we love. The new curtains. Grandma's birthday. The accounts in mother's shops. The distrust that had left Leo without a fabulous banquet in Ushuaia. Father's courses in DIY and business management. The tap in the downstairs loo that was still dripping. The landlord in El Calafate's terrible breath. Uncle Roque's latest bout of madness and Aunt Cris' irony. The fail in Maths and excellent in Literature. The medical discharge and end to appointments with the physiotherapist. And, in the middle, the word 'pretty' twice, 'treasure' four times and 'clever' another five to refer, in passing, to a certain Patricia that Roi had met during the camp-out in the Obradoiro.

'It sounds to me as if you might be falling in love, Roi.'

'None of that! I just find her interesting, that's all. She's the one who recommended the book I told you about.'

'You are a pedant, little brother. Has no one ever told you you sound like an old man, not one of those Ninis who party all the time?'

'I miss you, Leo.'

'Me too... But I still have another forty days of travelling and I'm not going to waste a single one of them. Where are you right now? In the library?'

'Obviously. Can't you see the books behind me? The Wi-Fi's free, and mother says we have to save down to the last penny. She says they're very hard to come by.'

'Would you look at that? The spendthrift finally worked out the value of things, whoever would have thought it?'

'Now she's the one who's working, things have changed a lot at home. Every single cost is weighed up and, best of all, there's no complaining. It's amazing!'

'I see there've been a lot of changes in my absence.'

'You can't imagine, Leo. You went off travelling, but life took us on travels of its own, you wouldn't believe it!'

When they said goodbye, Leo realized she'd been chatting with her brother for three hours. Never had they spoken so much in all their lives, never had they been so far apart.

The only thing Leo didn't say was 'sorry'. That incendiary outburst hadn't been against her brother but, as always, he'd had to put up with the reproaches aimed at someone else.

Someone else who went by the name of Martiño, a name Leo still refused to pronounce.

A new message from Lía suddenly appeared in her inbox, but Leo didn't have the strength or energy to open it.

> @ALeo90
> Back in my beloved Buenos Aires, the Patagonia wind has finally petered out. Back to autumn and the infinite city's bright lights.
> 28 May 2011 at 22:47

That was what Leo posted on Twitter before going offline. She then looked out of the window and realized night had taken hold outside. Blackness twirled around the metal shutters of the shops with an air of resignation and a heavy dose of tiredness. In that street of pastel palaces and one-eyed lamps, the day passed placidly, almost mutely, by.

Two perpendicular streets in another direction, the Plazoleta Julio Cortázar had turned into the eye of the storm for the laughter, music and Bohemian lifestyle that defined the neighbourhood of Palermo Soho.

But Leo decided not to go out. She was tired. The blasted Ushuaia wind was still blowing down her nape, and she had to admit she was a little afraid of the dark.

Tomorrow, she thought, tomorrow is another day. Tomorrow I'll resolve this issue once and for all.

But it wouldn't be tomorrow, either.

Oh, why on earth didn't she dare to write to Martiño instead of shouting at Roi?

# 32

Dolores was nice. Judging by her voice, she didn't sound so tall, rather short and stout. How stupid! When has a person's height ever been judged by their voice? But she had the voice of someone of average height, not of a woman who is as frail and infinite as a reed. She moved with amazing agility, no doubt in a previous life, before becoming a professor in molecular biology, she'd been a circus acrobat. Yes, Leo could almost imagine her holding a long pole while walking the tightrope. Three steps in front, a little jump, two steps back so as not to lose her balance. The drum roll would be deafening; the silence in the circus tent, dramatic. She would probably make do without the safety net, despite doing somersaults at a height of, how much would it be?, no less than ten metres. Perhaps even more, who could say? Yes, Dolores had once been an acrobat. There were her hands covered in calluses, the smooth skin on her face, as if there were still remains of the make-up from her last performance. Now she devoted herself to giving classes at the University of Buenos Aires, a far cry from the emotion of the tent, needless to say. In her free time, she did yoga, cooked *sorrentinos*, looked after bonsais and knitted kilometric, pink scarves. Of course, her unconfessable and obsessive secret was to do number puzzles. Putting the numbers in the Sudoku grids required the same sense of balance as walking the tightrope. A four in front, a five to the right, a three below… always in search of the perfect jump to round off a wonderful exercise. There was the fragile, crystal figure nervously awaiting the audience's reaction. Two, four, eight hands that start clapping timidly until the applause ripples throughout the tent. That was Dolores, a breakable object in constant need of recognition.

'Leo, are you there?' asked the woman.

The girl wasn't there. She was totally absorbed by the majestic to-and-fro movement of her host's hands caked in flour and water. That morning, the whole world had come to swirl inside the mass of pasta that was slowly being prepared in a house in Palermo Soho. Sunday's *sorrentino* was a sacred tradition in Buenos Aires families, and Dolores had wanted to offer her this dish. It was pouring down outside, and the leaves of the trees were dancing an abrupt tango among the lamp posts.

'Leo???????'

'I'm sorry, Dolores, were you addressing me?'

'Are you OK? You look a little confused. And your aunt told me you never stopped talking.'

'Talking? Me? Not at all. Don't you see Aunt Cris never lets me get a word in edgeways?'

'Yes, I think you're more like me. You prefer to do your own thing.'

They didn't need any more justifications or excuses after that, and the day passed peacefully and calmly amid knitting, bonsais, Sudokus, yoga and delicious *sorrentinos*. Outside, the storm cleared and, at nightfall, the moon regained its kingdom in the sky. During the afternoon, Leo spent a couple of minutes online, searching for an easy recipe for pancakes she could offer to her host. Dolores kept extolling the Parisian crêpes that Aunt Cris prepared, and Leo thought some pancakes would make a good replacement. She couldn't recall the exact amounts of all the ingredients. The Internet, however, failed to dispel her doubts, so she thought the best thing would be to improvise. Before going offline, she gave that unopened message from Lía a go.

What she read didn't please her at all. The Brazilian complained about the erratic direction taken by Ruth & Co. and the slavery imposed by majority decisions. 'I just wish,' she said, 'I had the courage to go off on my own like you. But I don't. I have the impression we all get on well enough but, if one of us were to disappear, the fragile good sense keeping us together would break forever with catastrophic results.' That was what Lía wrote.

'Shall we go out for a walk, Leo? It's stopped raining at last,' suggested Dolores.

The girl was still adrift in the contents of that message. The words left her with an unavoidably bitter taste, she wasn't sure why, it might have been nostalgia or sadness, but the taste was bitter all the same.

'Knock, knock, Leo... Do you fancy it or not?'

'No, no, excuse me, Dolores... I don't really fancy it. I prefer to darn some socks, if you don't mind.'

'Me mind? Not at all! I just thought since you haven't been out of the house all day...'

'Tomorrow, I'll go out tomorrow,' said Leo forcefully.

One eye remained attentive to the *sorrentinos* left over from lunch and heated up for dinner, but the other rushed towards the thick darkness growing on the other side of the kitchen window.

Tomorrow, she insisted, tomorrow is another day. Tomorrow I'll resolve this issue once and for all.

Needless to say, the pancakes never got made.

# 33

It was freezing cold, despite the fact Leo's watch showed eleven in the morning. She hadn't got up all that early, so she could wait for the first rays of sun. But what she really wanted was to escape the shivers she had been unable to banish from her body ever since the plane from El Calafate, which stubbornly increased with the onset of night.

Petiso Orejudo's shadow refused just to leave her alone, perhaps it was a little angry with her for abandoning that jar of wind on the seat in Jorge Newbery Airfield. So Leo had decided to get rid of it with the only course of action open to her: she would return the notebook to its owner. That was what she would do. She made her way to the hostel on Corrientes Avenue. When nobody was looking, she shoved the paperback under the door and pressed the bell. She then ran away and hid behind another building in order to wait. A few minutes went by, during which the cold decided to seize hold of her calves and heart and to chatter away inside her chest. Finally, the door opened, and the unmistakable nose of Luis, that clean, correct and elegant man she'd met only a few weeks earlier, peered out into the street. For a couple of seconds, he looked first surprised and then annoyed at not finding anybody there. He was about to turn around and ferry his wrath up the stairs again, but something made him look down. That was when he discovered the old notebook with its yellow pages which were about to be blown away by the gusts of autumn. The man bent down and lifted it carefully into his hands, like a relic, while searching anxiously for something. But his jar never appeared. When, reluctantly, he was forced to accept there was nothing else there, he raised his head and looked around. Leo shrank back a little more to avoid being seen. And yet, despite the distance and the walls shielding her from view, a damp shiver coursed up and down her spine. That look. That hatred. That desire. And those words in the book:

*Nobody understands us, Petiso, but it's best they don't know. Here, in Buenos Aires, we are safe because nobody recognizes us. Don't forget, it's not us, it's the head. Our head, your head, my head...*

*That is why, when they're least expecting it, we will kill again. All we need is to feel the chilly wind on the back of our necks. The Ushuaia wind. The wind...*

There was no way her landlord was getting hold of that wind. Leo wasn't going to feed his murderous madness any more, he could be sure of that.

One day earlier, in the airfield, a cleaner had celebrated the good fortune of coming across a rather lovely jar. He would give it to his granddaughter so she could keep her savings there, since it was her birthday soon. He didn't know that, as soon as he took off the lid, a monster would howl perpetually in the most intimate corners of his head.

Leo tiptoed away from there, relieved finally to have got rid of that devilish Petiso Orejudo. Without the book and the jar, that psychopath would find it difficult to stay anchored to her Achilles heel.

'Leo, how nice to see you!'

Leo almost fell over from fright. When she finally reacted, she came across the happy face of Adriana, the Italian girl she'd met during her first days in Buenos Aires.

'How was it in Patagonia? Are you coming back to the hostel?'

'Um... great... no... I mean, everything was fine in Patagonia, but I'm not coming back to the hostel.'

'I see. Yes, I realized. You were supposed to give something back to the landlord, weren't you?'

'Me? No!'

'It's all right. I know because he curses you every night for not coming back from Ushuaia as you'd promised. But I don't mind.'

Adriana was like a volcano. Sometimes she talked so much her innards spilled out of her mouth; others, she was quiet, jealous of her dark secrets. There was no middle ground with her, and sometimes she could be entirely unpredictable.

'Shall we have a coffee?' she asked out of the blue.

'I don't fancy it, Adriana, I've just had breakfast.'

'OK then. Let's go for a walk. It's a beautiful morning. Did you know? François, the Swiss boy, decided to hook up with the Argentinian girls, and they've all gone off to Mendoza. The idiot. If he hasn't gone and fallen in love with the short brunette. He failed to notice they're crazy about each other and all they were looking for in Greater Buenos Aires was the anonymity they couldn't find in Río Gallegos. The day they accept who they are and how much they love each other, François is going to get the surprise of his life! Ah, you find out all sorts of funny stuff in hostels, don't you?'

Yet again, Adriana's incandescent lava was capturing all the attention Leo had planned to devote to Buenos Aires. They opted to stay right there, in the district of Almagro, a hospitable area with clubs, libraries, civic centres and centenarian shops where the two girls whiled away the entire morning. Sometimes they talked; others, they remained silent, absorbed by the gentle traffic of the city. When Leo suggested heading down to the famous bookshop El Ateneo Grand Splendid, located in the old Grand Splendid Theatre, about which she'd read all sorts of wonderful things, Adriana shook her head.

'I'm not leaving Almagro. I have the sense it's going to happen one of these days, and I can't pass up the opportunity. I shall find the decisive clue any moment now.'

'What are you talking about?' asked Leo in surprise.

'My aunt Claudia, I told you her story,' answered Adriana, as if it was the most obvious thing in the world.

'Your great aunt who left Tuscany seventy years ago and whom you haven't heard from since?'

'That's right,' she declared. 'This district was taken over by Basque people to start with, and then by Italians, so I'm investigating whether Aunt Claudia lived here herself or someone can tell me about her.'

'I see. Tomorrow I'm going to Caminito, you can come with me if you want...' said Leo quickly, without thinking, to hide her astonishment.

'OK then. There was an important colony of Italians there as well. *Little path that time has erased, who saw us once walk past together, I have come for the last time, to tell you all my sorrows...*' sang Adriana softly in her unmistakable Italian accent. 'I try to go there occasionally. I might pick up Aunt Claudia's trail in those parts...'

'See you there then. Where exactly shall we meet?'

'On the corner of Caminito, you can't miss it. At eleven.'

Leo headed down Pueyrredón Avenue, leaving behind the ancient smell of the flower market that had made Almagro famous throughout the city. Its withered petals showed her the way to Santa Fe Avenue, in the district of Recoleta, where she came across the famous bookshop. Along the way, she thought Adriana had her work cut out if she was going to trawl all the places that had once been occupied by Italian immigrants. All the districts in the capital and in Greater Buenos Aires had roots in the Italian peninsula! That said, she was a little off her head...

The descriptions and rave reviews she'd read about the El Ateneo bookshop on blogs could not have prepared Leo for when she went in. She knew it was meant to be an extraordinary place, but she couldn't help letting out an awestruck 'ohhhhhhh!' when she reached the theatre's old stalls. It was a dream come true! The wonderful gilding on the walls, the seduction of the stage, the gentle, undulating shapes of the handrails and boxes and, above all, the comfortable seats where readers could retrieve and become lost in thousands of volumes left her feeling stunned.

That day, Leo forgot to have lunch. Her hunger couldn't tear her away from the tragicomic novel about composers of light opera she had pulled out of the second bookshelf on the fourth floor with a degree of curiosity and couldn't put down until she'd swallowed up the last word.

When she told the book group *Read, Read, What Are You Reading?*, they wouldn't believe their ears!

Night had fallen by the time she was forced to leave that magnificent theatre where the curtain never falls because there's always a story burning.

When she reached her borrowed hideaway in Palermo, she realized darkness had gone back to being an inoffensive animal that liked to walk around your legs and not a beast lurking menacingly in the shadows. She sighed. How glad she was to have returned that notebook about the devilish Petiso to its owner!

Having chatted with Dolores, had some consommé and two *empanadillas* for dinner and washed her underwear, Leo emitted her final tweet of the day:

> @ALeo90
> Read, Read, What Are You Reading? Have just found the most amazing bookshop! We could spend days there leafing through and commenting on books!
> 30 May 2011 at 23:13

Lying in bed, waiting for sleep, Leo came to the conclusion that Buenos Aires was more than a landscape or a state of mind. Buenos Aires nestled in the unremitting cramp that clung to her legs after she'd wandered along its long avenues. While walking, she didn't notice its fury but, as soon as she stopped, her muscles ached terribly!

She didn't know what, but Buenos Aires was something else.

Something told her, if she didn't find out soon, she would lose it forever.

And that was the first act of treason.

# 34

That was one of the great advantages of squatting in the house of a friend – or rather Aunt Cris' friend. The range of options was infinite: 24-hour access to the Internet, washing machine, fridge, en-suite bathroom, library, hot meals… And all for free! No money could pay for the pleasure of getting into bed without having to drive away the insects or having a shower without wearing flip-flops to ward off infections! The only thing Leo missed was the company of other travellers with whom to share the day's discoveries. And yet she couldn't complain. She'd never had such a generous and discreet host as Dolores! She was then immediately reminded of Zerdali and Iria in Istanbul, Rubén in Lisbon and her own Aunt Cris in Paris. They'd all welcomed her kindly into their homes, and she'd never written to them again. What could have happened to them once she'd left them behind on her way to somewhere?

When she got back home, she would send messages to all the people she'd met along the way and endeavour to reciprocate their hospitality. Inevitably, the whole of Ruth & Co. came into her mind when she encountered the metro stop. She'd managed to keep her sense of nostalgia at bay for several weeks despite the effort involved. The slippery Edmundo and the Les Eclaireurs Lighthouse had crashed into her protective wall unsuccessfully, and even Lía's email with its confessions hadn't affected her as much as she'd thought it might at first. But as soon as she entered the metro station to take line D, which would then connect with line C before she had to catch a bus to Caminito, she bumped into a group of boys and girls busking on the platform. She walked past, almost without paying attention, but when they struck up the chords of 'Alfonsina and the Sea' in Mercedes Sosa's arrangement, her body gave a turn. All her attempts to drive away Andrés' smile and the group's banter over the last few weeks slapped her on the face with the strength of a boomerang.

As she wandered into the lion's mouth of the underground, that melody nestled in her fireplace and lit the embers of her memory. *You're leaving, Alfonsina, with your solitude* (Rallie gives a jump), *What new poems have you found?* (Mayra's River Plate accent), *An ancient voice of wind and salt* (Ruth gives a lick), *Breaks your soul and carries it away* (samba in Lía's voice), *You're heading that way like in dreams* (Claudia's temper), *Asleep, Alfonsina, dressed in the sea...* (Andrés' caresses). So it was, one after the other, one after the other, she was visited by images of the group. The uncomfortable journey on the metro, slower and older than most she'd seen, wouldn't let her outrun them, and she had to succumb to the reflective embrace.

Damn, how she missed the shelter of the group! The happiness, consolation, energy, solutions, music, guffaws.

Nostalgia came looking for her treacherously when she'd least been expecting it.

As always.

The sound of tango that welcomed her to Caminito only increased the catastrophe of her sudden sadness, despite her attempts to push it away. The only thing that had a dissuasive effect was the visit to the La Bombonera football stadium. The shouts of the fans and unmistakable yellow flags of Boca Juniors swept her along on a wave of soccer passion.

'It's a beautiful street,' murmured Leo, admiring the prostitute who leaned arrogantly out over the tiny balcony of a fuchsia and green façade. Next to her, a similarly insolent fireman gazed lustily at her. The fact they were made of papier mâché didn't detract from the sexual passion.

Adriana smiled at her enthusiasm.

'That's right… They've managed to get the colourful sheets and buildings occupied by tourist businesses to practically erase the rotten misery of yesteryear. To start with, this was just a stream that led to Boca Quay; then it was a siding. On either side were the huts of black slaves, the quay's cheap labour force; then shacks belonging to European immigrants who'd come with the dream of building up the Americas. It seems tango was born here; Lunfardo as well, the language of the suburbs with its words derived from Spanish and Italian. They say at night, after a hard day's work, men and women would sing and dance, linked to nostalgia by their common places of origin, in amongst the layers of metal and mud. To drive away the dirt in their eyes, they decorated the façades with the remains of ship's paint, hence the brilliant, fragrant colours. If happiness couldn't command misery elsewhere, then it could at least run riot in the corridors separating this part of the port from the railway tracks. Years later, when the shallowness of the water prevented larger ships from mooring here, the port was moved north, to Puerto Madero, and all the stevedores abandoned this area as well. They left, but their Lunfardo soul remained. That is why I am sure my aunt Claudia's spirit is still alive in this place…'

Leo thought this business with Adriana's aunt was a little over the top, but she didn't say anything. What for? They soon headed in the direction of Puerto Madero, where it seemed the choicest neighbourhood in the city was being built between the Ecological Reserve and the district of San Telmo, next to the old quays now occupied by exclusive restaurants. 'That,' declared Adriana, 'is where we'll have dinner tonight. My treat.'

In effect, on that quay surrounded by shops and bars there arose a Buenos Aires made up of tall, luxury apartment blocks, fancy bridges, old, restored sailing vessels and lazy walkers. They had a sirloin steak washed down with a good Shiraz, which the Italian girl paid for without so much as blinking. The meal went down pretty well. But it would have been far more enjoyable if Leo had managed to drive away the images that had stuck into her when she was least expecting it.

So it was, half an hour earlier, just as they were leaving Caminito, a dilapidated bus took them along tracks that ran beneath large viaducts. At the foot of the pillars, the girl encountered hundreds of shacks belonging to the so-called *cartoneros*, men and women who survived by collecting discarded waste and whose very existence was often denied by the rest of Buenos Aires society. Inside that vehicle stuffed full of tourists, there was a strange, hostile silence. It wasn't fear that one of these ragged children or hunchbacked men might do them any harm. No. It was fury that this sight had come to dirty the colourful beauty of the Caminito they were leaving and the haughty exuberance of the Puerto Madero that was waiting for them. Between these two points of departure and arrival, misery had rubbed their noses in what had once been something else, a place nobody now wanted to remember. The sweat. The calluses from the ropes. The shouts of the stevedores. The bare feet. The mud. But poverty cannot just be hidden. It cries out. It is stronger than any number of coats of paint, however plastic that paint may be.

That was why the travellers on this bus hated those looks that sought them out from the sidewalks without asking for anything, simply asserting their existence.

And that was why, at midday in that choice restaurant of Puerto Madero, Leo's sirloin steak could have tasted a whole lot better than it did.

# 35

'I know Chacarita and Recoleta are pretty to look at, but I don't find any charm in them. Lots of people do that tourist circuit. With all the things there are to see in the city, and they have to go and visit the cemeteries. Boh! I hate tombs!'

Dolores was carefully pruning the branches and leaves of her diminutive apple tree.

Leo quickly scanned her mind and realized she'd visited several cemeteries during her trip. She immediately remembered Eyüp in Istanbul and the Jewish cemetery in Prague. She wasn't so sure what was wrong with visiting sarcophaguses, they sometimes even helped you to understand the land of the living more clearly. Of course, as a child, she'd gone with her grandmother Carmiña on every pilgrimage of the living and the dead there was in their area. The procession in open coffins of people who'd recovered from a serious illness in Pobra do Caramiñal had turned into a fixed annual engagement, but obviously the one that affected her most was the pilgrimage to Santo André de Teixido, where it is said you will go when you have died if you don't go when alive. She can't have been more than twelve when Grandma Carmiña insisted they make this trip to the end of the world and take the memory of her mother with them. Apparently, she'd turned up one night as a golden beetle, and now Leo's grandmother was terrified of not visiting the apostle who sleeps at the foot of Vixía Herbeira, one of the highest sea cliffs in Europe. She wouldn't go by car because she said it was too far, but she wouldn't back down, either, and she stuck resolutely to her devout plans. You bet she did. One day, she said she was going to visit a spa, she was tired, and Leo would go with her. 'An old woman like me, all alone, whoever saw such a thing, let the girl come with me,' she declared. And off they went. But instead of taking the coach to Lugo, which is where she was due to take the waters, they headed first to Coruña, then to Ortegal. It took them two days to reach Santo André and another two days to come back, but Leo remembered nothing of the tortuous journey or idle hours spent waiting in bus stations next to her stubborn grandmother. All Leo could remember was the exquisite beauty of the figures made of bread crumbs they bought when they arrived and the thick smell of wax being consumed next to wooden ships that had been offered for those drowned at sea. Also, taking great care not to tread on a single insect during their descent, which Grandma Carmiña insisted on doing on her knees, as required by tradition. Needless to say, on the way back, Leo had to put up with her complaints about the cramp and the wounds from the stones she'd encountered on her way down. Everybody guessed where Grandma Carmiña had really been, but not another word was said about the matter. From time to time, during the long and turbulent sessions over the dinner table, somebody would sardonically blurt out:

'That's the way it is! As true as the fact that Guitiriz is in Lugo province and has the finest medicinal waters in all the surrounding area. Isn't that so, Carmiña?'

'It may well be,' replied Leo's grandmother with a dose of humour.

Everybody was lying flat out, but nobody would offer their arm to be twisted, which made the saying 'when in the land of wolves, howl like the rest of them' famous in that house. Pure, distilled irony.

Leo never said a word about their excursion to visit the miraculous saint of the north-west. Only once did she want to show off her knowledge, and she hinted at it to her grandmother as she was sprinkling far too much salt into the cooking pot.

'Santo André de Teixido? You and me? No, girl, you must have dreamed it. The Lord protect me, Santo André, and what on earth would I be doing there, my darling?'

Damn family! Between the light and shade of its different members, it was impossible not to trip and fall down! Leo chuckled to herself at the memory, while Dolores cleverly brought the scissors to bear on the crowns of her carefully-tended bonsais in her pleasant house in Palermo Soho.

'But if you want to visit the cemetery, go ahead, don't let me change your mind,' continued Dolores. 'Whoever would have thought it, a cemetery… With all there is to see in the land of the living!'

She may have been right, but Leo, accompanied by Adriana once more, made her way to Chacarita and, the next day, to Recoleta Cemetery. While searching for traces of Italian emigrants on gravestones and in old people's homes, Leo came across a root she hadn't been expecting. The names of ancient establishments, streets and aliases revealed the existence of thousands of Galicians who had travelled to Buenos Aires during the previous century. Their presence could not be ignored. Every step she took, she discovered a familiar reference that spoke to her of intimacy. It was all so close it confused her sense of logic. It was difficult to comprehend the distance in time and space of that era when farmers from western Europe had set out to conquer the avenues of Buenos Aires. A reality that was present in the colourful *fileteados* of shop windows and advertisements, which simply refused to be swallowed up by the oblivion of the modern city. In old people's homes, her songful accent giving her away despite the fact it was an Italian emigrant she was asking after, dozens of daring hands clasped her own and asked about places she'd never even heard of.

'Garduñeira? Do you know Garduñeira, my daughter? How about San Paio de Abelenda? That's where my mother was from; my father was from Sas de Penelas. I'm from Sabaxáns. Carregal. Santalla de Devesa. Navallo. Uceira. Tabagón. Xurenzás. Larouco. Trez. Berdelle. Gulfariz…'

Never had she heard such a thing! She hadn't imagined she would come across all those names in an old people's home on Belgrano Avenue in Buenos Aires. They all had a Galician background. They all lacked a place of their own in which to die. They all clung to these names as if, by saying them out loud, they could spell out the key to the paradise they would never return to. Garduñeira. San Paio de Abelenda. Sas de Penelas. Sabaxáns. Carregal. Santalla de Devesa. Navallo. Uceira. Tabagón. Xurenzás. Larouco. Trez. Berdelle. Gulfariz…

It was in one of those old people's homes where Leo finally got caught up in Adriana's melancholy and understood her persistence. If she had an ancestor who was lost in the vast Humid Pampas, she also would endeavour to reach out to her in a foreign land.

So she could finally be at peace.

That said, Adriana was certainly off her head! No two ways about it!

# 36

Shortly after being infected with an Italian brand of nostalgia, or perhaps a little earlier, distrust put in an appearance. Leo couldn't have said exactly when a foreboding arose and took hold of her. She only knew it appeared with unusual violence and disarming clarity. In the last few days, the two girls had spent hours with old people's homes, cafés, merciless treks down long avenues, slices of stuffed pizza, roast meat, exhibitions in the best-known museums and most unlikely corners. Adriana always insisted on paying with a generosity that was as stubborn as the search for her aunt Claudia. Leo often wondered where the pocket of this woman who had been away from home for more than a year, with no obvious occupation, had its provenance. When she asked, all she got was evasive answers, and Leo gave it no more importance. But one afternoon, sitting on a bench in the Plaza de Mayo, Leo understood everything.

It wasn't so very cold. At dusk, the sky still shone while, in the shelter of buildings and trees, shadows lounged about at ease. Opposite, the Casa Rosada showed off its colourful appearance, somewhere between red and white, an unmistakable image on news programmes all over the world whenever the agitated political life of Argentina had something to say for itself. Everything had been crammed into that square: the Metropolitan Cathedral, the Cabildo, the start of the popular neighbourhood of San Telmo, the May Pyramid, the beginning of the unmistakable May Avenue that finished kilometres away in the Plaza del Congreso... Perhaps the quintessence of Argentina was not to be found in the outskirts, but in its nerve centre, where dozens of makeshift tents and banners demanded rights for a particular collective. It didn't matter which; once these had left, others would take their place. On the pink flagstones, inscribed with chalk, the white scarves of the Mothers and Grandmothers of the Plaza de Mayo mixed with those of their children, profiles of bodies beaten down during the unforgotten military dictatorship. Where the heart should have been, their names. In the Plaza de Mayo, memory, concerns about the present, were launched at the Casa Rosada to remind those in power, whoever they might be, of the popular demand for justice. Were this not the case, they seemed to say, we will occupy Mayo. Once again.

We will occupy Mayo.

This was undoubtedly Leo's favourite place in Buenos Aires. In the vicinity of demonstrators and beggars, there was a strange feeling that filled her with melancholy and comforted her despite the inevitable sense of disquiet. She didn't know why, how absurd, but that was how it was. As if a little maté had warmed her hands and heart.

Leo was so taken up with her own affairs she didn't notice that night had fallen. At this point, her permanent state of alert, more heightened than ever since her arrival in the vast expanse of Buenos Aires, sent out a warning signal on spotting several suspicious characters in the near vicinity. Very stealthily, she grabbed her rucksack with her feet and glanced around to try and understand what was going on. She then discovered strange movements of interaction between various individuals that worried her even more. She got up, openly now, and raced towards the brightly-lit May Avenue. She was just about to warn Adriana when she realized she wasn't there, but seemed to form part of the group interchanging things in the shadows. She scrutinized the darkness as best she could, but the distance prevented her from seeing what kind of merchandise it was. She had to wait at least ten minutes for Adriana to come back.

'Who were those people? What were you doing?' she asked her abruptly.

'That's my business. Shall we go and have dinner? I wanted to invite you to this amazing sushi restaurant that's just opened a couple of blocks from here.'

'No thanks. I'm tired, I'm going home.'

And Leo left without further explanation. It was Thursday 2 June 2011 when the girl decided to abandon Buenos Aires. She still had a thousand things to see, but wanted to escape from there before she was on the receiving end of more unpleasant surprises. That same chilling foreboding that disquieted her now had settled on her shoulders in Marrakesh with Edmundo. She hadn't been wrong then, and now everything seemed to fit. How could she have been so stupid! The invitations, the generosity, the insistence on visiting commercial centres and avenues full of people where she never stopped suffering sudden, passing attacks of torpor... There was something in Adriana that, behind her pose as a stubborn investigator, worried Leo, and she thought the best way to avoid her would be to put some distance between them. She had to get out of there before she ended up in a prison cell, being accused of illicit dealings! Besides, she was starting to be fed up of all this nostalgic past and searching for names on tombstones. She wanted to recover the lost pulse of her journey, the one that had been smothered by Dolores' hospitality and Adriana's routine.

Her head could be a real roller coaster; her will, a heap of inexplicable outbursts.

'I suppose the long-awaited moment has arrived.'

Knowing she would finally visit the place she'd dreamed about most, instead of moving her, shot her through with an endless melancholy that barely let her sleep.

It was decided. Tomorrow she would get the plane ticket.

After the bend in the roller coaster, the downward slope disappeared in front of her nose.

Leo felt she'd just denied the city of Buenos Aires an opportunity for the second time.

And that was the second act of treason.

# 37

'Where was that? Machu what?'

'Machu Picchu. In Peru. The capital of the Inca Empire. Don't tell me you don't know where Machu Picchu is!'

'Ha, Machu Picchu!'

'Well, I couldn't say Rome is…'

'It's better than Lisbon.'

'What made you say Marrakesh?'

It had happened on that long night of beers, coffee liqueur and rain, when the four of them had sworn on top of the marble table that, as soon as they had their degree certificates in their hands, they would embark on a great journey. Martiño said Lisbon. Inés opted for Marrakesh, Aldara for Rome and Leo for Machu Picchu. On the infinite map of that bar, the only borders were the stains left by the empty bottles. The cigarette ash and dirty serviettes formed mountains and other geographical features. The names of cities poured out on unmapped routes, and their suggestions travelled as far as the fuel of ingested alcohol would allow. How far away it all seemed now, so many years on and with so many disappointments on her shoulders! She had the feeling that centuries had gone by since that drunken night when, in a ritual without witnesses, they had sketched out what Leo had thought was the great project of their lives. A trip. For a year at least. That was the night when she woke up with Martiño, which they never talked about again, as if nothing had happened and the kisses had been a mirage of their hangover. When all that house of cards came tumbling down and the other three pulled out, leaving her all alone, she had hated them down to the bottom of her soul.

The song by Sés had turned into a kind of omen:

*Four by four, I sail on seas of paper,*
*dream a couple of verses by that captain*
*with whom I loved freedom, going after expeditions.*
*And the sea the boat and we ended up alone.*

That was right, she'd ended up alone. No sea, no boat, not even a bagpipe tassel to go with.

Now, so many centuries and kilometres later, the resentment was smaller, but the nostalgia was greater. How foolish they had been, how could they have passed up such an opportunity…? Now Machu Picchu was only a mouse click away, all those sensations intoxicated her again but, unlike the initial thirst for revenge, this time an unmistakable taste of triumph danced around her mouth. She was going to do it, she was going to discover the sacred city of the Inca Empire. At long last!

'Machu Picchu?'

My goodness, thought Leo, why are you all so surprised that I should want to visit Peru!

'Yes, Dolores, Machu Picchu. Don't you think it's a good destination?'

'A good destination? Are you joking? It's the most magical place in the world. There's an esoteric force up there that takes your breath away… Really, it's an inexplicable feeling that traps and changes you.'

There was Dolores with her spiritual outbursts. Just like Aunt Cris! They were as extravagant as each other. The woman had stopped knitting her endless pink scarf and was gazing at her with absolute envy.

'But you will come back, won't you? You still have a bunch of things to see.'

'Of course, I will. I have to catch my return flight here, so I'll come back a few days earlier.'

'You can't leave without discovering San Telmo Market and the nightlife in Palermo!'

'Don't worry, I will come back,' declared Leo.

What she wasn't so sure about was whether she would stay again in her house. Dolores had been a wonderful and considerate host, but Leo missed the liveliness of the pensions and youth hostels. With all the money she'd saved on accommodation and food thanks to Adriana's generosity, first, and then her underhand dealings, she had enough to indulge in a couple of whims in Peru! You bet she did!

The euphoria regarding her new destination overwhelmed her. Especially when she found out the ticket to Cusco the next day was less than three hundred euros, albeit with the inevitable stopover in Lima.

She was so content she decided to share her enthusiasm with the rest of the world:

> @ALeo90
> Off tomorrow to Machu Picchu in Peru!
> Before leaving BA, one last coffee in the Tortoni
> to celebrate my Inca expedition!
> 3 June 2011 at 10:27

She then sent emails to her mother, Roi, Sebastián from the book group, Aunt Cris. For the first time during her trip, she felt like dropping a line to Inés and Aldara as well, but decided not to. Needless to say, Martiño came into her mind, as so often before, and, as so often before, she pushed him out. The fact was she didn't know what to say to them.

That she didn't hate them any more?

That they were the ones who'd lost out?

That she missed them?

Deep down, all these options had an inevitable tang of revenge about them, so she let them be.

## 38

It was the tastiest coffee in the world. Not because of the fragrance, thick; or the foam, less than she usually liked; or the temperature, perhaps a little cold; or the sugar, a bit too sweet. As Leo drank from the porcelain cup, she swallowed down the romantic atmosphere that surrounded her. Perhaps the mirrors, the photographs, the attentive waiters, the plaques and busts with the names of artists who had sat at these tables, the piano, the red, velvet curtains, the Tiffany-style lamps and windows, the hidden rooms with their book groups, the wooden and leather chairs… everything oozed melancholy in the Tortoni. There, the nostalgia for a time when May Avenue was the epicentre of a cultural life promoted by Argentinians and exiles could be imbibed in small sips of coffee.

To Leo, it tasted just wonderful. She had been there for a while when a waiter suddenly came over to hand her a note.

'For me?' asked Leo in surprise.

'Yes, miss.'

Leo opened the note and took a couple of seconds to decipher those simple letters:

**i love you leo a.**

It wasn't such a difficult message to understand. It was just that it was unbelievable. Completely unbelievable.

'Excuse me.'

She couldn't help being a little abrupt with the waiter.

'Excuse me, who gave you this?'

'The note?'

'Yes, the note. What else would it be?'

'Someone at the table by the door. Just over there.'

His forefinger pointed to an empty space.

'Oh dear!' he seemed upset. 'They've already left. Was the note unpleasant?'

'No, no. Thank you very much...'

Leo felt like running after the table's occupant, but soon changed her mind. It was dark, and she would never catch up with them. She knew it would be impossible, so decided to stay where she was. Before paying, she went to the bathroom to recover from the shock, where, in the mirror, written in large, crimson letters, she came across:


## I Love You Leo A.


The ground fell out from under her feet, and she turned around without even opening the tap. Then, in the mirror next to her table, the same lipstick had written:


## I Love You Leo A.


And in the midst of the pages of a newspaper, a biro had inscribed the selfsame 'I Love You Leo A.' next to a headline about government measures that had infuriated large landowners in Rosario.

Anger beating against her face, Leo clasped her bag to her chest, put on her jacket and made for the door. Her path was blocked by a waiter.

'Excuse me.'

'No, no, don't hand me anything else. I don't want to know any more,' she snorted irritably, trying to find a gap through which to get a breath of fresh air.

'I didn't want to hand you anything. It's just that you haven't paid your bill,' smiled the waiter pleasantly.

Red with embarrassment and rage, Leo turned and paid for the coffee that had been the tastiest in the world before becoming the most bitter.

Outside, on a sheet hanging from one of those marvellous trees, could be read:

## I Love You Leo A.

But Leo didn't even see it. The girl had her heels against her bottom to reach the metro station and get back to Dolores' house in Palermo as quickly as possible, far away, so she thought, from all that madness that intimidated and overwhelmed her.

Fire and ice.

Clasp and slap.

All at one and the same time.

# 39

The night of 3 June 2011 was far too long for Leo. There was so much information careering around her head it was difficult to control its noisy flow. Having realized it would take her some time to get to sleep, she had chatted to Dolores until the latter decided to go to bed. Then she had gone online, checked the details of her ticket for the following day and embarked on a meticulous round of forums, blogs, travelogues, media and Facebook pages. Somersaulting from one to the other, Leo had gathered all the necessary information to undertake her visit to the Peruvian cities of Lima, first, and then Cusco. The lack of direct flights to Cusco at that time forced her to do a turn in the north, which was really stupid, since there wasn't all that much distance between Buenos Aires and Machu Picchu. It doesn't matter, thought the girl, that way I'll get to know the Pacific and the capital of Peru as well, they're probably really interesting. Despite her repeated attempts, there wasn't a single corner of the Internet that had good things to say about Lima, which everyone described as an insipid 'donkey's belly'.

She would soon find out why.

It wasn't just her head rushing along at a thousand kilometres an hour; her heart was also out of place. However hard she tried to avoid them, the sensations these 'I Love You Leo A.' had given her during a voyage that had already lasted five months kept shocking her. The first message had appeared in the month of February in Cádiz. How could she forget it? She'd never been so alarmed in all her life. Then they had appeared unexpectedly in the Sierra de Grazalema, in Granada, Marrakesh, Istanbul... They had turned into a caress waiting for her at any point in the world where she might set foot. Andrés' surprising reappearance had seemed to confirm something she already thought – and wished for – in the most intimate corner of her brain: that he was the author of this graffiti that pursued her all around the Mediterranean. It couldn't be anyone else. It had to be him.

With the evidence of this strung around her wrists, all the 'I Love You Leo A.' that shone throughout Italy were just noisy and repeated declarations of love about something she already knew: the Mexican was crazy about her. She was flattered, of course, but couldn't quite work out what she felt for him – except for the obvious sexual desire. Their farewell in Venice should have prepared her for what would come later. But feeling proud of her apparent control of the situation, she hadn't foreseen the emotional hecatomb that would follow. That was why Paris had appeared so large and so immense, so cold and indifferent, without any heart. For that reason, she'd written to Andrés and demanded his presence. She'd got to a point where she'd learned the email by heart:

> Hello, Andrés! I know it's you who's responsible for writing '*I Love You Leo A.*' Don't pretend any more, please. The game struck me as curious to start with, but I've grown tired of all those messages painted on façades, roads and bridges that catch me by surprise wherever I go. I want to see you and know you do too, so don't hang around. You once told me, 'You say "don't come", that means "come".' So now I'm telling you, 'Come, I'm waiting for you in Paris.'

But he replied that he didn't know what she was talking about and wouldn't come to the City of Light. Leo didn't want to believe it. What she had to believe – the fact was plain for all to see – was that he wasn't coming to meet her in Paris. All the indifference she'd used to build her sandcastle came tumbling down, and she was obliged to admit defeat. She'd almost downed tools and given up the whole journey. She was lucky her family had known, as always, when she least expected, how to give her encouragement with their sudden visit.

How stupid, she thought now, how could she have even considered giving up, just because Andrés refused to go to her in Paris?

Andrés... she hadn't even liked him all that much, boh...

What one day can look like a mountain some time later is just gravel on the road.

After that, the escape to Buenos Aires had been an ideal opportunity to put some distance between them and give the trip she had planned to finish only a week earlier a radical change in direction. So off she'd gone, rushing across the Atlantic, thanks to the accumulated air miles on her favourite aunt's gold card. She would visit Buenos Aires in Argentina, Machu Picchu, the city she dreamed of in Peru, and who knows what other destinations, all the ones she could afford.

She had thought, with that transatlantic journey, she would be leaving all those enigmatic 'I Love You Leo A.' messages behind.

So when she saw the first sign on the American continent in Ushuaia, her heart had almost burst. The terrible shock of reading the story of that serial killer called Petiso Orejudo had made her doubt. Had she really seen a message tied to a

Galician roadside cross in the southernmost city on the planet? No, she convinced herself, she couldn't have. It had just been her head, another of the tricks of that diabolical River Plate psychopath who had ended his days down in Tierra del Fuego, in the prison at the end of the world. Patagonia had had other surprises in store. Days later, on leaving behind the walkways of the Perito Moreno Glacier in El Calafate, she had come across another cryptic message wrapped around the railings of the paths that led to that icy front. But despite the fact she'd seen it quite clearly from the bus, it hadn't impressed her in the slightest. It was an insignificant and ridiculous object alongside the glacier's explosive, irreducible beauty. Leo simply turned the page, allowing the infinite glow of the blue of the icebergs and the different layers of pure ice to occupy all her emotions.

For that reason, the 'I Love You Leo A.' in the Café Tortoni had impressed her so much. There was no excuse she could use as a shield against the torrent of sensations that was suddenly unleashed on May Avenue. There was no incendiary arsonist or ice cathedral that could blur her mind. She was all alone before the obviousness of the message:

## I Love You Leo A.

Something deep inside her begged that the hand of Andrés might be behind this declaration of love. As a buttress against that centrifugal force, another, centripetal force shouted out no, it was impossible he could be following her wherever she went. And if it wasn't him… then who could it be? Who was the permanent shadow on her journey? She thought about somebody else, why not admit it?, but wasn't prepared to say it out loud even in front of herself. That was absolute madness, a crazy idea, how was it possible…? How could somebody pursue her across half the world? Rubbish. Stuff and nonsense. How was it possible…?

However hard she tried, there was just no solving this puzzle. Poor Leo didn't fall asleep until the early morning, when the noise of shutters announced the beginning of a new day in Palermo. That was the day of her trip to the world of the Incas!

At this point, the girl had no idea how close she was to missing her chance. Had her flight to Peru been delayed a mere couple of hours, she would have found it impossible to leave the Plate River estuary and been stuck in Buenos Aires for weeks.

As sleep took hold of her, a volcano's fury was banging about in the basement of the earth at a distance of several thousand kilometres.

Of course, Leo didn't know about that.

She just kept ruminating:

Fire and ice.

Clasp and slap.

All at one and the same time.

# 40

It must have been after three o'clock local time on Saturday 4 June 2011 when the Southern Andean Volcano Observatory sounded the alert. The scientists there told of the explosion of the Chilean volcano Puyehue and of a column of smoke five kilometres wide and ten kilometres above sea level, heading south at an altitude of five kilometres and south-east at an altitude of ten kilometres. This eruption had been the result of unusual seismic activity at the end of April in the Puyehue-Cordón Caulle volcanic complex in the Andes. The effect of the volcano was no more than four on the Richter scale, but its consequences were expected to be great owing to the vast cloud of ash and sand that was starting to be expelled from its belly. The most affected zone at this point was the Argentinian city of Bariloche. Barely half an hour later, Leo arrived at Ezeiza International Airport in Dolores' car. The news came through on the radio, and Dolores put her foot down.

'Get a move on, get your ticket as quickly as you can, go through security and sit in the departure lounge. Either I'm very mistaken, or this is going to be bad.'

'I don't understand,' protested Leo.

'The ash cloud. Doesn't that sound familiar? A few years ago, I was in Paris when Eyjafjallajökull erupted. I was trapped in France for weeks because substances expelled by volcanoes, which include silica, are very dangerous for jet engines and can cause air disasters. Just pray your flight isn't cancelled.'

Leo said goodbye in a rush to stop her saying any more but, she muttered, it couldn't be all that bad. Used as she was to

Dolores, like Aunt Cris, inhabiting the realm of exaggeration, the girl thought a simple Chilean volcano could hardly lead to the cancellation of her flight.

At that point, Leo could not have known the volcanic cloud caused by Puyehue's seismic activity would shut down airports in all the world, from America to New Zealand. The economic and environmental consequences in the southern hemisphere would be considerable. Its devastating effect would go on for weeks owing to the rain of dust and stones, the lava and electrical discharges. But she would only find this out later on, once she was safely in Peru. The extraordinary coincidence of her flight being at five in the afternoon, and not later, saved her an unpleasant aerial mishap. When the plane took off and left behind the sprawling mass of Greater Buenos Aires, Leo only had eyes for her numbers.

The back of her notebook looked more like an Egyptian pictogram than an account book. If her mother had seen it, she would have shouted out in anger, being as organized as she was! But numbers, which were so boring and revealed all her expenses, caused her discomfort, and Leo tried to hide them behind amusing drawings. This time, thanks to Dolores' hospitality and Adriana's generosity, the addition and subtraction gave her the most joy she'd had all journey. She had landed in Buenos Aires from El Calafate with 1,240 euros for flights, 925 euros for living and 42 days' travelling in front of her. She did her sums and, in her week in the Argentinian capital, all she'd spent was the equivalent of 71 euros! Having taken off this amount – and 294 euros for the flight from Buenos Aires to Cusco – she still had 946 euros for flights and 854 euros for living. Amazing! She closed her notebook with a feeling of immense happiness and turned to the newspaper the air stewardess had given her. Normally this business with the numbers took her an age and she had no time for leafing through the news, but now there were barely any mathematical calculations to make she used this opportunity to catch up on recent events. Her brother, Roi, would have been proud.

Her eyes danced across headlines that for people like her, unfamiliar with Argentinian life, were rather difficult to understand: 'The Turbulence at River Continues and Even JJ Has Lost His Cool', 'Bets: Referee Who Oversaw Nigeria-Argentina Under Suspicion', 'Cristina and Berlusconi: Pure Feeling, Pure Wave', 'Massa Paves the Way for Re-Election of Scioli' and 'La Cámpora Lands in La Plata As Well'. All this struck her as irrelevant until she came across a tiny headline at the foot of the page, in the section of accident and crime reports: 'Search Continues for Six Chilean Andinists Missing in Torres del Paine'. In five short lines of text, it said they had last been seen at the entrance to the National Park, Laguna Amarga, the previous Monday and, despite being warned of the dangers of bad weather, had insisted on making the ascent.

Leo shivered from tip to toe. Was this a reference to the crazy gang she'd met at the hostel in El Calafate? There were no more clues in the article that permitted her to confirm her suspicions but, as the plane ate up miles over the forest, her head kept turning the matter over. Could they have been foolish enough to set out for the furthest lakes in Torres del Paine at that time of year? Felipe, Carlos, Laura and Néstor, perhaps not, but Fabián and Marieta... With the shadow of doubt still hanging over her, she managed to sleep for a while.

That would be the last she heard of them.

An hour later, she woke up to the sound of the senior flight assistant asking passengers to fasten their seat belts and put their seats in the upright position.

Lima lay under a thick layer of cloud beneath their feet.

It was getting dark. Excitement beat against her cheeks and brought her to.

That night, she'd decided to sleep at the airport.

# 41

The blame belonged to a website Leo came across by chance via a backpackers' forum. The link described various airports in the world and assessed their suitability for spending the night according to such criteria as safety, vending machines for snacks and beverages, noise, sanitary services or cleanliness, and other things. Jorge Chávez International Airport had received a wonderful mark in 2010 – nothing short of a golden pillow – and Leo decided to take the risk. She couldn't spend the night in a hostel when the time between her flights was less than twelve nocturnal hours. Besides, her large rucksack had been checked in through to Cusco, which meant even her luggage wouldn't be a problem.

As soon as she got off the plane, Leo wandered through the departure lounge to a place far away from the main escalators, where there was a constant stream of people. On reaching the spot the surfers had cited as the most peaceful and the most suitable for sleep, she got a major surprise. There were at least twenty people there, in their sleeping bags, hidden away behind their rucksacks. She soon realized she wasn't the only experienced traveller who'd looked out this possibility online and they must all be transit passengers waiting for the early-morning flight to Cusco. With a touch of disappointment and a heavy dose of resignation, Leo searched out her own little cranny, right next to the window, between a middle-aged couple and five girls who, judging by their accent, must have been Australian. She distributed a few discreet smiles in search of some complicity and got an enthusiastic response from all her neighbours on the floor.

Until midnight, immersed in noise, Leo did her best to

read a book by Bryce Echenique that Dolores had lent her as soon as she'd learned about her Peruvian destination. The book told the story of a boy, Julius, who grows up in a Lima that is divided according to class and who must live with all the contradictions that bump into his innocence day by day. Leo then jotted down some things in her notebook, ate a few biscuits and brushed her teeth. Her initial reluctance to sleep in a public space surrounded by strangers vanished as soon as she fell asleep. She didn't even hear the sound of the floor-cleaning machine, or the passing of the security guards, or the landing of several untimely aircrafts. She might even have missed her flight had it not been for the middle-aged couple who woke her up with barely half an hour to go before boarding! The shock sent her reeling, and her heart took several minutes to return to its normal rhythm. Fewer than the minutes it took to board, however, because of successive delays that plunged her into despair. 'All that haste only to spend an hour and a half in the queue!' snorted Leo. She used this opportunity to exchange a few words with the couple who'd ensured she was awake and ended up laughing out loud at the remarks of those two Argentinians from Tucumán who were eager, like her, to discover the most intimate secrets of the Inca Empire.

Half an hour later, she was online, using the Wi-Fi on their electronic devices. She made the most of this opportunity to send out a quick tweet:

> @ALeo90
> I passed the test. The night in Lima airport
> was surprisingly calm. Heading south.
> Cusco awaits!
> 5 June 2011 at 9:30

When it seemed all the suffering at the airport had come to an end, on catching the bus that would take her to the steps of the plane, Leo collided with the luggage trolley. She collapsed like a basket. Her first reaction was to get up again and wave her hand to play down the incident, so the other passengers wouldn't laugh. She fought back the tears of pain as best she could because she had in fact received a nasty knock on her left arm and leg.

And, on top of that, she'd severed one of her boots.

This was no laughing matter. The blow had succeeded in separating the heel plate from the rest of the shoe, and her sock was visible for all to see.

She would now be forced to spend some money at the cobbler's or on some new footwear.

# 42

The business of the broken boot lasted a couple of days and, much to Leo's dismay, embittered her initial experience of the incredible city of Cusco. As soon as she got off the plane and retrieved her luggage, she dragged her left leg to the stop of the bus that would take her to the centre.

The other passengers were breathing in and out to see whether the famous altitude sickness had affected their respiratory apparatuses.

Nonsense, thought Leo, you can breathe perfectly well.

Cusco welcomed her with a chilly temperature at that hour of the morning and an incredibly blue sky. Just as Leo had read, it was a time of drought and significant temperature swings between day and night. She had finally managed to get away from the storms of wind and water that had pursued her all over Argentina. At the airport, she changed half a dozen euros into soles so she could pay for the bus ticket. A euro was equivalent to four Peruvian soles, or almost, so she should divide every amount by four if she wanted to know the equivalent cost in euros. That was only a rough idea, since exchange rates and commissions, as she'd found out to her chagrin all over Argentina, could vary enormously depending on the exchange bureau.

What with the pain in her limbs and the fear of ending up barefoot, the bus trip seemed to last forever. The girl was so upset about her fall she was incapable of admiring the arid geography all around her. The little houses lined up along the hillside revealed a city of ochre roofs and white walls that had their roots in Inca constructions. The city is said to have the shape of a puma, one of the central and most venerated figures in Inca cosmogony. On the side of one of the mountains, an enormous message challenged the sky: 'Long Live Glorious Peru!' None of this mattered to Leo. She got off at the last stop, Plaza de Armas, the heart of the Inca Empire's old capital, declared a World Heritage Site on account of its beauty. But neither the colonnades, nor the magnificent colonial buildings, nor the walls of monumental, angular stones, nor the cathedral, nor even the indigenous physiognomy of its inhabitants, so different from what she'd seen until then, managed to capture her attention. All five senses were focused on salvaging her left boot so she wouldn't have to buy another one!

Her understanding, not always correct, of the inversely proportional relationship between price and the distance of a hostelry establishment from the tourist centre made her walk a couple of kilometres through a confused grid. She ranted and raved for half an hour before another backpacker, feeling sorry, no doubt, for the lamentable state she was in, led her to the address the hostel had given. She was so exhausted she wasn't sure she'd be able to climb the stairs to her room on the first floor. The room was tiny and sparse. The only decoration was a highly visible sign that showed where the room was and how to evacuate the building in case of earthquake. Buf. She seemed to be out of breath, and the pain in her limbs was getting worse. Leo collapsed on the bed. She felt really down in the dumps. This had been far too much effort for one day and, on top of that, the effects of sleeping rough on the floor of the airport were beginning to be felt. She dozed for an undefined period of time and then awoke with a palpitating heart and a desire to throw up. Lying in bed, the world started spinning as during a drinking spree. Her headache was unbearable, and she was forced to drag her mistreated body to the communal bathroom so she could eject the last drop of liquid that lingered in her stomach. The little sense she had left to try and control the situation made her realize if she didn't die then and there, she wasn't far from doing so. Perhaps it was something she'd eaten, or an insect bite, or contaminated water... she couldn't tell the real reason for her malaise, made worse by the bruises, but she was sure it wasn't good. She rummaged in her rucksack until finding the international health card her mother had insisted she take with her, but the cloud of sensations in her head prevented her from making out the numbers. Just as she was about to lose consciousness, she rang down to reception.

Minutes later, she came across the bemused look of the man who'd given her the key to her room an hour earlier.

'What? Are you dying?' he asked while putting a cup of aromatic tea to her lips.

'Could you call for an ambulance, please?' implored Leo. 'Here's my international health card number.'

'Ambulance, my foot! This isn't going to kill you!' laughed the man again.

'What do you know? I must have picked up some bug... My mother always told me, "You're no good for leaving home, what with all the illnesses there are out there." Do you have cases of malaria?'

The man's guffaws echoed around the room.

'Malaria? You must be joking. What you've got is *soroche*, my little girl. You need to ingest lots of liquid, some tea, this pill, and try to eat something. You'll be fine in a couple of days.'

'*Soroche*? What's that? Is it contagious?'

'Have you any idea where you are?' The man, who had been laughing until then, suddenly turned serious. 'You tourists are an incorrigible lot. You get on board a plane without the slightest idea of where you're going and then you pay the consequences... So clever when it comes to buying a cheap ticket on the Internet and so stupid for other things,' he sighed.

Leo's state of exhaustion went some way to calming his anger, and he regained the pleasant tone he'd used before.

'Let's see. Have you really never heard of altitude sickness? Cusco is situated more than three thousand metres above sea level. That causes a reaction in some people who aren't used to the altitude, known as *soroche* or altitude sickness. The symptoms come in all shapes and sizes: vomiting, diarrhoea, headaches, dizzy spells, nausea, loss of consciousness... It depends a lot on the body. But once the body grows used to it, the symptoms go. They simply go.'

'Yes, yes, I read all about altitude sickness!' Leo came out in defence of her traveller's pride now that she'd recovered a little thanks to the ingestion of some tea. 'But when I got off the plane, I didn't notice the lack of oxygen. I didn't notice anything at all. This malaise has to be something else. There must be some kind of virus...'

'Boh!' The hostel owner showed signs of growing tired of the girl's stubborn attitude. 'Why do you all think you'll be out of breath as soon as you get off the plane? There's no less oxygen here than anywhere else, the only difference is in the pressure. It's up to you, but the best thing you can do is rest and drink lots of maté until you feel better. It would be a shame to come this far and then have to turn around without seeing the sacred city!'

Leo wasn't convinced, but she clung to the hostel owner's explanation in the hope of getting better soon. It was that or continuing to believe in some mortal virus, and she preferred this so-called *soroche* as a diagnosis.

For two and a half days, Leo didn't leave the hostel. She spent the first twenty-four hours lying in bed; the next, trying to catch her breath and making a huge effort to reach the dining room, where she was served soup and porridge to replenish her emaciated body. When her strength finally put in a timid appearance and she looked in the mirror, she almost fell over from fright.

'Ah, how awful! I look like Bella Swan from the *Twilight* series. I can't switch on the camera to talk to my mother, or she'll send the cavalry to come and get me. What a disaster!'

Towards the end of Tuesday, her usual good humour returned, and she decided to plan out the details of her forthcoming visits. She read all the guides in the hostel library until soaking herself in Inca imaginary and determined that Wednesday would be a good day to begin her fascinating journey to Tawantinsuyu.

> @ALeo90
> Still alive despite the altitude sickness. Bad grass
> never dies! Tomorrow outside these walls at last
> Cusco city the navel of the world awaits.
> 7 June 2011 at 22:30

# 43

'Shit on a stick!' exclaimed Leo angrily. 'Shit, shit and double shit!'

In the two and a half days she had been ill in the hostel, she hadn't taken off her disguise of pyjamas and flip-flops and had managed to forget all about the inconvenience of her footwear. Now she would have to put off her planned visits and look for a cobbler to repair the heel of her left boot unless she wanted to end up with a bare leg and foot at any given moment. It was clear that Cusco wasn't going to succumb all that easily.

'Ah, you're alive again!' smirked the hostel owner. 'I have to confess I was beginning to wonder. It's not usual for the effects of *soroche* to last so long and to be so aggressive. Take it slowly and get used to making an effort unless you want to end up back in bed...'

'I have no choice, I'll have to go slowly... have you seen the state of this boot?'

The man almost fell over laughing. Leo didn't know whether she was just funny or she looked like a silly puppet, so she didn't say any more. She left with clear directions to a cobbler's and again had to go round in circles before coming across the shop of a little man who repaired the broken heel with some superglue. This solution looked like it would be more temporary than permanent, and Leo decided she'd be happy if it lasted a month until she got back home. When she finally took her eyes off the flagstones on the ground, Leo encountered a wonderful city that had been invisible until then owing to her various mishaps.

As she'd read in the guides, Cusco meant 'navel of the world'. This was the starting point for four paths that led out into the universe. There was no doubt the ancient Inca Empire lived on in the bases of the city's walls. Owing to their oblique position, the enormous blocks of stone set at impossible angles had survived all the earthquakes history had thrown at them. The only earthquake that had almost caused their definitive disappearance had been the arrival of Spanish colonists who, blinded by their thirst for gold, had destroyed all the temples and emptied them of their idols and jewels. Religious and economic greed swept over the navel of the world like a plague and practically stripped it of its magnificence. On top of funerary monuments and Inca homes, the Spanish nobles built tall palaces with colonnades, upper floors and ornate wooden galleries to show just who would be in charge of things around there from now on. The temples of ancient gods and goddesses were renamed and turned into convents and churches in which Cusco painting and altars with precious stones took the place of Inca offerings and mummies. God ceased to be the Sun and became the Catholic Christ. In the name of his Cross, the most terrible massacres among the indigenous cultures of all America were committed. Walking down the streets of Cusco, you could feel the weight of history in your pupils. It wasn't necessary to read so much to find out about the chronicles of yesteryear. You just had to look at a wall for it to spit out its truth and reveal the greedy lust of the Spanish conquistadors' spears. Leo thought this was the prettiest city she had ever seen. Not only because of its architecture, but because there was something there whistling a lullaby that emerged from the conch of time. As if History were alive and had come to talk to you.

The men and women she bumped into in the street – who showed who had inherited that earth – also talked. Low of stature, dressed in bright colours and large sombreros, their dark skin didn't capture Leo's attention so much as their language, a guttural language, the words of which scratched the flesh before crossing the border of air. Quechua was born from the deepest part of the throat to explain the world in words that didn't exist anywhere else because they were only needed here. As if it hurt to speak in this city where everything spoke from the magnificent silence of Coricancha to the Plaza de Armas, ancient threshing floor of the Inca Viracocha. Leo simply listened to its litany, rocked by the coming and going on Hatun Rumiyoc Street.

She had a month to go before returning home, and her hunger for travelling just kept on growing.

# 44

The emotions multiplied by Leo's discovery of the city and *soroche*-imposed isolation created an unusual need to talk to somebody. She didn't think about it twice. She got back to the hostel and went online, intending to proclaim her fascination to the four winds. The first email she came across was from Mayra, and she opened it at once. How she would regret this rash decision! The Argentinian's words caught her off guard, and Leo's pride took a good beating. Her enthusiasm fell down to her feet. Or perhaps even lower.

Mayra said that Ruth & Co. had just abandoned Greece with their tails between their legs. Their involvement in demonstrations and strikes had not had the desired effect on the group's state of mind. She insisted everything was still great with everyone, but they'd decided to spend some time apart so as not to overdo it. What was more, the Mexican brother and sister had fallen in love once again and, when this happened, it was better to rush ahead to avoid laments later on. Claudia, it seemed, had hooked up with a civil servant who was angry about the Troika's cutbacks, and Andrés had lost his head over a lawyer who defended paperless immigrants. They both seemed to have come straight out of a novel by Petros Markaris, Mayra joked, and it wouldn't last more than the time it takes a cockerel to crow. But that's the way Mexicans are, she remarked ironically; when they're infatuated with somebody, there's no tearing them away. So, Lía, Paul, Astrid and she had abandoned the idea of going to Jerusalem and had headed for Bulgaria by train. Apparently Paul wanted to see the St Alexander Nevsky Cathedral in Sofia above all else! Strangely enough, she had nothing to say about Edmundo and his northern adventure, and Leo understood more from her silences than from her words.

There was no doubt this email didn't marry very well with the messages she'd already received from other members of the group, but the girl refused to chew it over too much. So, by good fortune and contrary to what had happened in Paris, Leo reacted bravely. She wasn't going to let them embitter Machu Picchu with their stupid fallings in love or anything else. No way. Stuff Andrés and all his lovers, she swore, before glancing around in search of some heroic exit that would enable her to overcome the treacherous blow she had just received. She was in luck. Next to her, a couple was leafing through the guides, and she decided surreptitiously to hook up with them. They both opened their eyes wide and let her talk her head off. How things had changed! At the start of her journey, she hadn't dared to address anybody, but necessity can create real miracles. Her timid and shy nature had been overwhelmed by a chatty Leo.

'… so that's my story,' she concluded, feeling rather proud of herself. 'Five months away from home, and one month in America left. How about you?'

She described her trip almost without taking a breath. Of course, she avoided all reference to the Mexican and Ruth & Co. and emphasized her bravery in crossing the world without a lifeline. Then, encouraged by Leo's communicative voraciousness, these two told their story as well. They were both from Taiwan, a place the girl could never guess because she couldn't distinguish certain Asiatic features from others, despite the fact they said they were completely different. Their names were María and David, but she couldn't tell which was which because their androgynous features had left her feeling completely confused. About as much as their ability with the language. They spoke Spanish correctly! There was no doubt this couple had a great mystery hidden away.

'Excuse me, but how is it you speak Spanish so well? And what are you doing so far away from home? And how is it possible that you're called María and David?'

The two of them burst out laughing.

'We're no further away from home than you are, what do you think? There are no distances nowadays. We finished our degrees two years ago and decided to come to South America on different projects with international cooperation agencies. María's with an NGO in Cochabamba, Bolivia, researching aquifers, and I'm helping at the school of an indigenous community in the forest bordering Ecuador. Let's just say I like a bit of movement. I'm in the territory that belongs to the FARC. We've been here a while, and a knowledge of the language helps when it comes to learning.'

'So what are you doing in Cusco? Are you on holiday?'

'Of course we are. Every six months, we take a fortnight off and meet up somewhere in the southern hemisphere. We've been to Cartagena de Indias and Manaus, and now we've decided to visit Machu Picchu.'

'But… are you really called María and David?' asked Leo.

'Boh, that's just an obsession of our Spanish teachers, who insist we use a common name that's easier to pronounce…'

And again they laughed out loud. In the time Leo would spend with them, she would discover that when María and David laughed, they weren't always happy and when they cried, they weren't always sad. Contact with different cultures teaches you that even facial expressions are not universal. The only universal thing is feelings, not the way you express them.

She would find that out when María and David turned into Lunmei Hsu and Chen Chou. Not before.

Two hours' conversation was enough to confirm that the chemistry between them worked a treat and they could definitely conquer the Sacred Valley together. The symbiosis between the three of them was perfect. Leo gained company, and they gained a greater ease for communicating with the locals. Despite their linguistic knowledge, communication wasn't always easy for them. The three of them would save money by sharing services.

'For our purposes, we need a fourth passenger,' murmured the one who could have been María or David, glancing over at an absent-minded backpacker who had just handed in his passport at reception.

That night, they switched to a triple room, and Leo had to admit, as well as the saving involved, it was pleasant not to feel so alone.

When she fell asleep, she still wasn't sure who David was and who María was, and whether they were a couple.

Never again would she recall Mayra's email and the succession of slaps to her pride.

Boh, Andrés... what did it matter what that goofball got up to?

# 45

'So who's David and who's María? Excuse me, but I can't work it out...'

Leo was amazed by the abruptness of this tall, slim man who replied to the name of Manfred and whom they approached over breakfast with the aim of securing a fourth passenger for the Sacred Valley. The Taiwanese couple responded with absolute normality.

'Don't worry. Leo's been with us for twelve hours, and she still doesn't know,' mocked one of them, who turned out to be María. 'That's David.'

They quickly told him their plan, and Manfred nodded. All of this in basic English with some words in Spanish and lots of signs.

'It may well be a wonderful plan, but give me at least another two days to get to know Cusco. I can't set off right now.'

They agreed to leave for the Sacred Valley in two days' time. The plan was perfect. Public transport didn't facilitate freedom of movement between the various Inca ruins and cities scattered around the Urubamba Valley, the so-called Sacred Valley of the Incas, at the upper vertex of which was the sanctuary of Machu Picchu. So they decided the best thing would be to hire a car with a driver that would take them to Ollantaytambo with a stop anywhere they fancied along the way.

'I have one condition,' warned Manfred. 'I like to do my own thing, so I'm just going to share the cost of the car, that's all.'

Having pointed this out, Manfred seemed like an ideal travel companion, and they agreed to meet two days later over breakfast.

Leo hated haggling. She really hated it, and yet she had no choice if they were to get a good price for the trip to the town of Ollantaytambo about eighty kilometres from Cusco. The Taiwanese couple's apparent innocence almost led them to arrange a car for three or four times the amount recommended on forums. The girl stepped in just in time and persuaded herself that from now on she would be the one to arrange payments. They finally hit on a middle-aged man with a pleasant smile who conquered them with his loquacity and the 160 soles he would charge.

Leo had been in Cusco since Saturday, but had to admit that the city never ended. It seemed to grow every day, offering up new and surprising places. Having carefully studied all the entrance tickets she would have to buy – it seemed you had to pay for everything – Leo opted for the tourist ticket that gave you access to seventeen important places for a student rate of 70 soles. The ticket was valid for ten days and allowed her into such unmissable sites as Coricancha and Sacsayhuamán together with others she would never have chosen had she not had the ticket. Coricancha, temple of the ancient sun god, known as the golden temple because its walls were once covered in this precious metal that made it shine from far away, left her reeling. Here, she encountered the Inca walls that had been revealed by an earthquake under the Convent of Santo Domingo and came across clues that fed her voracious curiosity. She was so absorbed she didn't notice Manfred drawing in a notebook at her side. That afternoon – it might have been Thursday or Friday – she devoted to searching online for more information about the chronicles of Pedro Cieza de León, Felipe Guaman Poma de Ayala, the Inca Garcilaso de la Vega and an enigmatic Juan de Betanzos, who described the city of Vilcabamba.

When David and María returned from their visits, Leo couldn't resist sharing her discoveries on the Internet with them.

'Did you know Juan Diez de Betanzos was a chronicler who came to America at the hands of Pizarro and, by learning Quechua, wrote *Narrative of the Incas* in the sixteenth century? In the few fragments that have been preserved of this manuscript, he talks of a city, Vilcabamba, which has yet to be discovered. During the twentieth century, numerous expeditions were launched in search of this lost city but, so far, nobody has managed to find it. Some say it's the remote ruins of Espíritu Pampa, but others insist it still lies hidden away in the dense undergrowth of the forest. Don't you get it? Juan de Betanzos! Betanzos is a town in Galicia. He must have been Galician – like me!'

The two looked at her with cramp in their legs and minds.

'Shall we go and get some pizza?'

Leo ignored them and decided to send out a tweet to her book group. They would know what she was trying to get at.

> @ALeo90
> Read, Read, What Are You Reading? Heading for
> the Sacred Valley in search of the lost cities
> described by ancient chroniclers.
> Come with me to the Inca Empire!
> 10 June 2011 at 18:30

On the way back from dinner, with the smell of firewood from the mud oven still impregnating their clothes, the bells of the cathedral rang out for the last Mass of the day. At that point, Leo discerned some familiar letters in the middle of the Plaza de Armas. The handwriting was tortuous. The ink, yellow. The message, unmistakable:

### I Love You Leo A.

After her anger at Mayra's message, Leo felt completely indifferent.

'Up yours!'

She could be heard saying in that starry night.

'If it's you, Andrés, then up yours! If not, then up yours anyway.'

At that moment, it didn't occur to her that Mayra's message, like so many other things, might just have been a red herring. That would come later. Her sense of indignation only allowed her to say:

'Up yours!'

A little further on, David and María argued over the price of a bead necklace.

# 46

It was a luminous morning on Saturday 11 June when they decided to conquer the Sacred Valley in the back of an old banger driven by a chatterbox. They'd agreed on the price of 160 soles. That meant 40 soles per person, a much cheaper and more convenient rate than the successive changes of bus required when taking the route from Cusco to Ollantaytambo with a stopover in Pisac. The Taiwanese couple laughed at all the driver's jokes while Leo gazed out at the green of the chlorophyll growing vigorously on the other side of the window. Next to her, Manfred slept the whole way with a hangover that smelled of pisco sour, a delicious cocktail with high-proof liquor and a difficult digestion.

Behind them lay that 'I Love You Leo A.' which Leo insisted on forgetting.

Shortly after setting out, they stopped in the little town of Pisac to visit the local market, gaze at the trinkets bought by the Taiwanese couple and drink some coca tea at the suggestion of their talkative driver.

'Drink slowly and breathe deeply. Coca's good in tea. If you'd like to chew some leaves, just ask me for them. It's the best cure for *soroche*. It's not a drug, don't look like that! We all consume unprocessed coca leaves to avoid headaches and tiredness. Believe me, you'll need the energy for what's waiting for you in the Archaeological Park,' he smiled maliciously.

In effect, what was waiting for them was way too hard for all of them. When the old man lifted the handbrake in a parking space on the side of a mountain a couple of kilometres from the village, they all stared at him in amazement.

'You must be joking!' sighed María.

No, he wasn't joking. The remains of Inca walls trailing up the mountain told them the climb would be complicated, not so much because of the effort involved as because of the difficulty of breathing. The agricultural terraces and various lookouts offered privileged views of the Sacred Valley, which had been sliced open by the furious knife of the River Urubamba. Walking from one terrace to the next became an arduous task that required constant breaks. The distance wasn't great, but the arduousness of the climb was. Leo had the impression she was fading whenever she took a step but, seconds after breathing slowly and calming the unruly beating of her heart, she recovered the strength to keep going. The visit took them seven hours. They could have done it more quickly, but preferred to go slowly and enjoy the wonderful views and buildings that sprouted at their feet. On the summit, the Intihuatana – or ceremonial centre for astronomical observation – and military outposts gazed at the sky and the chasm of the Kitamayo River. From there, nothing of the earthly or celestial world could have escaped the condor-like sight of the priests and guards.

'Goodness me! This must be as fabulous as Machu Picchu!' murmured Leo on reaching one of the defensive bulwarks that afforded a panoramic view of the valley.

'Wow, and that was just the peasant farmers,' confirmed David, 'just imagine what it will be like when we get to the nobles…'

Manfred, two terraces further down, leaned against a wall and drew in his notebook, his eyes lost on the horizon. He didn't have lunch with them, and they had to wait half an hour after the agreed time before they could continue to Ollantaytambo.

It was dark when they arrived. The cold had descended from the realm of the apus on the peaks of the Andes and taken hold of that last Inca city before the sacred sanctuary. David, María and Leo opted for a triple room in the hostel next to the main road. Manfred, however, stayed in his tent in the back garden. His tiny rucksack held a tent that gave him the freedom to sleep almost wherever he liked.

That night, a grandiose spectacle awaited them up in the sky, where thousands of stars twinkled in a way Leo had never seen before.

# 47

The noise woke Leo very early – far too early. The constant passage of vehicles roaring past and horns of tourist buses speeding down the narrow streets of Ollantaytambo didn't let her go back to sleep.

'What a racket…!'

The day had yet to dawn when hordes of tourists started pouring down the tracks that led to the station, where they would catch a train to Aguas Calientes and from there to Machu Picchu. It was the usual, most convenient way of reaching the sanctuary, which meant thousands of people huddled together at that untimely hour in a corner one step away from the northern forest to board the earliest trains. Leo heard David and María snoring and slipped outside. The first rays had yet to warm the atmosphere, and she decided to take refuge in the garden. As the droplets of light melted the early-morning dew, Leo discovered brightly-coloured trees and flowers she had never seen. A strange hum, as of a swarm of bees, reached her ears, but she couldn't detect an insect anywhere. What she did discover a little further on, on a bush of mallows, was the vertiginous flapping of a hummingbird's wings. Her heart started racing. What a beautiful sight! With its lively tongue, it sucked the nectar of the flowers, oblivious to her presence. Its blue chest glinted against the damp green of the broom, and Leo let the minutes go by, transfixed by this charming creature. Suddenly a low noise frightened it away, and it flew to a creeper on the other side of the garden. When the girl sought out the source of the noise that had startled it, she noticed a movement behind Manfred's tent.

He was a very strange guy. All they'd learned was that he lived in Stockholm and worked for a design company. What they didn't know, despite their repeated attempts to find out, was exactly what he designed. With their angelic expression of being permanently at a loss, David and María tried on several occasions to pull on the thread of his life, but to no avail. Whenever they tugged too hard, Manfred would shoo them away by softly whistling 'Moon River', the signature song from *Breakfast at Tiffany's*. What would the boy do when they got to Ollantaytambo? Once they'd paid the driver, their travelling pact was over, so it seemed likely they would never see him again.

Or perhaps they would.

On the other hand, the unlikely trio of Leo and the Taiwanese had decided to continue their adventure together for at least another couple of days. They would spend two or three days in Ollantaytambo to visit the Inca ruins there and go cycling in the vicinity. Once they'd had breakfast and the noise of vehicles had stopped echoing down the main street, the town regained its warm tranquillity. Leo wasn't sure why, but she was fascinated by this place. Perhaps because she hadn't been expecting it, or else the virtual absence of visitors gave her a much better chance of admiring the magnificent beauty of the archaeological remains that, to her surprise, were located only a couple of metres from the hostel. How could they not have noticed them the day before! They comprised a series of almost vertical terraces, with steep stairways and paths that led to the ceremonial centre of the sun god. It was smaller than the one in Pisac and no doubt more modest than the one on Machu Picchu, and Leo felt especially drawn to it. She spent the day hiding out on the summit, at a bend in the hill where Manco Inca Yupanqui had succeeded in warding off the advance of the Spanish conquistadors towards the sacred mountain. The fortress was unassailable, dominated by large stones that revealed the architectural prowess of their makers. From up there, having struggled to get over her vertigo, the girl closed her eyes and let herself be cradled by the tepid sun of an Andean midday. Not far away, Manfred also remained in a contemplative position.

Perhaps this boy had more to do with her than she imagined.

The following day, rocked by the pleasant temperatures, they decided to go on a bike ride by the River Urubamba. It was nice to have the freedom to go wherever they liked – or wherever their energy would take them. Turning the pedals was much harder than they'd envisaged, and they never lost sight of the defensive walls of the Inca settlement. In the distance, it looked like a small fort, a knot that tied the valley so the Incas could protect their precious treasure of temples and dreams. Leo, David and María didn't dare go further than common sense allowed, in case they had to hire a car to get back.

When they returned, exhausted, but with gleaming smiles on their faces, Manfred's tent was still in the garden. They decided to call him so they could go and have dinner together in a bar.

The night was longer than they could have imagined. To start with, they treated themselves to quinoa soup, potatoes, fried pork and Peruvian corn with cheese. They drank plenty of beer and, at the tavern-keeper's insistence, sampled *chicha*, an alcoholic drink made from fermented corn that rushed into their heads. They laughed out loud and, hours later, let the words come tumbling out. They were as drunk as conger eels.

There was a moment when their inebriated state led each of them to talk in his or her own language and, strangely enough, they all seemed to understand one another. Perhaps the communication problem at the Tower of Babel was because they hadn't drunk enough *chicha* or made a big enough effort to get on. When people want to understand each other, they do. No language prevents this. That was the only bright idea Leo could capture on a night of mist that nurtured a rather painful hangover.

When Manfred went to get the others from their room the following day, the coming and going of tourist buses had ceased some time earlier, and the city had descended into its putrid calm. It seemed the night before they'd agreed to hire a car to go to Maras and Moray. Nobody apart from the Swede could remember this but, even so, they got up and went to arrange a car. They agreed to pay 100 soles for the outing. They would have given another 30 soles, and the driver would have done it for 30 soles less, but in the business of negotiation nobody ever shows their cards. The hammer of ethylic excess banged against Leo's temples the whole way. The high speed of the vehicle as it climbed and descended hills, dodged children, bikes, llamas and lorries, didn't help much. At the top of a ridge, the driver stopped and with a brief nod indicated the way. When they leaned out over the precipice, Leo almost died.

She might have been moved by the descending structure of large, concentric circles emerging at her feet, but all she felt like doing was crying at the thought of the effort involved in going down and back up.

'Can't we just look at it from here?' she stammered as the rest of the group skipped merrily along the path.

'You must be crazy!' laughed David. 'After extensive research, historians have concluded this structure on various terraces in the form of a bowl was a kind of agricultural laboratory where they tried out different temperatures to extract as much as they could from the cultivation of cereals. A kind of greenhouse, in short.'

'And? So?'

'Well, what's interesting about this place is experiencing the different temperatures on each level, woman. Come on!'

'Ohhhh, my head... It's so hot!' snorted the girl as she carried on walking.

In effect, and surprisingly enough, the temperature did vary on the various platforms of the enormous swirl of fields. Leo found this out when, in a gust of heat, she collapsed in the central circle. She thought she'd never make it back to the car and in all probability she wouldn't have, had it not been for the help of the rest of the group. David and Manfred pulled her along the whole way while María insisted she take little sips of water.

It was obvious these travel companions of hers were from another world because they possessed an unnatural ability to put up with altitude sickness and hangovers. Either that, or they'd drunk fewer glasses of *chicha* than her. She felt a little stupid and tried to remain calm but, when they got back to the car park and found their taxi-driver wasn't there any more, she just slumped on the ground.

What a moron! He'd pushed off and left them there, in the middle of nowhere. It was David's fault – he had kindly offered at the petrol station to pay part of their fee up front. And now here they were, on a green ridge, suffocating and surrounded by horses and tourists. Just great. Manfred went off for a while, and the Taiwanese couple started shouting angrily at each other, so Leo decided to have a sleep. She was tired… When she woke up, the taxi-driver had returned.

After an unlikely excuse about having some urgent matter to attend to, they all got back in the car and headed for the open salt ponds of Maras. By this time, Leo was so exhausted she had no strength left and decided just to look from the road. She only got out of the car to buy some water. She might also have been afraid that the driver would abandon them again and leave them to walk back to Ollantaytambo.

I'm never going to drink again. Never.

When they all talked of taking the night train to Aguas Calientes to visit the sacred city the following morning, she shook her head vehemently.

'Not for anything in the world. I just want to sleep and recover from this blasted headache.'

She wasn't expecting much so, when David and María laughed out loud and postponed their visit to Machu Picchu so they could wait for her, Leo felt a warm sense of comfort. That was the closest thing to Ruth & Co. she'd come across in South America. Manfred silently watched a boy chasing a sheep.

When you sleep at an inconvenient time, you run the risk of waking up at an inconvenient time. So when Leo woke in the early hours of the morning, she again cursed that drinking spree that had been bothering her all day. On top of that, her room-mates were snoring, so she had no way of going back to sleep. She decided to get up and visit the common room, where she could go online. At such an ungodly hour, there wouldn't be a queue, and it might be days before she had the chance to check her email again. She used this opportunity to send messages to her mother, Roi and Aunt Cris, and to access some online media. There, she found out that Greece was facing another day of strikes with street protests and there would be a total lunar eclipse. These two news items inevitably led her back to Andrés and Mayra's email. What a scumbag! He had a different lover in every country he went to in order to escape the unwelcome visits of solitude. He probably deceived them all with the same endearing, but empty caresses. Boh! Damn fool! How was the rest of the group? Ruth & Co. were a bunch of unpredictable lunatics; anything seemed possible in that group of stateless people with more flags than sense. Were they OK? Leo tried to drive away these pointless worries, but she was inevitably reminded of the moonlight on the Galata Bridge, when Andrés had gone looking for her at a time when it seemed they loved each other, but really it was only desire. That full moon lying on the waters of the Bosphorus between Asia and Europe had been the most beautiful she'd ever seen. Now she thought about it, with this new eclipse, she'd be able to see the stars in Ollantaytambo better.

She emitted a cheerful tweet to hide the rage she felt at her wounded pride:

@ALeo90
I just love Ollanta and hate chicha. Tonight
train to Aguas Calientes to wake up tomorrow
in Machu Picchu. Did I tell you
how much I hate chicha? Ohhh!
15 June 2011 at 6:11

It was just about to dawn when Leo went out into the garden to await her friend, the little hummingbird. But instead of the bird, she came across Manfred lying in his sleeping bag. As she approached, he hid what was in his hands and greeted her effusively.

'Hey, sleeping beauty…'

'Sleeping beauty can't sleep,' retorted Leo.

'Ah, what nonsense, you just had a little too much *chicha*. That will pass.'

'Yes, the *soroche* was supposed to pass as well. I feel like a disaster. Peru will be the end of me before I ever get to Machu Picchu.'

Leo tried to keep the conversation going, but to no avail. The boy had taken refuge behind an unassailable wall, quite unlike David and María, about whom she knew pretty much everything. David was twenty-four, had renal colic, beautiful, smooth, black hair and six pairs of trousers that fitted in the most ridiculous rucksack. He was tall, hairy, and had, shall we say, an exotic beauty. María, on the other hand, had just turned twenty-three and had promised herself a condor tattoo on her buttocks. By popular demand, one night of drunkenness, they had persuaded her to include a snake and a puma in her work of art so she could complete the sacred trilogy of Inca cosmogony. She weighed more than eighty kilos, so space on her skin wouldn't be a problem. The Taiwanese girl cared little or nothing about her appearance. Ever since they'd met, she hadn't taken off this revolting red and green jersey, while a cap with ear flaps made her look even more outlandish. Manfred, however, gave little away with his physical appearance. Normal complexion, normal height, normal-coloured skin… the Swede was really insipid. And by not talking, he didn't do anything to make himself more attractive. And yet there was something mysterious about him that drew Leo's attention. Nothing annoyed her more than a secret she couldn't fathom. Perhaps that was what made her so insanely curious.

After breakfast, they booked their train tickets to Aguas Calientes for the end of the afternoon, in the category of Backpacker, which was the cheapest. After that, everyone chose what to do with their time. Leo had learned her lesson from Ruth & Co.: every now and then it was necessary to split up in order to be able to carry on together; no group can endure more than five days' permanent cohabitation. It's exhausting. So, every once in a while, it's necessary to go off and do whatever you feel like without giving explanations, free of the tyranny of majority decisions. The girl used this opportunity to visit a laundry, air her clothes, read some guides about Machu Picchu and have a walk in that town whose walls and water channels were a noisy relic of Inca times. On one street, she came across David and María, who had just climbed up to some ruined granaries scattered along a gully, from where they said the views of Ollantaytambo were exceptional.

With less than an hour to go before the departure of the train, Leo went to get her clothes from the laundry. But it was closed! She banged as hard as she could on the door and carried on knocking, but nobody answered. A neighbour told her the owner of the business lived in the town of Urubamba and had left two hours earlier, so there was nothing they could do. Leo was startled at first, and then dumbstruck... She had been left without any clothes! She only had what she was wearing! Her head started spinning around. No, she definitely couldn't waste the money she'd spent on the train... It had cost an arm and a leg. In a couple of minutes, she reached a decision: she would leave for Aguas Calientes and pick up the clothes on her way back. Yes, that was what she would do. Surely they'll keep them till I come back, she reasoned.

Surely.

The night train stopped them contemplating the extraordinary views of lush vegetation as it advanced along the railway towards Aguas Calientes, a city born in a ravine for the sole purpose of serving tourists to Machu Picchu.

The darkness did not detract from the emotion of the journey, it just turned it into an odyssey in which anxiety, nerves and happiness were mixed in equal parts. There were only a few hours to go before she accomplished her great dream of visiting the sacred sanctuary.

It would be a lie to say that Leo slept at all that night.

# 48

The clickety-clack of the train disturbed the valley's silence. Like a knife, it sliced through the luxuriant forest and competed with the roar of the river that leaped down the hillside. It was midday, and the world had put on a luminous mantle. For Leo, however, it had yet to dawn.

She still couldn't believe what had happened in the last two days.

Uncertainty gnawed away at her and ached in her chest.

She just couldn't believe it.

She was so exhausted, physically and mentally, she couldn't even rest.

Two days earlier, they had undertaken this selfsame journey in the opposite direction, from Ollantaytambo to Aguas Calientes. It had been night-time then, and she hadn't slept a wink on account of the emotion of discovering Machu Picchu. How could she have guessed what would happen next? How could she have guessed?

And all because of that stupid message.

# 49

The previous day had passed at a dizzying pace, and events had rushed along in a waterfall that had taken Leo from happiness to the most awful dismay. It was only a few hours since she had travelled on that selfsame train in the opposite direction. The emotion of visiting Machu Picchu had enveloped her from head to toe. David, María and Manfred wouldn't stop wittering while sinking submarines drawn on sheets of paper. Anything sufficed to pass the time and banish the darkness that held sway in that carriage. It was Wednesday 15 June, the day of unrest in Greece and of the total lunar eclipse, when the four travel companions left Ollantaytambo on their way to Aguas Calientes, the last stop before the sacred sanctuary. The following day, they would wait for the sunrise at Inti Punku, the Sun Gate, on the last stretch of the famous Inca Trail.

And so it turned out. It was night-time when they took a taxi in Aguas Calientes to climb up to the sanctuary with their torches. Leo's mother had been right to include a small LED flashlight in her rucksack. The darkness meant they couldn't see a thing and, almost in silence, the four of them slowly ascended the royal path that led to the Sun Gate, just behind the hut for the funerary monument's guard. They had read all the information in great detail, and there could be no doubt. They wanted to reach the gate so they could gaze out at the wonder of the unassailable fortress that nestled against the limits of the forest. Manfred had insisted on doing it because, as he confessed when they were walking up, step by step, his primary desire had been to do the four-day Inca Trail, but he hadn't managed to get a permit. It seems the Inca Trail is one of the most famous treks in the whole of South America and the world. It crosses Andean mountains and valleys full of Inca remains and then sinks into the luxuriant tropical forest where hummingbirds and wild orchids blossom beside the stone trail. It's only forty kilometres, but the harsh steepness of its terrain and the altitude (Dead Woman's Pass is 4,200 metres above sea level) make it an exercise in resistance for the chest and joints. On top of that, there is no warning of bad weather because the Andes can be a little treacherous. It can rain heavily or the sun can burn in the space of a couple of hours. It is supposed to be the final stretch of a royal road that linked Machu Picchu with the other four provinces of Ancient Tawantinsuyu, which stretched from present-day Ecuador to Chile.

Manfred's voice encouraged the other members of the group up the slope. Around them were only shadows and the Swede's rage at not obtaining a place on the Inca Trail. Apparently, access is limited to a few hundred people each day and, in high season, you can't get a place unless you book several months ahead. Manfred hadn't done this, hence his constant litany as they ascended the slope. What a pest! He'd said the walk would take no more than half an hour, and they'd already been trudging along for an hour with no sign of that blasted Inti Punku. Suddenly, they heard a murmur, and dozens of glow-worms loomed out of the night. It took them a few seconds to realize these were the earliest risers who, like them, had wanted to be there to greet the sun.

Manfred gazed hungrily at their rucksacks, dirtiness, tiredness and cramp, and promised he wouldn't return home until he'd done the trek himself. Or else his name wasn't Manfred. He didn't say this out loud, of course, but Leo had learned how to interpret his enigmatic silence.

The darkness of the night gave way to some soft shadows and sighs of amazement. There is a brief moment when, because of the process of thermal inversion, the blanket of mist covering Machu Picchu at dawn suddenly dissipates. It's only a moment but, for that tiny instant of time, it's worth getting up early and arriving at the Sun Gate out of energy. When Leo began to glimpse the forms of the sacred city, she felt an emotion in her chest that was difficult to describe.

Fulfilling a dream is wonderful, but it also pushes us towards the precipice.

And there, surrounded by strangers, she trembled like a green reed.

She'd done it. She'd reached Machu Picchu all on her own. She was right at the crest of the wonderful dragon's back whose tail she had glimpsed in Ushuaia. The Andes range, backbone of the American continent, daringly scratched the stars in southern Peru. Perched atop its spine, you could feel the huge Andean beast's heart beating down in the sacred citadel in a systole and diastole of oblique walls and trapezoidal windows. Nothing had stopped her.

And that same sense of certainty showed her the beginning of the end of her journey was nigh.

Suddenly, as had happened at her departure, though this time without anger and with plenty of nostalgia, she missed Aldara, Inés and Martiño. She didn't hate them any more. She felt no rancour at the way they'd abandoned her at the last minute. Now she only wanted them to be there so they could gaze out with her at that wonder raking the sky from the peak of the so-called 'Old Mountain' of the Andes, right at the foot of the leafiest, most impenetrable forest where the Incas are said to have hidden Vilcabamba.

She wished the three of them could have been there to see it.

'Come on, peanut, let's be off.'

She had been so absorbed in her thoughts she'd forgotten all about David, María and Manfred, who were staring at her in alarm. First of all, they made fun of her consternation but, as they went down the stony path, Leo saw the emotion dancing in their pupils as well.

Machu Picchu leaves nobody indifferent.

David wanted to rush ahead so he could access the famous Huayna Picchu. This mountain has a complicated path, not suitable for people who suffer from vertigo, but the guides all said it was worth the effort because of the extraordinary views of the sacred city. The Taiwanese boy, agile as a snake, insisted he was going to climb it, and that was what he did. Manfred, María and Leo continued their visit to the enclosure, the limits of the sacred place now flooded by all the hikers and hordes of tourists from Aguas Calientes. And yet Machu Picchu is so large you can still feel alone, especially after midday, when the furious flocks of cameras abandon the mountain as quickly as they came on their way back to Cusco.

Leo had the whole day in front of her and didn't plan to run after anybody. She took out her reams of notes and started exploring the sacred city. First, the agricultural terraces, granaries, Temple of the Sun, springs, Room of the Three Windows, the Intihuatana or solar observatory... The whole citadel spoke of a mysterious world which investigators have been unable to fathom. The various theses about the meaning and function of stones, sanctuaries, walls and granaries, have given rise to conflicting explanations of a city some consider a military refuge, others a ceremonial centre, others a town, most a palace, others a stash of Incan gold.

It doesn't matter. Machu Picchu is a treasure all to itself which cannot be summed up in a rational explanation of its purpose. Leo recalled the words of Dolores, Aunt Cris' colleague in Buenos Aires:

'It's the most magical place in the world. There's an esoteric force up there that takes your breath away… Really, it's an inexplicable feeling that traps and changes you.'

Reluctantly, she had to admit that she was right.

There was something up there that took away your senses. The oblique walls and trapezoidal windows failed to stem the flow of thoughts that crashed against the leafiness of the forest rustling mysteriously below. Yes. There was something that went beyond logic and beauty and hurled you into the abyss of the unknown.

There was nobody there when they abandoned the sacred enclosure and returned to Aguas Calientes. On the bus link, in silence, all four of them chewed over the emotion of the enigma that surrounded the lost city.

They reached Aguas Calientes when it was dark. Exhausted and hungry – having lunch inside the enclosure was forbidden, and the restaurant outside was way too expensive – they decided to have dinner before returning to the hostel.

Leo was dying to get away so she could go online. She needed to express the surprising joy of that visit and to tell Aldara, Inés and Martiño she had missed them. She had missed them a lot.

But she didn't do this. That blasted message came and messed up all her plans.

## 50

It was nine o'clock in Peru when, facing the computer screen, Leo decided to write to her friends. She opened her email and, to her surprise, came across a message from Aldara that said:

> I'm so sorry, Leo. At a distance, I suppose it's all that much harder to take. You have all my support.

The girl couldn't understand what she meant and read the message without a great deal of conviction. What was Aldara referring to? It never occurred to her that it might be something serious. She had to read the message four or five times to realize what it said and, as she went over the text, anxiety started to take hold. No, no way... It couldn't be... Aldara said how sorry she was to hear about Grandma Carmiña, she knew how close they were, and it must be hard being so far away from home. She added she'd learned about it in the papers and her family was strong enough to recover from the blow. That was all. Aldara said nothing else. She assumed Leo knew all about it and just expressed her support, sending her a hug to soothe her pain in the distance. Her heart pinching her chest, Leo desperately searched for the time. It was half past nine, local time, half past three in the morning at home. She couldn't call and she certainly couldn't leave Aguas Calientes. She had no way of making contact and, however hard she tried, it would be at least two days before she could get back home to... No, no way... Not Grandma Carmiña... After the fright, the confusion, the anxiety, the pain, came the tears. She felt she couldn't breathe and went out into the cold of the

Andean night. Next to her, the turbid waters of the Vilcanota River tumbling over the mountain stones roared along. No, no way… Not Grandma Carmiña… What could have happened? Why hadn't her mother told her? A message, a tweet, anything. Why hadn't anyone thought of her? Grandma Carmiña…

Leo was conscious that life continued its course in another part of the world. Nothing stops, and she wasn't the only one experiencing things. It can happen, life continues and everything changes while you're away. The trip, her brother, Roi, had said, wasn't hers alone.

'What is it, Leo?'

Manfred the Swede had come out to smoke a cigarette and discovered her disconsolate downpour in the night.

'Leo, calm down. What is it?'

'My grandma, Grandma Carmiña…' sobbed Leo.

'Try to speak, Leo. What has happened to your grandma?'

'I don't know, I don't know…'

'Then why are you crying?'

'Because a friend wrote to me and expressed her support for what's happened. Only I don't know what it is! And I can't call home at this hour!'

'I understand. Breathe deeply and try to calm down. You don't know what's happened, so why imagine the worst? It's just possible…'

'But why didn't anybody tell me? Why?' The constant tears obstructed Leo's words.

It was a long, strange night. David, María and Manfred didn't leave her silence, which was interrupted by sighs, murmurs and laments. To begin with, they tried comforting her with jokes and games to divert her embittered thoughts, but Leo was not to be consoled. She only had thoughts for Carmiña, and the feverish spate of memories of her grandmother raced past as noisily as the river outside.

No, there was no way her grandma could have left without saying goodbye. No way...

The hours sifted through the Andean night. In that dark gully, the murmur of the water and night birds disturbed her mood even more. When it was two in the morning, eight o'clock at home, Leo grabbed the phone and called.

It was undoubtedly the most painful phone call of her life. She didn't know what voice would answer, nor what they would tell her, but she was sure it wasn't going to be nice. Prepared for the worst, Leo listened to the ringtone until she heard her father's sluggish voice.

# 51

'Hello?'

'Good morning, papa,' wept Leo.

'Leo, daughter! What is it? Is something up?'

'No…'

'Leo, what is it?'

'What's happened, papa? What's happened to Grandma Carmiña?'

There was no sound on the other end of the line.

'How do you know about that, Leo? Who told you? We agreed not to inform you.'

'Then it's true, papa? Tell me honestly.'

'The accident? Yes, of course it's true. But until we find out how she is, we didn't want to worry you.'

'How she is?' Leo suddenly glimpsed a shaft of light at the end of the tunnel, an unforeseen light she hadn't even imagined during the long hours of waiting.

'Leo, what have you heard?'

'Then, she… she isn't dead?' A tiny thread stretched its way across the ocean.

'No! Who told you that? It was a fairly spectacular accident and got everybody talking, but she's OK.'

'What happened then?' Leo's voice was now one of anxiety.

'She fell out of the fig tree. That blasted old tree! It's been a curse on the women of this family! You know how stubborn she is. The first figs appeared, and she climbed up the tree until a branch broke and down she went. You've a grandmother who thinks the years don't go by for her. She's not a young whippersnapper any more. The problem is she was lying on the ground for almost a whole day until Maruxa da Chousa heard her and called for an ambulance. Now she's in hospital, but it's only a broken hip, hypothermia and several bruises. She'll be home in a couple of days. You know how crazy she can be!'

'It's just that I thought… I thought…'

'We didn't want to inform you so you wouldn't be alarmed without reason. In the end, it wasn't anything at all. It all came out in the papers, but it's just been a fright. Are you OK, Leo? Not long to go now before you come home!'

'Yes, I am now,' whispered Leo, feeling a little lost. 'Tell mother to call me when she's with grandma in hospital. I want to talk to her myself.'

'To who – mother?'

'No, Grandma Carmiña. Tell her to call me as soon as she can. I'll have the phone on. Take care, papa. We'll see each other in a couple of weeks. Lots of kisses.'

Leo collapsed when she put down the phone. Next to her, David, María and Manfred were waiting expectantly. They hadn't understood a word she'd said, but her sudden serenity told them that perhaps things might not be so bad.

'She's in hospital. She's going to get better,' announced Leo eventually.

She was surrounded by applause and hugs. Leo would never forget that, when she thought she would be attending her grandma Carmiña's wake at a distance, a Taiwanese couple and a Swedish boy showered her with consolation and affection. They decided to go to bed for a couple of hours, even though all the emotion had been too much for them to fall asleep.

When they got up to take the first train back to Ollantaytambo, Leo hadn't slept a wink. She wouldn't believe the news until she'd spoken to grandma herself.

That was why the return journey, with the brightly-shining Andes and warm sun caressing the world, was so protracted. Leo had no coverage on her phone and she knew it would be at least another couple of hours before she heard her grandmother's longed-for voice.

Ah, how stubborn she was! Climbing a fig tree! She'd been warned a bunch of times it could be dangerous, it was a treacherous tree! She'd learned nothing from the time Leo and Aunt Cris had fallen down at the local festivities, when Leo had received that wonderful book of maps!

But her granddaughter knew her beloved Carmiña wasn't dotty.

Fig jam was Leo's favourite. She was sure her grandmother had climbed the tree just so she could have some ready for when Leo came home.

This certainty filled her with guilt.

The sacred sanctuary of Machu Picchu was left behind. It would be several days before Leo recalled the emotion of that place, which had been totally eclipsed by the news about her grandmother's accident.

And by the guilt that gnawed away inside her.

## 52

They got off the train in Ollantaytambo and immediately linked up with a bus that would take them to Cusco. Leo was so focused on her mobile phone and the call that just wouldn't come that she forgot all about the clothes she'd left at the laundry. At that moment, nothing mattered to her except hearing Carmiña's voice. She could see the rainbow on all the local flags and the bulls of Pukara presiding over the roofs of the city-navel of the world when she finally heard the longed-for sound.

'Grandma!'

'What's the matter?'

'Grandma, are you OK?'

'Of course I am! Praise be to God! What a scandal in the parish, it's all anybody talks about! It even appeared in the papers! I've kept a cutting for when you get back. It says, "Old Lady Lies Wounded for Twenty-Four Hours at the Foot of a Tree." Blasted journalists, I'm not an old lady! And I'm not crazy either! All I did was slip out of the fig tree, and now they've got me here in hospital as if I was sick... You know how stubborn your mother can be. All I want is to go home. What's up with you?'

'Nothing, grandma. I'm on a bus.'

'Whereabouts?'

'In Peru, grandma dear. I've just been to Machu Picchu.'

'Macho what? So you liked it, then?'

'Yes, a lot. Are you sure you're OK?'

'Here we go again. I'm fine, don't waste your money on me. Go on, off you go.'

'Grandma, we'll have to cut that fig tree down, don't you think?'

'Another cow in the cornfield. What makes you think the fig tree's to blame! You lot! Come on, hang up now, don't waste your money.'

'Grandma!…'

'What?'

'I love you a lot.'

'I love you too, little one. Now be careful… And make sure you eat properly!'

And without further ado Grandma Carmiña put the phone down without even letting her talk to her mother. Leo felt so relieved she went weak at the knees. The world had done a flip and a half in only two days, and her body was paying the price of so much emotion.

Finding accommodation that night in Cusco was rather complicated. It seemed the tourist season was reaching its zenith with the celebration on 24 June of the famous Inti Raymi, the winter solstice in Sacsayhuamán, and there were hardly any free beds. Having done the rounds, they ended up in the private house of a woman who lived at the top of the district of San Blas. A very steep slope led to this neighbourhood that was home to craftsmen and artists and had wonderful views of the city. The coats of arms on the colonial houses filled the streets with colour, but the hovel they'd ended up in had nothing luxurious about it. Manfred, who'd always refused to share a room, had no choice but to give way and unite his dreams to those of the others. But even having to have a cold shower out of the washbasin didn't bother them that much after the difficulty of finding a place in that heaving city.

After everything that had happened, the symbiosis in that group was strange. They had started out being simple strangers sharing a taxi and little by little, without any of them realizing it, they'd been carried along by the convenience of having company. It was easier like that to share experiences, to organize trips, to negotiate prices, to find somewhere to eat. Of course, everybody had their different tastes, moods and foibles. David and María would stop at every single stall to buy whatever was on offer, be it pottery, silver or rag dolls. They filled their rucksacks, which seemed to have no bottom. Manfred, on the other hand, was always lightening his load. Every day, his luggage became more discreet. That said, the Swede was a vegetarian, which limited the restaurants they could go to.

That evening, Leo connected with her mother and Roi on Skype. They spoke for the half hour they were permitted in an Internet café full of people demanding their own time online. It was enough. Leo just wanted to hear their voices on that day when she'd felt so vulnerable. That may have been why she sent out the following tweet:

> @ALeo90
> Today was far too long, but all's well
> that ends well. Back in the navel of the world
> I can only say I miss you all so much!
> 17 June 2011 at 21:45

# 53

'As far as I'm concerned, we can leave straight away.'

'Me too. Another day, and my good memory of this city will be completely ruined.'

'Well, if no one's against the idea, let's get out of here.'

The four of them were in the middle of the beautiful citadel complex of Sacsayhuamán, about two kilometres from Cusco. This huge open area surrounded by ancient towers, terraces, different-shaped stones, sanctuaries, water channels, tunnels and granaries, was presided over by the Inca throne. Conceived as a large, ceremonial fortress, its shape represents the head of a puma from Incan mythology, and its main features correspond, it would seem, to a perfect alignment with Coricancha and other relevant places in the centre of Cusco. And yet what surprised them most about Sacsayhuamán was not the function or vastness of the enclosure, but the enormous stones that evoked the shape of animals and the angular perfection of the rocks that were welded together like an exemplary set of teeth.

Despite its beauty, however, the four travellers couldn't help feeling ill at ease. So it was a relief when David expressed what they were all thinking: this place was like a market. The proximity of the feast in honour of the sun god the following week had turned it into a hubbub of tourists, benches and rehearsals. It would have been nice to see the people of Cusco dressed up in Inca costumes, performing the sacred rite of Inti Raymi, had it not been for the hordes of cameras following their every movement. It was clearly time to get away from there. They had planned to visit other nearby Inca sites – Qenko, Puka Pukara and Tambomachay – but gave up on the idea. This human activity was all but unbearable.

That afternoon, they spent hours poring over the map. Nobody was sure where they wanted to go or keen to make a proposal that might displease the others. So, when David and María suggested Puno on the shores of Lake Titicaca, everybody accepted at once.

Nobody said what they were really thinking.

Least of all, Leo. She would never have told the others her initial plan had been to take the plane from Cusco to Lima without visiting anywhere else in southern Peru.

Even so… Puno? What was interesting to see in Puno?

Suddenly, the girl realized she didn't want to part company with the others, and that more than made up for the destination.

She used that afternoon to buy herself a T-shirt, some trousers and underwear, so at least she had a change of clothes. That would be a lot cheaper than going back to the laundry in Ollantaytambo. How could she have been such a dumb trout and left all her clothes in the Sacred Valley! At this rate, she would end up going home in the nuddy.

But this setback, which at the start would have ruined her whole journey, didn't bother her all that much so, to say goodbye to Cusco, she visited the cathedral.

Never had she seen a more moving Crucifixion than the humble Lord of Tremors, the city's patron and defender against earthquakes.

Never had she seen a more beautiful altarpiece than the Altar of Forgiveness with the glistening Lady of the Nativity, the so-called Ancient Virgin, flanked by the beauty of Cusco painting and goldwork. That said, the greatest gleam probably derived from the fervour with which the locals venerated the image.

Grandma Carmiña would have loved to say a prayer in that place.

The night before leaving, the floor of the kitchen in San Blas delivered up some unwelcome guests.

# 54

Leo emitted her final tweet in Cusco before getting on a bus that was strikingly modern. David and María had been arguing in that peculiar way of theirs, one voice never rising above the other, with a sweetness that resembled a caress rather than a reproach. Next to them, Manfred was sleeping off his pisco-sour hangover. It seemed the nightlife in Cusco was impressive, and the Swede hadn't wished to pass up the opportunity of partying until dawn. He would sleep the whole trip.

The girl opened up her notebook and did her calculations for the last few days. At the back, where she kept her figures, it was difficult to go back to doing sums. She had arrived in Peru with 946 euros for travel and 854 euros for living expenses, a budgetary marvel. Unfortunately, she had yet to include her costs over the last two weeks. The resultant shock could be considerable. And so it was. What with taxis, accommodation, train and bus tickets, entry into Incan sites, clothes, medicine, drinks and food, she had spent... no way, it wasn't possible!... She had spent 636 euros! More than 40 euros per day!! She added up, took away, multiplied and divided several times, but there could be no doubt. All she had left for daily expenses was 218 euros, with another 20 days' travelling ahead of her. Would you believe it! At least she'd put on a couple of kilos thanks to the fortune they'd squandered in restaurants and on drinks. What a disaster! How could she have been so careless! Suddenly, a bright idea shed some light on the affair. 'Now we've got this far,' she pondered, 'why not combine both budgets and simplify matters? If I factor in the money for plane tickets, I have a total of 1,164 euros. That's the figure I'll use from now on. I just have to keep enough back for the ticket to Buenos Aires, and the rest will become obvious. That said, you can forget about any more aerial destinations,' she murmured to herself.

The horror of her accounts did not stop her jotting down at the front of her notebook her final impressions of Cusco, which, as usual, were taken from the book *Invisible Cities* by Italo Calvino:

> *For those who pass it without entering, the city is one thing; it is another for those who are trapped by it and never leave. There is the city where you arrive for the first time; and there is another city which you leave never to return. Each deserves a different name; perhaps I have already spoken of Irene under other names; perhaps I have spoken only of Irene.*

In the meantime, the bus passed through the suburbs of Cusco with their lowly shacks protected by the bulls of Pukara, clay figures that blessed the houses and invoked good fortune for their families. Once all the rainbow flags, diagonal Inca walls and noble shields had been left behind, the plateau with its glistening yellow grass and blue sky oversaw their advance over the furrow of the River Urubamba, flanked by the snowy peaks of the Andes range. On either side, the llamas prevented Pachamama, Mother Earth, a fertility goddess, daring to challenge the omnivorous power of her husband Pacha Kamaq, orderer of the universe along with the deity Viracocha and god of the sky.

'Oh damn, I've got lice!'

# 55

The eight-hour bus trip from Cusco to Puno was really terrible. The ascent to an even higher altitude above sea level – the La Raya Pass was at 4,335 metres – again caused them vomiting and headaches. On top of that, Leo had this annoying itch all over her head. She was waiting for the moment to go down to Puno and buy a tonic at the chemist's that would eliminate those blasted parasites.

It was getting dark when they reached a leaden city with an equally ashen atmosphere. Leo didn't know whether it was her own discomfort or the city's geography placing its feet in the vast Lake Titicaca, on the border with Bolivia, and climbing the hills in small mud and straw shanties to the Kuntur Wasi viewpoint.

When they went to bed, in a pension that was cheaper and more comfortable than those in Cusco, they all thought that perhaps they shouldn't be there. With this uneasy sense of remorse, they spent the whole night making frequent visits to the bathroom and the box of medicines.

> @ALeo90
> We still don't know Puno but are eager
> to leave. Before that we'll sail on Lake Titicaca
> and visit some islands. Brrr, it's cold!
> 20 June 2011 at 9:30

They awoke in a strange mood. Manfred had got up at least two hours earlier and gone for a walk with his usual secretiveness. David and María wouldn't stop arguing about a technical term, and Leo wandered the streets in search of a pharmacy. Either she got hold of a tonic or she would have to rip her head off her shoulders because that itching was getting really bad. An hour later, she was violently scratching her head while Manfred explained about the excursion he'd just arranged.

'On the boat, we'll visit the floating islands of the Uru and the community of Taquile. If anyone wants to visit Amantaní, they should go on another day because it's a long way.'

Now that they were there, they were hardly going to dash off again, so Leo accepted the proposal, albeit without much enthusiasm. Lake Titicaca is situated on a plateau and forms the border between Bolivia and Peru. There, the weight of the Aymara tradition of the south comes into contact with Quechua culture, forming a hybrid culture where gods and humans combine religious rites and ways of living. Leo understood this as soon as she set eyes on the bowler hats and colourful clothes of the indigenous women, nothing like the ones she'd seen in Cusco. The overcast sky deposited ash on the world, and the lake reflected this sadness in the atmosphere like a mirror. Something wasn't right because everything produced a negative sensation in Leo. She didn't even get off the boat to visit the floating islands of the Uru. They were undoubtedly one of the main tourist attractions in Puno, but the girl concluded they were a rip-off. It seemed communities lived on the lake on artificial islands made of totora reeds that the men would anchor and tend every day. On these wicker islets, they built wicker huts. The children flew their multi-coloured kites in the grey sky, and the women worshipped the gods of tourism with their beads and handmade cloths. Leo gazed at them from the boat with distrust, while Manfred observed the monumental effort of a boy to fly his plastic device. David and María haggled over a thick-ribbed cloth and climbed on to a shaky vessel to take some photographs.

No, thought Leo, it's obviously not my day.

And she scratched her head.

The visit to Taquile Island didn't do much for her either. Having climbed five hundred steps, she realized, because of the light and gleam of the waters, it was like being on a Mediterranean island rather than a plateau thousands of metres above sea level. The red earth glinted on the terraces in stark contrast to the mercurial, almost solid, surface of the lake. At the top, in the main square of the village, dozens of tourists dealt in ponchos and soles at the communal cooperative, while children secretly begged for money. Leo felt a bit awkward. In Cusco, the pressure on tourists had been far greater, but it had been easier to escape the epicentre of such trickery in the Plaza de Armas. Perhaps because of their austere appearance, nobody bothered them too much, but it wasn't pleasant watching middle-aged Americans and Germans with airy pockets get accosted. She spent the rest of her visit carefully observing the barely audible dialogue between two old men who'd sat down next to her. They were speaking a plaintive Quechua that was less voluble than the Quechua she'd heard on other occasions. Leo couldn't understand what they were saying, but their glances and clothes were the only real thing in that square where genuine articles were being bought and sold.

Leo was convinced they were laughing at how idiotic people could be.

Because of those two ironic old men, it had been worth sailing across Lake Titicaca. But she didn't plan to waste another day in that place. She most certainly didn't.

To her surprise, though, not everybody was of the same opinion.

# 56

'Don't be ridiculous, Leo!'

The steam from the coffee cup made their cheeks boil.

'David, don't tell me you believed anything you saw today,' retorted the girl.

'Why not?'

'Oh come on, all they need is a sign to say they're being sponsored by a soft-drinks company.'

'Leo, don't be so sceptical.'

'I'm convinced they don't live there, they head out early in the morning on their motor boats to perform their theatre. Listen, I'm not saying it's bad, it's a way of earning a living just like any other. It's even quite exotic. But I refuse to believe it's real.'

'I'm not so sure,' intervened Manfred. 'Besides, we see everything through the lens of a traveller; in that sense, we're always attending dramatic scenes that have been created just for us and wouldn't be there without our presence. That's happening here and in any museum in the world, don't you think?'

'Of course it is! I just don't like feeling deceived…'

'Everybody runs that risk. I'd even say they have the right to deceive themselves and be deceived. Don't think about it so much.'

At this point, Leo started thinking their shared voyage might be nearing its end. That was fifteen seconds before María then said:

'David and I are planning to spend a few days on the island of Amantaní. We found today's experience on Taquile with the indigenous community very moving. They say in Amantaní, further to the north, that sensation is multiplied and can change your life, so we've decided to spend a few days in their houses. I've read out there, in the middle of the lake, you can almost touch the stars with your fingers. We'll probably then head over to Copacabana, in Bolivia, so we can visit the Islands of the Sun and Moon from its shores.'

'Oh, what nonsense!' exclaimed Leo with a feeling of boredom. She immediately regretted her remark, she had no right to question the motives of others. 'Excuse me, I'm just tired and don't know what I'm saying. Manfred?'

There was a pleading tone in Leo's voice.

'How about you?' The Swede returned her question with a lack of enthusiasm.

'I prefer to visit Arequipa. This place doesn't... I don't know. Doesn't do it for me. It must be my fault, I'm sorry, I just don't want to stay here.'

'I'll come with you.'

Amazing, just amazing. All the guilt was abruptly swept from Leo's conscience. If Manfred didn't want to stay, then maybe she wasn't so blind. When they reached the hotel, they put everything back in their rucksacks and prepared to say goodbye. They searched for a happy, colourful restaurant on Jirón Lima Street and used the hours available to them to drink in the border-town spirit of Puno. On the way back, as they hummed a strange song a folklore group had performed over dinner a few hours earlier, Leo thought there was something strange about this place, an unsettling beauty that mingled with the obvious ugliness. It was freezing cold, and they huddled together, seeking the comfort of bodies and unexpected affection. As they hugged in the street, it happened.

'My name is Chen Chou,' said the one they'd known as David.

'And mine is Lunmei Hsu,' declared the one they'd called María.

'Please don't ever forget our names,' they asked with a hint of embarrassment and a great deal of humility.

Leo forced a smile. Just to find out their real identities, it had been worth experiencing the highlands, the lice, the headaches and those truly ridiculous islands.

## 57

When Manfred and Leo left for the bus station, Lunmei Hsu and Chen Chou were still sleeping peacefully. The cold breeze from the mountains turned their breath into locomotives that filled the darkness with warm air. Early-morning workers trudged silently towards the fields and mines. They were almost there when Leo spotted, quite clearly, some blue graffiti on a clay wall:

**I Love You Leo A.**

The message had come looking for her as far as the shores of Lake Titicaca.

On the way to Arequipa, she thought about nothing else. A few rows behind her, with the excuse of stretching his legs during the rest of the journey, Manfred seemed to be writing something in his journal. Or reading a book. Leo wasn't sure, but he was clearly holding something that occupied all his attention. Every time the girl changed seat to share some water or have a chat, the Swedish boy hid whatever was in his hands and stopped her discovering his secret. Well, that was his business! All that mystery over nothing!

The trip from Puno to Arequipa wasn't as spectacular as the Cusco plateau had been. Passing through Juliaca, a large city of underhand dealings, border smuggling, popular markets, colourful bicycle rickshaws, tin roofs, noisy motorbikes, brick walls, tangles of cables and large electoral slogans, left a bitter taste in their mouths. The dangerous hubbub of the streets had a magnetism that was washed away in the immensity of the Salinas y Aguada Blanca National Reserve, inhabited by thousands of vicunas and alpacas. The horizon resembled an unreachable line and yet, five hours later, the sugary peak of Misti Volcano appeared.

'Welcome to Arequipa, the white city,' mused Manfred.

The descent to an altitude above sea level that was less than it had been in recent weeks gave them a surprising amount of energy. Otherwise, there would have been no understanding their patience while searching for an acceptable hostel during more than three hours. Luckily, their rucksacks were light and didn't weigh too much.

Leo thought the less you have, the less you need. Had she known this, she would have travelled with her hand luggage!

After lots of walking about, they ended up in a sweet little pension with a large garden surrounded by electrified wires. Manfred asked for a corner where he could put up his tent, and Leo opted for a single room with its own shower. There were still a few lice crawling about her head, and that was company enough. Sharing a room with Lunmei Hsu and Chen Chou had been fun and cheap, but it was time to regain her own space so she could smarten up and sleep properly. When they went out for a walk at sunset, they realized they'd practically seen the whole town while trawling for accommodation. Well, maybe not that much, but it had been an effective way of finding their bearings in the historic centre. The liveliness of the streets excited Manfred, and Leo knew she would return to the hostel on her own. The Swede's nocturnal devotion was absolute, far greater than his persistent taste for trekking. In the struggle between the tandem of music-drinks and several hours' walking, the former would always win, even though his mouth was always extolling the latter.

His now famous pisco-sour hangovers had become a classic of their Peruvian adventure.

The last time Leo saw him that night, he was sidling up to an Australian with perfect skin and a cleavage so large it made you dizzy just to look at it.

# 58

The sky was a little cloudy, but Leo was confident it wouldn't rain. She left the hostel with the intention of wandering the streets for a while and observing the city's rhythm in the first few hours of the day. The paved ground and white walls of volcanic stone blinded her eyes. In the Plaza de Armas, the pearly cathedral proudly surveyed its porticoed courtyard of porous rock. The signs informing what to do in case of volcanic eruption and earthquake revealed this was an ephemeral city that rose and fell according to the capricious will of the earth's uncontrollable hiccups. Some time before, the volcano's fury had swept away the city's suburbs in a matter of minutes and reached the heart of the city almost without encountering obstacles. As many times as it had been destroyed, it had been built up again with extraordinary pride. The morning passed peacefully beneath a tepid sun. Leo used this opportunity to read the information she'd printed a few minutes earlier and be rocked along by the whispering silence of the fountains and turtledoves. The volcanic stone of the buildings ranged from soft pink to muddy white, while the façades seemed to rival the purity of the volcano Misti's gleaming white peak. As if the city were a threshing floor permanently covered in snowflakes that stubbornly ignored the soaring daytime temperatures.

When the sun got too hot, Leo decided to take refuge in the little citadel of the Convent of Santa Catalina. She didn't always trust the guides and forums. Sometimes words exaggerated; others, they weren't enough. At the start of her journey, the girl was always railing against what she considered to be falsehoods but, as the days and destinations went by, she realized everybody spoke of the fair as things went with them there. No two travellers, and therefore no two travel experiences, are the same. Everybody adores or hates according to their taste, and it's good to analyze proposals carefully so you can make the most of them. Whether it's a question of accommodation, restaurants or tourist sights. All travellers agreed the Convent of Santa Catalina was the most fascinating place in Arequipa, and Leo decided to set aside her prejudices and pay the entrance fee. From outside, the walls weren't particularly remarkable but, as soon as she passed through the gate, the girl knew she'd entered another world.

Inside, she found nothing to remind her of the servitude, asceticism and religious vocation so common to monastic life. As she passed through the tall, thick outer walls, Leo entered a miniature town of streets, houses, basins, churches, cloisters and markets that had been founded in the sixteenth century for the exclusive use of the daughters of the richest Spanish families in the city. A world of women, for women, where material wealth and fine living didn't necessarily contradict their religious passion. She wandered past wells, houses, vaults, oratories, wood ovens and alleyways with familiar names – Córdoba, Toledo, Burgos, Seville – and had to admit this was one of the most surprising places she had ever visited. So much so, she decided to spend the rest of the day there.

At mid-afternoon, in the cloister of orange trees, the girl came across a familiar silhouette. Manfred was seated in a corner with his inseparable journal in his hands. She was about to greet him openly, but held back so she could watch him for a while. The boy was flicking his eyes and fingers from a fixed point in the patio to his journal. With patience and greed, he was gathering forms and colours from outside and bringing them together on that small sheet. Leo couldn't help smiling. The lover of pisco sour and trekking was also a devoted artist. The Swede was clearly a box full of surprises!

'What, did you triumph yesterday or not?' said Leo, eventually going over.

The boy quickly closed his notebook and gave her a blank stare.

'The Australian, Manfred. How did it go?'

The Swede chuckled, and Leo realized the previous night had been long. As the next would be. After dinner, the girl let herself be convinced to go to a disco with this amazing upper terrace and astonishing DJ. Well, it certainly wasn't a bad place. At the high point of the night, Leo descried the Australian woman's cleavage advancing through the crowd of devoted dancers and decided it was time to retreat.

'I'm going to the market tomorrow!' she shouted at Manfred.

'You what?'

'The market! Tomorrow!'

And Leo left before the invincible armada captained by a single, powerful, southern ship could sink the nutshell of her northern majesty.

As she walked, laughing, back to the hostel, she wished Andrés could be there.

Yes. In spite of everything, she wished he could be there.

She then thought she glimpsed a shadow chasing her in the darkness of the distance and ran so hard she had no time to dwell on the Mexican's caresses.

# 59

@ALeo90
Today I shall meet Juanita, just in time for her name day.
Jump over the St John's bonfire three times for me!
Happy summer solstice from Arequipa!
23 June 2011 at 11:15

Leo was still having breakfast when she caught sight of a blond silhouette sneaking between the bushes in the garden. There was Manfred's companion running away like a vampire with the first rays of the sun. The Swede's sullen face appeared at breakfast. He didn't say a word for ten minutes.

'The market, then?'

Leo smiled. When you're travelling, the best company during the daytime isn't necessarily the same as at night.

'The market.'

In the midst of that hotchpotch of colours of juices, fruit, potatoes, hens and animals sliced open, Manfred pulled out his notebook. Surprisingly, he didn't hide from Leo's curious gaze and started drawing. They spent the whole morning there, watching a woman dressed in traditional clothes, with a weathered face, on top of a mound of potatoes of every imaginable colour and shape. She rubbed her hands on a red apron that covered her chubby legs. Behind the tubers, some feet tied in sandals made of car tyres slept a siesta. On her head, a black hat concealed the start of two tight plaits that met at her waist, their tips strung together to prevent her hair swaying from side to side.

The seller gazed out at a market full of merchandise, voices and tourists. Beside the mound of potatoes, she had her own thoughts and was oblivious to the morning hum. Curiously, as the woman took shape on Manfred's blank sheet of paper, her silhouette grew slimmer. The strength of the drawing was such that it gradually erased the woman in front of them. By the time it was finished, her dignity traced in two lines on the paper, the lady wasn't looking at her earth-coloured tubers any more. She was shining on the piece of card.

Leo knew then that Arequipa would always be the potato woman.

When they met Juanita, the emotion of Machu Picchu came looking for them in the icy interior of the museum. Apparently, on various expeditions to the summits of neighbouring volcanoes, historians had encountered the remains of human sacrifices offered by Incas to the apus in the hope of assuaging their fury after an eruption or earthquake. The mummy Juanita had been found on the side of the volcano Ampato and was proudly displayed in a museum that told her story. Neither of them said it. Not Manfred, nor Leo. But both realized that Inca fever had nestled in their brains. The Swede, however, refused to paint the little mummy. For his collection of prints, he preferred the noisy bustle of the market to the glacial silence of that girl offered up to the gods of the mountain.

When they left the chill of the museum rooms, they bumped straight into the Australian, who, judging by her reaction, was decidedly keen on Manfred. She had exchanged her dizzying nocturnal cleavage for endless legs in sandals with impossible heels. Manfred greeted her with the coldness of the mummy and quickened his pace.

'Leo, I was thinking we could go to the Colca Valley tomorrow. There's nothing left to see in Arequipa. What were you planning to do?'

Nothing, Leo hadn't been planning anything. As the days rushed along towards the end of her trip, the girl realized a mute paralysis had taken hold of her will. There was something inside her that stopped her making haste. As if the simple fact of slowing down her visits might slow down the implacable passing of the hours until she had to return home. That was why her body experienced a constant struggle between the desire to see things and the temptation not to do so. Perhaps that would help her make time grind to a halt once and for all. Wretched time…

'OK then. Let's go to the Colca Valley.'

That night, neither of them wanted to leave the hostel, and they took refuge in the electrified garden until the early hours of the morning. One was trying to escape a southern grip that wanted to curtail his freedom; the other, a feeling of nostalgia for the bonfires of St John.

It was her favourite night of the year. The shortest in the calendar; the longest in terms of bonfires, ashes, bitter wine, sardines and bagpipes. The shadow of June exams during her degree, in that brief interval, enjoyed a moment of fun. In the early morning, as was their tradition, she would wait with Martiño for the magical dance of the sun from the top of the Alameda. They hadn't managed to see it yet, but that didn't make it any less real.

On this occasion, Leo was experiencing not the summer, but the winter solstice. The darkness of the white city of Arequipa concealed her strange longing to love and not to love.

Neither knew how or why, but the two of them ended up sleeping in Manfred's tent. Perhaps it was because you could see the stars infinitely better from there, and they both needed to chase away the coldness of that icy princess called Juanita.

# 60

'Leo?'

'What?'

'Why do you always insist on travelling by plane?'

'To be honest, because of fear.'

'Fear?'

'I never imagined I'd end up travelling on my own. I'd been planning this trip for years with three friends. When it was time to leave, they all decided their savings deserved a better destination and pulled out. I also thought of not going because fear was stronger than I was, and yet this was the dream of my life! One day, I found myself rearranging all the routes and destinations. I had to rethink the whole thing. If I was going to go on my own, then I couldn't hitchhike or share a room or use any form of public transport that struck me as unsafe. Before leaving, I thought if I was near an airport, I could always return home if something bad happened. Pretty dumb, huh? Whatever happens, you're always on your own, and home is far away. I learned that when we had that scare about Grandma Carmiña because it was the longest night of my life. Five months ago, there were only fears and insecurities. Now look at me – I've just slept in the tent of a complete stranger!'

There wasn't even an awkward silence. As if this had happened because it had to be, without thinking about it or giving it special importance. Outside the bus taking them to the Colca Valley, the suburbs of Arequipa stretched and yawned. The roads filled with men and women heading somewhere else apart from their modest mud and straw shanties. Only the uralite challenged the inclemency of the sky.

Manfred gazed at the arid ridges with curiosity, while Leo carried on talking. Perhaps this would enable her to silence the shouts of that

## I Love You Leo A.

she had seen on the wall of a colonial house near the Plaza de Armas. The darkness and their hurry hadn't stopped her reading the firm writing in black letters that challenged the pride of a family's coat of arms on that pearly wall.

The vomiting and headaches of the other passengers kept them company for the rest of the journey.

On top of a cairn devoted to the apus or gods of the mountain, Leo asked for her most intimate desire.

A day and a half later, they were sharing guffaws and applause with this fun group they'd met on their way to see the proud flight of the condors that floated on the warm currents of air in the deepest part of the Colca Canyon.

Leo didn't know why, but at this point she realized she had to change direction. It was 25 June 2011, only thirteen days before she had to return home. The clever tactic of not thinking about it had not succeeded in slowing down time, and now she needed to apply a little common sense. If she went any further, she wouldn't be able to get back.

That night, in the town of Chivay, there was a huge hullabaloo on account of the local festivities. Music and brightly-coloured grotesque masks entered and left the church to the amusement of hundreds of spectators. When the music was at its highest and two dancers flashed their ribbons and rattles, Leo shouted:

'Manfred, I have to go back!'

'To the hostel? Are you mad? This is fascinating! Just look at those colours… Leo, stay!'

'Not to the hostel. To Buenos Aires.'

'What are you talking about? What made you think of that?'

'I have to go back, I'm sorry.'

The rest of the night was swallowed up by the coming and going of dancers, musicians and images of the Virgin with large, conical skirts that were reminiscent of the mountains and carried out of chapels on people's shoulders. Dragons, Turks, Cocos and saints. Leo didn't stop dancing until dawn, but that wasn't enough to allay her sense of nostalgia.

# 61

'Then it's decided, Leo. You're going back to Buenos Aires.'

Chivay offered them that morning a serene feeling of peace. They hadn't done it deliberately, but that was how it was. Perhaps it was the silence, or the pure mountain air, or the will of the apus, who can say? A whole day of confessions and farewells that ended up telling them the more walls you erect, the more rubble and noise they make when they come crashing down. Luckily, it didn't hurt too much.

'Yes. I'll take a flight to Lima, and from there to Argentina. My time is running out. How about you?'

'Well, from here I'll go to the Cotahuasi Canyon. I need to draw the flight of the condors! And from there I'll climb up to Choquequirao. Did I tell you I got a place on an organized trek for four days that takes you to the remains of this Inca city hidden away in the middle of the forest? Amazing! I'm finally going to do some walking! After that, I don't know. I feel like entering the jungle from Puerto Maldonado and seeing the Nazca Lines, but I haven't decided yet. What's for sure is I'll have to go back to Ollantaytambo.'

'Then you can get my clothes!' laughed Leo as she spread the map of Peru out on her knees and traced the Swede's destinations with her forefinger. 'By the way, you must be barking mad. Your route doesn't make any sense.'

'Why?'

'Well, look at the zigzag you're going to do. Wouldn't it be more logical to decide on a particular destination without going in alternate directions?'

'Logical? It's not always the best logic that saves you

kilometres. The direction of a trip has to be judged by weightier reasons than that.'

'Right.'

'Leo?'

'What?'

'I wanted to show you something.'

At this point, with a timidity the girl hadn't seen before, the Swedish boy opened his notebook and gave it to her. Leo turned the pages with a sense of perplexity. The white city of Arequipa fitted entirely in those drawings! The well in the Convent of Santa Catalina, the Misti volcano, the Australian's cleavage, the fruit in the market, the potato woman, the pearly cathedral, the shacks on the periphery, a girl hugging a sheep... Suddenly, Leo went as red as a beetroot. She had just come across her face sleeping inside a tent!

'Manfred, you're a real artist! Goodness me, you work with a whole bunch of different techniques!'

'Each scene asks for a different way of being told, and I try to seek the one that suits it best in that moment.'

'Watercolours, charcoal, Indian ink... You have a go at everything!'

'Go on then, choose one before I change my mind,' whispered Manfred.

'You what?'

'Tear out whichever page you like.'

'You must be crazy! How do you think I'm going to rip your journal? It's a real gem!'

'No, my travel journals never stay with me because an image never replaces the memory of what it was. That's why my journals are hidden away in the places that meant the most to me.'

'You mean you discard all of your work?'

'No… I always keep a scanned copy. I just hide the original in case I go back there one day and want to get it back. That gives me a really good reason to return. Go on, choose one.'

Leo didn't hesitate. The potato woman. That would be the image that would accompany her home.

They were in a stony area on the way to nowhere. From here, Leo would take a bus back to Arequipa, and Manfred would continue his journey to the Cotahuasi Canyon. The girl was the first to get on board. There were no hugs or kisses so everything could be easier but, even so, they couldn't help the odd tear betraying their pact of indifference. As the bus disappeared around the bend, Manfred took a placard out of his rucksack.

'My name is Olof Brodde Lindberg.'

Leo turned up her nose. Why did everybody on this voyage conceal their real identity? Besides, that handwriting struck her as somewhat familiar, she wasn't quite sure why, but it was definitely familiar.

When she reached Arequipa Airport, she was welcomed by a sheet in the departure lounge with a familiar message:

### I Love You Leo A.

Misti's snowy peak had been the white city's first sensation and, from the runway, it also became the last. When the volcano's sugary lips gave her a fond farewell kiss, the stretch-marked back of the Andes also shivered a little.

# 62

The shortest tweet of the journey was sent from the strange dawn of an implacably leaden and noisy city. Heavily influenced by advice she'd picked up on forums, Leo had chosen a hostel on the most central street in the select neighbourhood of Miraflores, in the Peruvian capital. Warnings and recommendations about security, in particular with reference to women travelling on their own, also had a bearing on her first experiences. On landing the previous evening, she'd taken an official taxi and headed straight to the hostel. Outside the taxi window, dusk was falling on the promenade, a tortuous road full of traffic that separated the city's red gullies from the Pacific Ocean. The humbler quarters of the outskirts gave way to luxurious lofts and malls overhanging the sea. People bustled about in the Lima night, but Leo decided to go to sleep. She was really tired. She was dying to have a good shower and a sandwich.

When she woke up the following morning, she had to reconcile her numbers before taking any new decisions. She'd left Cusco on 19 June with 1,164 euros in her pocket. The towns of Puno and Arequipa had swallowed up 253 euros, what with excursions, food, accommodation and the ticket to Lima, which left her with a budget of 911 euros. The money was speeding away! How annoying! She would definitely have to give up on the crazy idea of the northern beaches, otherwise she ran the risk of not having enough money for her return flight to Buenos Aires. There was a time, when she'd dreamed of going to Peru, she had included the warm Pacific beaches in the north of the country among her possible destinations. She'd gone over various names until hitting upon one that attracted her attention: Piura. It wasn't the most highly recommended by travellers on forums, but Leo thought, if she was going to visit a beach, then it had to be Piura. It was several days before she understood the reason for this decision. Piura was one of the settings in the Peruvian writer Vargas Llosa's novel *The Green House*! During the ever-passionate discussions of the book group *Read, Read, What Are You Reading?*, the novel had grown powerfully inside her head, along with the extraordinary cast of characters: Don Anselmo, Sergeant Lituma, Fushia and 'Wildflower'. The novel referred to Piura, a dusty town in the desert, and to Santa María de Nieva in the Amazon rainforest. It wasn't these places Leo was after so much as the enormous beaches. Never mind. The evocation of the name was enough to make you want to go there.

Piura – you only had to say it to feel desire.

But all these projects of bathing and sun were left hanging in the air because of her obvious budgetary restrictions. She could risk it, of course, but what if she didn't have enough money to get back? She had always been a bit of a coward when it came to financial affairs and wasn't going to change now. Cowardice or pride, she wasn't sure which was the best description, but she preferred to do without the visit rather than having to go cap in hand to her parents. She'd sworn she would do this trip on her own, and that was the way things would be. Aunt Cris' ticket to Buenos Aires was the exception that proved the rule.

Leo was immersed in matters of finance, but couldn't help entertaining another thought. It was large, weighty and twisted. She couldn't get it out of her mind. She'd been chewing over that devilish doubt ever since parting company with Manfred – or Olof, or whatever the hell he was called – at that arid crossroads in the Colca Valley. Before heading out to visit the historic centre of Lima, the girl returned to the computer with the intention of going back online. She had to wait more than an hour because there was a German couple that seemed to want to write to their whole family... When it was finally her turn, she inserted that name into the search engine. There were dozens of references to him and a website named after him! She opened it at once to find his fantastic drawings filling the screen. She couldn't understand a thing, so selected 'English' in an attempt to unravel the Swede's story.

She was so stunned she didn't know how to react. He was one of the most renowned illustrators in northern Europe. As he himself explained, he travelled the world armed only with his notebook and an iPad that allowed him to upload his works of art. The website had thousands of visitors from all over the world; each notebook had luxury editions on paper that disappeared from the market as soon as they were printed. There were long waiting lists for each new edition and destination! The last one Manfred – or Olof, or whatever the hell he was called – had put online was the notebook dedicated to Cusco. As she flicked through the virtual pages, Leo came across Chen Chou's hair, the sunrise at Inti Punku, a hummingbird in the garden at Ollantaytambo, a beetle in a barn, the lower terraces at Pisac, a tattoo on Lunmei Hsu's buttock, a girl embracing a sheep in Moray, a panorama of the salt ponds in Maras... This diary contained the most intimate secrets of their voyage, and Leo felt naked in front of the world. And yet it wasn't shame she felt, but rather pride at forming part of something so wonderful. The few words on each page summed up feelings she had also experienced, and she was sure, if she ever forgot them, she would be able to find them again in that place.

Ollantaytambo appeared majestic in numerous images, and Leo understood why Manfred had to go back. Suddenly, her curiosity was too much, and she started flicking through the other notebooks. There were all kinds, detailing all sorts of different journeys. From the never-ending beaches of Colombia to the deepest recesses of the equatorial rainforest, his fingers had drawn prints that cost an arm and a leg in high-quality reproductions. So that was how he paid for his erratic zigzagging across the globe! An interactive map allowed her to view the places the Swede had visited when, to her surprise, she came across a star on Santiago. She couldn't believe it. He had been to her city and not told her! When she opened the notebook, she found a place that was both recognizable and not. The curved mouth of a gargoyle with pointy horns. Shadows down a blind alley. A cluster of light in an arch of the archbishop's palace. The prophet Daniel's smile. The hands of a woman selling turnip tops. A channel of water on some paving stones. An angel's glasses. A satchel anchored to a student's hip. Three drops of Barrantes wine merging with some oil on a paper tablecloth. A panorama of roofs. Two old people holding hands on Bonaval Hill. A man raising a flag. A small girl watching it pour down from an arcade.

*Compostela: The City Where Umbrellas Dance*. That was the title of the notebook.

And Leo realized that places are the eyes that look at them.

An American woman's cough reminded her she had been on the computer for two hours. She said sorry and emerged into the strange Lima day. It was one o'clock in the afternoon, and the light was the same leaden light of three hours earlier.

She was beginning to understand why the sky in Lima was described as a 'donkey's belly'.

# 63

The city that had been nicknamed 'Lima the Horrible' was, in effect, totally overwhelming. The smell of tar, the dirt, the racing past of minibuses, the itinerant hawkers, the crazy traffic and thousands of people wandering from side to side enveloped Leo in a suffocating cloud. That grey sky prevented her from knowing whether it was getting light or dark. The contrast between the capital and the warm tranquillity of the south was shocking. 'Arequipa! Arequipa! Arequipa! Arequipa!' was the deafening shout emitted by vendors of tickets for the shared taxis that lined the city's main artery. No doubt the name was meant to be a tribute to the white city, but such filthy pollution only tarnished its memory. The girl, stubborn like all the women on her mother's side, swore she would find a charming side to this South American capital. But, four days after having landed from the south, she had to admit that, if there was one, it was well hidden away in all the persistent dampness. 'Arequipa! Arequipa! Arequipa! Arequipa!' She tried every way she could. She visited the historic centre with its cathedral made of hollow wood as a defence against earthquakes, the catacombs with thousands of skulls, the red dragons of the Chinese Quarter, San Cristóbal Hill with its shacks painted bright colours to disguise the misery. The cut-off head of Pizarro, founder of the city, chased her around as she snaked between the churches and pastel colonial palaces of the centre and even when, against all possible advice, she visited the neighbourhood of Callao, the ancient port from which all the American gold had departed and which was now a hideout for fishermen. But however far she walked, that strident and humid litany just kept going faster: 'Arequipa! Arequipa! Arequipa! Arequipa!' It was after trying some delicious seafood and stuffed peppers that she understood why the travellers she'd met considered Lima an essential gastronomic stop-off before heading in the direction of Cusco. None of them ever got so far as to unpack their bags. And they were stunned when she expressed her intention of staying there for a couple of days more.

'Here? In Lima? Whatever for?'

But no, despite her insistence, the Peruvian capital failed to charm any of her senses: her sense of smell, her sight, her hearing – her taste just a tiny bit. Of course, Leo wasn't expecting much in the way of touch, and that was where the city with the ruminant's stomach conquered her in the end.

'Does the sky never change here? Is it always like that, grey and bad-tempered?'

'In winter, this ashen mist called *garúa* never leaves us.'


Leo had bought a return ticket to Buenos Aires for the 'modest' price of 350 euros for 1 July, the next day. The sun was shining behind the blanket of mist, and Leo, against all recommendations, decided to go for a walk on the beach on the other side of the promenade, beneath Larcomar Park. Fearful though she was, the girl was fed up of all these controls and warnings of danger. Whatever she read, whoever she asked, every sentence began with 'Take great care', but she was not to be daunted. To start with, she'd only taken official taxis, not spoken to anybody, not walked more than a hundred feet without looking behind her and taken refuge in the fortress of her hostel before it got dark. Like Cinderella's golden carriage, she ran the risk of turning into a pumpkin if night caught her out on her own on the streets of Lima, from where no doubt there would come vampires, gangsters, muggers, rapists, thieves, aliens, kidnappers and werewolves, all anxious for a taste of her youthful blood. The caution she'd always taken pride in – for no other reason than that she really was a bit of a coward – didn't seem to be enough in this monstrous city, and Leo upped all her precautions. But as the days went by, the girl finally managed to discharge ballast and relax until she overcame her initial fears. This wasn't enough, mind, to make her want to stay in a city where she was paying 25 euros a night to sleep, something that could only be done in a safe hostel in a residential area that was well lit and crawling with police officers and security guards.

In effect, all this pressure took away her wish to remain there, so her ticket to Buenos Aires was more like an escape than a return.

Also, she had to admit out of the corner of her mouth that Peru without Olof, Lunmei Hsu and Chen Chou – or whatever the hell they were called – was no fun.

That was until she went down to Costa Verde Beach, also called Waikiki by the locals, in the district of Miraflores. There, the Pacific stretched lazily towards the horizon, and dozens of surfers danced hesitantly on the back of that meek ocean. It wasn't particularly cold or hot, but she didn't let the winter temperatures, around twenty degrees, or the threat of pollution put her off. She went ahead, got quickly undressed before her common sense told her not to and had a dip in the water.

Ahhhhh, it was wonderful... how she had missed this... The sea! If she wasn't going to make it to Piura, then at least she could feel the Pacific in Lima! She closed her eyes and let her body be rocked by the waves. She loved to play dead and listen to the soft hum of the ocean's entrails. She tried to scrutinize each sound so she could differentiate that lullaby from the murmur of the Atlantic. They sounded exactly the same! Ah, that damp rocking allowed her to forget everything that made her mad when she was on land. She only had a few days' travelling left, and yet the world insisted on spinning around her like a mad top. The dizziness got too much. But here, her skin encased in a layer of salt, Leo managed to stop her little head gyrating for a moment.

When she came out, who knows how much later, she realized someone had stolen her wallet. She rummaged through her clothes to make sure it hadn't just fallen in the sand, but finally had to accept that someone had made an unpleasant visit to her belongings. Leo smiled. Luckily, all it contained was fifty soles and a copy of her passport.

She may have been stubborn, but she wasn't stupid.

Had her wallet been stolen at the start of her journey, she would have suffered a panic attack, but now nothing bothered her all that much.

She walked back to the pension. Darkness had taken hold of the pavements and traffic lights, and only the tips of the skyscrapers still glowed in the fading light. She was soaked through and started trembling.

Boh, of course Lima was worth the effort.

# 64

@ALeo90
Going back to Buenos Aires though
Tawantinsuyu will stay with me forever.
Arequipa! Arequipa! Arequipa! Arequipa!
1 July 2011 at 12:11

The 'donkey's belly' or whale's maw that described the sky in Lima persisted stubbornly beneath the also grey belly of the plane. It had been an insipid, somewhat sad ending to a wonderful country. And yet Leo realized that Lima was not to blame. Its constant *garúa* had only served to dampen her already low spirits.

She had 386 euros left, with less than a week to go.

Her trip was coming to an end, and that was all there was to it.

Two days later, back in Buenos Aires, in the nostalgic market of the popular district of San Telmo, Leo rummaged through the paraphernalia in search of a maté gourd for her father.

For Roi, she had taken a photo with a papier-mâché figure of Mafalda on a cold, sunny bench. In her hands, she held a box of *alfajores* for Grandma Carmiña.

Behind her, an old couple danced the tango while two men argued over the price of a copper basin.

But Leo didn't notice. The shadow of her return hovered over each and every one of her thoughts.

# 65

Leo never imagined her last hours in Buenos Aires would be so nostalgic. She wanted to see her family, of course, but the thought of going home was too much of an uphill struggle. Never had she enjoyed so much freedom as in the last six months, and all the experiences she had undergone huddled together in the lean-to of her memory now that her journey was coming to an end. She had no more money and, on top of that, she had to keep her word. That was what she said to Dolores when the latter came to fetch her from the airport. Of course, she'd thought of spending her last week in a youth hostel but, on perusing her accounts, had decided not to. The house of a friend of Aunt Cris' in Palermo Soho was far too comfortable a refuge to ignore.

'So your journey's almost over.'

'That's right.'

'Can I ask you why?'

'Because I promised. I said I'd be back in six months, and I will.'

'That's all well and good. Every journey has its end. But you can always come back one day.'

'I don't think so! It's not so easy.'

'But you're very young. You have the whole of your life in front of you.'

'I know. May I have another piece of steak? It's really very good.'

Leo had learned that all conversations can be avoided by a touch of irony or an allusion to food. She didn't feel like discussing this with Dolores. She didn't feel like discussing anything with anybody.

And she certainly wasn't in the mood for preparing pancakes. That would have to wait.

Leo spent the last few days of her stay in Buenos Aires walking compulsively around the never-ending blocks of eternal pedestrian crossings until her muscles were exhausted and she got cramp again. Having totted up her accounts, she chose not to cross the Plate River estuary to Montevideo, as had been her intention, and not to visit the Tigre Delta. She would devote her money to the sweet pleasure of not thinking about it and to satisfying her body's whims. That said, when she came across some smart mountain boots in a shop window and decided it was time to replace her old ones (the heel plate that had been stuck in Cusco had opened again and wouldn't last long), she almost fell over. The equivalent of eighty euros! That was her budget for four days! Needless to say, she didn't buy them. What a dumb way to throw away your money! The ones she had would get her home. Of course, she forgot all about the times she'd spent a great deal more on an overcoat, some electronic device or a designer T-shirt. Since she hadn't been paying and it had been on her father's card, that had been a different matter entirely.

As she notched up kilometres in the capital's asphalt jungle, Leo thought she had paid her debt to the city and all she had to do now was enjoy. Of course, there were hundreds of places she hadn't visited and had noted down in her journal, but she didn't feel like searching out anything new. She only wanted to reacquaint herself with the city where she'd enjoyed so many positive moments and not go around making new appointments. What she'd seen was enough. She didn't need any more. The list of monuments, statues, parks, attractions, buildings, museums, streets and establishments of every kind had reached its quota. This comfortable nook was enough to love the city with all its undiscovered, melancholy folds. Breathing in the warm air of May Avenue was sufficient. Ah, Buenos Aires, she hadn't left yet, but already felt nostalgic, perhaps because of the strange sensation she was missing something and hadn't penetrated its skin. It may not have been the city betraying her, but her betraying the city with her indifference at every step.

That Wednesday, she jotted down:

> @ALeo90
> Buenos Aires rocks me in its warm cradle
> of farewells. Catching the plane tomorrow at 18:00.
> Will be home on the 8th as promised.
> 6 July 2011 at 10:11

'Are you sure you have everything? You're not missing something? There's nothing else you wanted to see? It's your last day here,' Dolores had asked insistently.

'No, thanks, Dolores. I'm ready to go.'

She had been preparing for this moment ever since she'd left home six months earlier. To start with, she'd thought it would be a long time; now she was sure it wasn't enough. She had just left, and now it was time to return! If it was up to her, she'd go home, do a quick wash, give everybody a resounding kiss and head off again as quickly as possible. Whatever the destination might be.

She hustled this naughty thought out of her head. No, she couldn't, it was impossible, and besides she'd promised.

Overcome by nerves about her return, she decided to spend the last day with no fixed direction again. She wandered erratically, following the direction marked out by noises, lights, music, accents. Unable to focus on one thing, she struggled to give herself a clear objective. The third time she passed in front of the same shop window on Rivadavia Avenue, she became aware of her compulsive movements and had to admit:

'OK, I'm finding it difficult to leave!'

She sought refuge in the shops of San Telmo to avoid retracing her steps and ended up in Dorrego Square, the nuclear centre of the neighbourhood, where the previous Sunday she'd visited a wonderful and entertaining popular market. She liked these little shops that mixed the decadent nostalgia of an ancient establishment with the latest advances in fashion.

Suddenly, as she reached a crossroads, she spotted her.

In the bar El Hipopótamo, there was as much nostalgia as in its next-door neighbour, the bar Británico. Both of them, their names painted in exquisite *fileteado* on the window, with their old wood, marble tables and eager waiters, represented that River Plate life of select pleasures and unending conversations.

Overwhelmed by this feeling, Leo went in.

# 66

'Hello!'

The other looked back with all the astonishment of someone who's just seen a ghost.

'Hello!'

'May I sit down?'

'Of course, *nomás*.'

The initial surprise of Adriana, the Italian girl Leo had met several weeks earlier in the hostel in Corrientes, had given way to affectionate curiosity. By this stage, neither of them believed in accidents, so they avoided all reference to the stubborn arbitrariness of a chance event that had brought them together again in a café in San Telmo. The girl stared in affectionate silence, waiting for what would come next.

At this point, Leo started talking with a voice she'd never heard before:

'It was 8 July, practically half a year before my departure, when it happened. For months now, papa had been bad-tempered and taciturn on account of some affairs to do with the building company, which he only ever hinted at with mother, hardly anything at all. He never explained what was going on. You didn't have to be particularly intelligent to know it was something big and things weren't going at all well with the family business. The company had never lost money and had grown considerably thanks to a seafront development that papa was particularly proud of. And yet we had barely seen him for months and, when we did, he spent the day swearing and cursing people and subcontractors the company had always been on good terms with. We didn't understand a thing but, to tell the truth, we didn't care much either. Neither my brother, Roi, nor me. We were used to this kind of thing. Papa was never there, and mother had her own affairs to attend to.

'It was a Friday, the eve of the feast of Our Lady of Mount Carmel at Grandma Carmiña's house. I had just finished my exams, and mother had asked me to go with her to help prepare the family meal. We spent the afternoon with laughter and the excessive salt grandma always put in the soup. Night had fallen when mother's mobile rang. Her dramatic expression told me something really terrible had happened. An accident. Papa and Roi. It seemed they were OK. Papa had lost control of the car on a bend – he doesn't know what happened. A write-off. They were in emergency. In the hospital. His shoulder had borne the brunt of the impact. Roi had received a multiple leg fracture, and they were operating on him at that moment.

'I don't recall very well what followed: mother's hysteria, Grandma Carmiña's strange calmness, the rush to the hospital…

'A few hours earlier, papa had filed for bankruptcy with a court in Santiago. At the time of the accident, he'd been driving over the speed limit, and the car had crashed into a barrier. It was a miracle they weren't killed.

'And yet something of papa remained on that curve.

'After that, our lives changed radically. Without the income from papa's company and with all those debts on our backs, we had to seek other ways, and mother decided to rent out some business premises. Papa and Roi embarked on a painful circuit of rehabilitation and operations that kept them shut up at home for months. From one day to the next, mother opened a shop for clothes and luxury accessories thanks to the unconditional support of Aunt Cris. Papa, meanwhile, went from bad to worse. He'd always been financially responsible for his family, and finding himself defenceless, both physically and professionally, plunged him into a terrible depression.

'All of this happened six months before my departure. For weeks, my mother rebuked me for my alleged irresponsibility and lack of solidarity. She said I was a bad daughter for not paying attention to her difficulties. I only thought about myself. I couldn't do this, leave her there on her own with two injured people and an unsteady business.

'But I left, all the same.

'And now I must keep my promise to go back after half a year, on the anniversary of the accident and the eve of the feast at Grandma Carmiña's.

'I just wanted to tell you that day, in the Plaza de Mayo, I left because I didn't like your turbid dealings with those delinquents. I don't know whether you were stealing, or trafficking, or selling, it doesn't matter. I went through all of that with Edmundo and, put quite simply, I felt let down. I just wanted you to know. I don't hold it against you. You were a good friend when I was at my loneliest in Buenos Aires. Thank you for that.'

Leo came out with this speech almost without pausing for breath. She needed to get rid of all this ballast from the other side of the sea because she couldn't go back with such a heavy weight. It would sink her without trace. Something told her that Adriana was the right person to listen to her story of fear and guilt. After all, the Tuscan girl had shared her own story almost as soon as they'd met. Having finished her confession, Leo felt a huge sense of relief. Adriana spoke softly, almost imperceptibly:

'Those "delinquents", Leo, were young people helping me locate my aunt Claudia. When I turned eighteen, my mother informed me there was an inheritance worth thousands of euros from the sale of my aunt's lands. My aunt had named me as the only beneficiary, as appeared in a strange document at the solicitor's in San Gimignano. None of my family knew about this will until I became an adult. With that money, I could do whatever I liked. It was mine. I didn't have to provide any explanations or share it with anybody. And yet I decided I didn't want to live my whole life on the back of my unknown benefactress. I went looking for her. My trip and stay in Buenos Aires are funded by her generosity. There are no shady dealings, or thefts, or smuggling. Just the inheritance of my aunt Claudia, who died all alone in these vast Humid Pampas where I am going to find her. I know I will take her ashes home. Sometimes, quite randomly, I come across information about someone who disappeared during the dictatorship and pass it on to the Mothers and Grandmothers of the Plaza de Mayo. To tell the truth, I often suspect that was my aunt's only wish: to collaborate with those searching for their loved ones... Who knows?... Who knows?...'

It was the evening of Wednesday 6 July, a day before her return, when Leo learned we shouldn't always trust our instinct. It can sometimes turn into our cruellest enemy. As she walked slowly along Defensa Street, arm in arm with her Tuscan friend, both freed of the weight of responsibility that had been burdening them, she knew there would be no third act of treason in Buenos Aires.

Suddenly, in that drizzly night, Leo and the city made their peace and loved each other like never before.

Leo thought Adriana would be the last surprise of the day. What nonsense.

As she crossed the Plaza de Mayo to accompany her friend to a concert and catch the metro back to Palermo, she found her name inscribed in large chalk letters on the pink flagstones:

### I Love You Leo A.

And that wasn't the last surprise of the day, either.

# 67

She wasn't expecting him.

No way.

Not him.

Leo reached Dolores' house when night had fallen, the gusts of cold wind slicing her lips like a knife. Her host had yet to get back from the university, and Leo started packing her rucksack. It didn't take her long because she wasn't taking much back. Once she'd finished, she went online to print out her boarding pass for the flight the following day, 7 July 2011, departing from Buenos Aires, destination Santiago de Compostela, with a short stopover in Madrid. She mechanically introduced the details, got a seat towards the front, next to the aisle, and waited for the sheet to emerge slowly from the printer.

This really was the end.

Suddenly, a message flashed up inside her inbox.

Andrés.

She couldn't believe it! How could he be so ill-timed?

The Mexican boy had this to say:

> Hi, Leo! Since we last saw each other, the world has chopped and changed. The disturbances in Greece ended up unsettling relationships in Ruth & Co. After some of the group travelled to Bulgaria, where things didn't go all that well, we decided to hook up again and start from zero. Lía, Claudia and I retraced our steps and went back to London, our departure point. There, certain events made us take the decision to abandon Europe. There's a whole lot to tell, but I don't have the time. The important thing is we're now in Brazil, at

Lía's house. I want to see you and know you do too, so
don't hang around. You once told me, 'You say "don't
come", that means "come".' So now I'm telling you,
'Come, I'm waiting for you in Salvador da Bahia.'

Leo had to read and reread the message dozens of times
to understand, or rather accept, what it contained. Barely
a month earlier, she'd heard from Mayra, and her version
of events in Greece didn't coincide with what Andrés had
written. What a rogue, he had omitted all reference to the
Greek lawyer! But the most surprising thing was that, in less
than a minute, Leo had already pressed the magic keys in the
computer's search engine.

'Thursday 7 July 2011. Flight Buenos Aires-Salvador da
Bahia. 230 euros.'

Twenty euros less than she had in her account.

It would be a lie to say she didn't think about it. Leo was
only a click away from altering the course of events for good.
One hour earlier, she had felt she was bringing her adventure
to a close with that unexpected confession to Adriana in the
café in San Telmo. And yet now she had the sensation the
ending remained open, there were opportunities to be had,
last-minute surprises.

For several, long minutes, she caressed the mouse button
with her forefinger. She only had to press it to continue her
journey and meet up with Andrés in Brazil. The ticket would
be the act of madness that finally put paid to her economic
solvency, but she would find a way to survive. The last few
months had shown her that survival was sometimes more a
question of ingenuity and will than good fortune. And yet her
reason reminded her again and again of her promise to return

home in six months. After everything that had happened, her presence there was required. But Andrés was only a short distance away, a few hours by plane. If she left, the ocean would come between them forever.

What shall I do? wondered Leo, what the hell shall I do with my life?

And Leo did what she thought she had to.

Dolores' pancakes would have to wait. She had no time now for batter, griddles or bagpipe tassels!

It was all she could do to control the whirligig of her head.

# 68

The plane was less comfortable than Leo had imagined. There weren't enough toilets, the food was sparse, the air stewardesses were particularly irritable, and the earphones for the music didn't work. All of this, on a transatlantic flight lasting more than thirteen hours, is extremely inconvenient. But Leo didn't mind.

She had enough to do trying to calm the incessant motion inside her head.

There wasn't a minute on the return journey when she didn't think she was making a mistake and in fact she should have gone to Andrés in Brazil. Pride, the certainty she wasn't all that crazy about the boy, fear, insecurity and the lack of money had convinced her she should go back home. And yet, in limbo, so many feet up in the air, in the cruise ship that was the plane's belly, all those reasons struck her now as absurd. A terrible doubt gnawed away inside her and stopped her contemplating anything else... What if this had all been a red herring? What if the messages from Ruth & Co. had been a pretence, the Mexican had actually been following her all over the world and this had been their final appointment?

Weren't all those 'I Love You Leo A.' a sufficient token of love?

She'd always imagined the return journey would be full of recollections and nostalgia, not those troublesome cirrus clouds that had seeped into her brain.

As she ate up the air miles and contradictory sensations in equal parts, it became public knowledge that somebody had stolen the Codex Calixtinus from the Cathedral of Santiago de Compostela.

# 69

'Mother!'

As Leo kissed her mother's warm face with unfeigned euphoria in the arrivals terminal at the airport, she looked around.

'And the others? Papa and Roi?'

'Oh, daughter! They weren't free. They said they'll see you at home. What is it? Are you limping?'

'No... Well, yes... My boot split open, and I'm afraid it's going to fall apart.'

'Oh... Well, come on, my little darling.'

They were, exactly six months later, at the point of departure. The girl gazed at the scene, and nothing seemed to have changed all that much. The same hurry, the same suitcases on wheels, packages, discarded newspapers, bins, kiosks, coffee and water machines... exactly the same coldness that is the non-place of any airport. It could have been the airport in Granada, Ushuaia, Prague or Lima. Nothing, except for the facial features, distinguished them all that much. And yet Leo had eyes not for the space, but for the absences. When she'd left, papa and Roi had been there to say goodbye. At that time, she'd missed the brave presence of Aldara, Inés and Martiño, it had hurt that none of them had turned up to wish her a good journey. But now the girl couldn't help feeling disappointed.

Once again, none of them, neither the rest of her family nor her friends, had wanted to welcome her back.

She dragged her battered rucksack and superglued boots to the car park. Suddenly, she saw her own image reflected in a window and got a real fright.

'Oh, mother, how awful I look!'

'Don't talk about it, Leo. You're as thin as a rake, to say nothing of that hair and those frayed trousers. You look dreadful. I didn't want to say anything in case you started protesting... Well, you won't mind the sun, Leo! When you left, it was freezing cold, and now you're back just in time for the summer!'

In effect, everything was strangely different. Leo couldn't take her eyes off the world that bustled about on the other side of the car window. The city seemed like a welcoming place, and yet also unreal. She was so absorbed by the landscape she didn't notice the car was taking a different route home. She didn't realize until her mother stopped the vehicle.

'Here we are.'

'What? Where are we?'

'Take a look.'

Leo looked. On the other side of the street, she observed a large, well-lit window with several mannequins dressed in shiny clothes and a sales sign. There were lots of people inside and, among the unknown figures, she caught sight of the familiar silhouettes of papa and Roi. Her father was taking money behind the counter, and Roi was arranging jumpers on a shelf. Leo was both startled and confused.

'The other shop soon became too small, and we decided to rent some more central, suitable premises. It's the sales, that's why papa and Roi couldn't come up to the airport to meet you.'

'That's wonderful, mother! The business is going really well! And they say there's a crisis!'

'Ah, daughter, the crisis only affects majority sectors. The luxury sector is doing very well. You know how it goes, the rich get richer and the poor get poorer.'

'Right. Shall we go? I'm dying to make fun of Roi. Look what a smart shop assistant he makes!'

'Just a moment, Leo. We have to talk.'

'What about?'

Leo couldn't have made up what she heard next. She could have invented strife, recriminations, rebukes, relief, welcomes, hugs, acknowledgements... but not what reached her ears.

'Leo... I'm not sure where to start.'

'Mother, you're making me nervous, and I've only just landed. Has something happened to grandma?'

'Let's see... I know before you left, you had to put up with a lot of pressure. I wasn't fair to you, my daughter. The business with the accident and filing for bankruptcy was a heavy blow for your father. And I wasn't able to react. From one day to the next, I found myself with a family and financial burden I wasn't sure I could withstand. I fell into a pit and I swear, Leo, I couldn't see a way out. And you suffered the consequences. Indirectly, I know with all my reproaches I made you feel very guilty, as if everything that had happened was your fault. I unleashed all my tension, fears and insecurity on you. Leo, I'm very sorry. I'm sorry you left with that burden and had to put up with me. I'm very proud of you and of the fact you decided to leave all the same. It was your dream, and you went ahead and fulfilled it.'

'Thanks, mother,' murmured Leo, a little overwhelmed by shame and surprise. 'Come on, let's go. It's over now, you won't want me to start crying. I've only just arrived!'

'Just a minute, I haven't finished. Forget it all.'

'What?'

'Everything you promised before leaving, forget it all. It's not your responsibility.'

'What are you saying, mother? Have you gone mad?'

'Listen to me. I made you swear you'd be back in six months and help me with the shop. That was the deal. You'd finished your degree and could lend a helping hand to get the business up and running. Well, I don't need you.'

'You what?'

'I don't need you, Leo. I can do it on my own. Over the last few months, I've learned we can survive, we have enough strength to keep on going. Papa and Roi are recovering very well. Your brother has to take his school certificate, and papa's learning all about fashion. You have to decide your future for yourself, without any kind of pressure. We can't put our mistakes, doubts and fears on your shoulders. It's your life, Leo. Your life. You know where we are, but you're the one who has to decide. And whatever you do, we'll always be with you.'

In the end, her mother's voice was reduced to a trickle. It was useless trying to stem the tears, and she ended up shaking from emotion. There, she'd said it. Everything she'd thought for weeks and imagined she wouldn't be able to say to her prodigal daughter had just escaped from her mouth. In that car, opposite a glittering shop window, Leo also started crying. Suddenly she felt enormously relieved of a weight she hadn't known she'd been carrying for a year. That blasted responsibility was far more uncomfortable and painful than she'd ever imagined. She'd been used to its inevitability and irrevocability for so long she hadn't realized what a terrible burden it had become.

'One thing though!' warned her mother, wiping away her tears. 'You're not to go very far! No Japan, Senegal, Russia, Nicaragua or any of those out-of-the-way countries. I've been scanning the international pages of the newspapers for months, and there's been nothing but misfortune! Attacks, earthquakes, volcanoes, accidents, revolutions!'

'One thing after another, mother! Come on you, agony aunt, I don't suppose in that wonderful shop of yours you've got some nice clothes I could put on?' laughed the girl.

'Leo, does your head smell of anti-lice lotion?' exclaimed her mother, bringing her daughter's hair closer to her nose. 'My goodness, it stinks!'

'Oh, come off it, mother! Lice! Whatever were you thinking?' mocked the girl, pushing her mother away affectionately.

And the two women – mother and daughter – got out of the car with the strange sensation that their bodies weighed less than a few hours earlier.

'Look at you, little sister! What a sight! Is it me, or are you limping?'

That was Roi's welcome while her father mustered a timid smile.

## 70

The affairs of the shop kept them busy until late. It was necessary to count the day's takings, to remove new stock from the boxes, to refill the shelves and tidy up the shop window. So it was half past ten on 8 July 2011 when Leo finally crossed the threshold of her house, exactly six months after her departure. She'd been so immersed in Roi's nonsense and the strange story of the maths teacher who'd got confused doing an equation on the board that she didn't notice the wall opposite their building. At that precise moment, her father was wittering on about a cube root, and her stubborn brother was insisting it couldn't be three, it had to be nine. That was why Leo didn't notice the wall. Had she been more attentive, she would have seen those tiny letters painted bright orange:

**i love you leo a.**

The girl thought, when she entered the house, she would throw down her rucksack, take off her clothes, have a good shower, eat her mother's croquettes (as requested days earlier by email), her favourite ice cream as well, put on her summer pyjamas and stretch out on the sofa to watch some daft programme on TV while replying to all kinds of questions from her family. That was how she'd imagined her return.

But none of this happened.

'You've a parcel, Leo. It arrived a few days ago,' said her mother, putting down the keys and removing her high heels. 'Grandma's prepared a soup for the festivities tomorrow. Shall I make you some croquettes?'

'That would be great, mother. What's in them?'

'The remains of the stew.'

'Mmmm… Delicious, I can't wait!'

But Leo wouldn't even get to taste them.

# 71

It was Leo's unhealthy curiosity that made her – before the shower, the summer pyjamas, the croquettes, the ice cream, the sofa, the TV programmes, the stories – pick up that parcel.

It had no sender's address.

This increased the sense of mystery, and Leo lay down on the bed to open it slowly. Ah! How she had missed her mattress and the smell of clean sheets!

As she scratched at the flap with a little nervousness, the mystery grew bigger. Inside, Leo came across a handwritten letter in blue biro and another, smaller parcel in an envelope where it said:

'Open after reading the letter.'

So her eyes turned towards the letter. What she read there, she would never forget.

Ever.

*Leo, please, please don't tear up this letter. I'm asking for one last opportunity. I know you don't open my emails or, if you do, you don't reply, so I thought this would be the only way to reach you. You once told me the Internet had done away with all the ancient charm of traditional letters, those someone writes and they really travel the world to reach their destination. They would pass through hundreds of hands, but their contents would remain secret until someone opened the envelope and the magic of communication took place. Remember? You said envelopes were better off than their recipients because they themselves travelled for miles. They saw the world. At that point, I should have understood that travelling for you was a necessity, a dream, a goal, not just some crazy whim, but I was dumb. I didn't see it, Leo. I didn't see it. That was why, when I pulled out, when we pulled out, I couldn't understand your angry reaction. I was convinced you would pull out as well. If neither Aldara nor Inés nor I were going to go with you, you wouldn't be able to do it on your own. I was selfish and stupid to believe that my decision could prevent you from fulfilling your dream. Once again, you have shown me that, when you set out to do something, there is no human force that can stop you.*

*I started to realize this when I went up to the airport to say goodbye, but didn't arrive in time. Knowing that you'd left, the ground fell out from under my feet, and I had to accept that I'd made a mistake, I should have plucked up the courage and gone with you.*

*That was when I understood that I couldn't live without you. I love you, Leo, and whatever excuses I come up with and cling on to so as not to suffer on your account are just a stupid waste of time.*

*But then it was too late: you'd left, and I had to accept it. I started writing emails you never replied to and had to make do with your tweets, those precise geolocators. Thanks to them, I learned of your passing through Lisbon, Barcelona, Granada, Marrakesh, Istanbul, Prague, Italy, Paris, Latin America... At the most unexpected moments, your remnants on the clothes line of Twitter served to position you on the map and imagine what you were doing. That was how my own virtual journey began, following in your footsteps. Anxious to learn what you were learning, to see what you were seeing, I started seeking out photographs and descriptions of the places you were visiting. One of* my main sources of information was the blogs and forums where other travellers would record their experiences. Remember? When the four of us were planning our trip, we talked a lot about the usefulness of these first-hand accounts by other backpackers. At that time, I was doing my exams at the Official Language School so, to put my knowledge to good use, I started surfing the forums of German travellers and practising my language. That was where the idea came from. You were in Barcelona at that point. In the forums on Catalonia, people talked about the wonders of Gaudí. And I decided to ask them. I had to make use of all my communication skills to explain that I was head over heels in love with this young woman with wheat-coloured hair and honey-brown eyes who was travelling on her own with a green rucksack. I begged them to help me take my declaration of love to wherever it was you went. All they had to do was write in a visible place:

## *I Love You Leo A.*

The graffiti had to appear in a touristy part of the city or at a transport hub (a road, a railway, bus or metro station, an airport) so you would see it. It wasn't easy to start with. When you were on your way south, I asked travellers in Andalusia to paint your name on the roads entering Córdoba and Cádiz and in the Sierra de Grazalema. I'm not sure if someone managed to do this in Granada as well... I had to demonstrate that this wasn't harassment, it was just an innocent declaration of love, sending you kisses from a distance. It involved lots of explanations in private messages and overcoming all sorts of susceptibilities, but *in the end I achieved this. Over time, I became known as the anonymous lover of the forums. This heightened the interest of backpackers and their willingness to help with the messages. As soon as you said you were in some place, I would hook up with people travelling through that area and all kinds of social media in order to throw my bottle into the sea. Always in German, of course, so you wouldn't know about it. People put messages in the most incredible, beautiful parts of the cities you visited and, I suspect, of those you never set foot in, I was never quite sure where you would be. I never expected the initiative to take off the way it did and confess that, in the end, the sense of expectation started to become a bit too much.*

*I never meant to pester you or bother you. If I hadn't dared to go with you, I had no right to watch over you from a distance. I just wanted you to know that somebody loved you from far away, Leo. Wherever you might be, I wanted to tell you this over and over again so you would never feel alone or that you were being watched. That was why I asked anybody who came across you not to talk to you and not to tell me about it. I had to respect above all your wish not to answer my emails. Not to hear from me. I didn't want there to be unpleasant interferences. The girls from Munich on the hill of Montmartre in Paris almost messed the whole thing up when they found you and risked taking a photograph with you. Also, the group that greeted you at the railway station in Rome. And your brother went a little over the top painting all those cryptic '.AOEL UOYEVOLI' on the RER carriage in Paris! I'm glad to say you didn't realize. Probably I've lost you for good but, like this letter, my words have gone looking for you, travelling thousands*

*of kilometres at the hands of a large group of travellers
who, for no reward at all, have been willing to carry my
message to you to the ends of the earth.*

*I don't know which signs you saw, and which you didn't. I
trust you saw some of them but, just in case, open the other
envelope. This is what travellers sent me by email. Thanks
to them, I also travelled with you so that I could say, again
and again:*

## *I Love You Leo A.*

The girl's hands were trembling so much she almost couldn't
read that tortuous handwriting. When she'd finished, she took
the other envelope and, on opening it, was unable to contain
her amazement. Inside, there were hundreds of photographs
of places all over the planet with signs of every kind, on
different backgrounds, in different styles and colours, even
with spelling mistakes. There were big ones and small ones.
In green, black, red, yellow, blue. On sheets at the airport, on
tarmac, cardboard, walls, T-shirts. Next to the messages, faces
of every race, age, gender and condition that had one thing
in common: a large grin because of the naughty thing they'd
just done to please an anonymous lover's stubbornness. Leo
couldn't believe it! She'd seen very few of these messages –
and some she had seen were not even there! The one on Notre-
Dame, by the mosques in Istanbul, on the walkways of Perito
Moreno, in the Café Tortoni in Buenos Aires, on the Charles
Bridge in Prague, on the Milvian Bridge in Rome… There she
was, with the girls on the steps of Montmartre! Here were the
yellow letters in Cusco's Plaza de Armas! And the muddy wall
in Puno! The tarmac in Grazalema and the quays of Cádiz

and Eminönü! Then there were others she hadn't seen or that had been in places she hadn't visited. Someone had placed a message on top of the Empire State Building! Others had left it in Moscow's Red Square or in front of the Opera House in Sydney! It was completely unbelievable.

The last photograph was a snap in front of the Brandenburg Gate in Berlin. Martiño was holding a placard in his hands on which was written in large, black letters:

## I Love You Leo A.

And, on the back, it said: 'I left in the end because I also want to fulfil my dreams. If you ever get tired of the monotony of home and need to recover your travelling spirit, you know where to find me. Or, better still, name any other point on the planet where I can find you.'

Overcome by emotion, Leo glanced at her old, worn rucksack and smiled. She had learned that quote from the book *Invisible Cities* by heart:

*'Forgive me, my lord, there is no doubt that sooner or later I shall set sail from that dock,' Marco says, 'but I shall not come back to tell you about it. The city exists and it has a simple secret: it knows only departures, not returns.'*

Indeed, beloved seafarer, once someone leaves, they never return.

No, they don't.

Read more titles in the series  published by Small Stations Press!

## Rosa Aneiros, I LOVE YOU LEO A. DESTINATION SOMEWHERE

Leo went through the security archway with far too much insecurity in her feet and restless pumping in her heart. That may be why the civil guard ordered her to take off her boots and passed the metal detector over her nervous body. Had it been able to measure her heartbeat, that little device would most probably have exploded as soon as it reached her chest. But it didn't explode, possibly because such instruments know nothing about the comings and goings of the soul. Meanwhile, the X-ray machine was closely examining the contents of her rucksack. The rucksack didn't seem exactly comfortable with its contents. It had gone from carrying sheets, folders, books and notes to holding lists of Internet addresses, descriptions in different languages, a passport, a brand-new debit card, some socks and a scarf.

After university, Leo is due to go travelling for six months with her friends Aldara, Inés and Martiño, but at the last minute her friends pull out and Leo is left to travel on her own. Her first stop, in Lisbon, Portugal, is a rain-soaked disaster. She is dragged around the city by her overbearing host and only really gets a feel for the city during the final few days, when she is cooped up in his apartment. But everything changes with her next destination, Barcelona, where she meets up with a group of friends from Latin America who call themselves 'Ruth & Co.' and busk for a living. Romance, excitement, frustration, appalling and luxurious living conditions, familiar and foreign cultures, follow as Leo travels to Granada, Córdoba, Seville and Cádiz in Andalusia, Marrakesh in Morocco and finally Istanbul. In this first instalment of Leo's travelling adventures, Leo discovers that she must learn how to leave a place before she can truly enjoy her experiences, and how travelling can bring you back full circle. She is also mystified by the graffiti that keeps appearing along her route: 'I Love You Leo A.' Who is it that has scrawled this graffiti wherever she goes, and what do they want? Only by continuing with her journey and not giving up will Leo find out the answer to this riddle!

ISBN 978-954-384-040-3

## Rosa Aneiros, I LOVE YOU LEO A. TRANSIT STATION

The sun beat down, and all the passengers hurried to get off the vehicle. There were lots of middle-aged women carrying large packages and half a dozen children with grubby cheeks and translucent eyes who went from crying to running around, sulking and laughing almost without noticing. Right next to a petrol pump, two men stood smoking and, over on the other side, another four were playing draughts. In the distance could be seen the city, which spread over the stony hill with its yellow and white buildings of no more than four floors. Humble houses with their belly of misery surrounded the current political and administrative tummy button of Turkey. Leo sighed. They had been travelling for hours! The succession of events over the last two weeks made her feel dizzy. The young man next to her also got off and invited her to a cup of tea with a brief gesture of his hand. She accepted and smiled. Beforehand, she asked permission in the station to use a computer and post a public message on Twitter, as she had promised her brother before leaving home on that distant 8 January. It was the quickest way to let her family know which part of the world she was in.

In this second instalment of Leo's travelling adventures, Leo, a university graduate, has been travelling on her own for three months. She finds herself on the outskirts of Ankara, the capital of Turkey, after visiting the famous rock churches of Cappadocia. She returns to Istanbul, hoping to find her current boyfriend in the hotel room where she left him. A moment of panic causes her to lash out and buy a one-way ticket to Prague, where she hooks up with a group of Americans, practises her English and tours Bohemia with its ups and downs. She then dresses up as a Vestal Virgin to see if she can fool the man of her dreams in the Roman Forum. Another misunderstanding almost leads to disaster, but the other members of Ruth & Co. — the group of buskers who are a joy for the pocket and a heaviness for the heart — prevent this, and together they travel to Siena, Bologna and Venice in Italy before Leo decides it is time to visit her favourite aunt in Paris. Along the way, Leo continues to come across graffiti that says 'I Love You Leo A.' — who is the anonymous author of these messages that pursue her wherever she goes?

ISBN 978-954-384-055-7

Andrea Maceiras, EUROPE EXPRESS

Only when I got to the hotel and observed the postcard under the magnifying glass was I fully aware of everything. Of the fact that what's happening is the greatest coincidence or most unbelievable stroke of destiny in my life and necessarily has to mean something. I can't stop gazing at this postcard, although, every time I look, a new shiver runs down my spine. I visited this city when I was still a teenager, but how could I ever have imagined I'd be here again ten years later? And how could I ever have thought I'd find them again, my old school friends, in a postcard? That summer we spent travelling around Europe was amazing, but it all ended in tragedy. At that time, winter entered our lives and never left. We barely kept in touch.

Nico is a computer programmer from Coruña in Galicia. On a business trip to the city of Bergen in Norway, he visits the quays of Bryggen, a place he has been to before. He buys a couple of postcards from a shop there and, much to his surprise, discovers that one of them has captured the moment when he and his friends visited Bergen on an Interrail trip after leaving school ten years earlier. There they all are: Óscar in his Deportivo football shirt with Bea; Nico with the slightly pretentious Mía, poring over a map; the Italian exchange student, Piero, a few feet behind them. But where is Nico's girlfriend, Aroa, and his best friend from school, Xacobe, the other two members of the group? Nico is shocked to find  that they are in a corner of the postcard away from the others and are kissing. He resolves to unearth all the mystery surrounding that trip and the bitter month of September that immediately followed, when a tragedy occurred, a tragedy that split the group apart and from which no one has recovered. He will invite all his friends to a school reunion and, by gauging their reactions to the postcard, finally learn the truth of what happened.

ISBN 978-954-384-090-8

## Antonio Manuel Fraga, TARTARUS

'I want to propose a deal: we'll divide your class time into two parts. If you invest a minimum amount of effort in learning to play the klavia, I'll tell you a story – a good one, too. It's about a girl just like you, perhaps a tiny bit older. It begins on the day she went to one of those clubs in the nabrallos. I think you'll like it.'

The matter was clear: I either had to sit for two hours in front of the hated klavia or do so for less time and put up with the old woman's ravings. It didn't take me long to make up my mind.

'I like stories with magic in them,' I confessed.

'Oh, this one has plenty…'

When Guiomar Brelivete, a thirteen-year-old schoolgirl who lives in Audierna, is told by her parents that she must start attending klavia lessons in the old quarter of Plugufan and miss training sessions for maila, her favourite sport, she is understandably annoyed. But her teacher, Mastrina Xaoven, turns out to have a sense of humour and agrees, in return for Guiomar learning to play the instrument, to tell her a story about a girl called Attica who is a member of the politically powerful Gwende community. The traditional inhabitants of the land, the Malluma community, have been confined to the nabrallos or suburbs, where Gwendes are not supposed to go. But one evening Attica boards a train to the nabrallo of Bragunde, hoping to attend a concert in one of the famous hicupé clubs, and there she meets Fuco, a Malluma boy who claims to be a firewalker. The nabrallo has been overrun by a plague of scorpions, and the children resolve to consult the witch Onga, Queen of the Cemetery, about this. They will learn that a far greater evil lurks beneath them, in the lost underground world of Nigrofe, where the balance between good and evil has been obliterated by the removal of a sacred tree, and it rests on them to restore that balance if only they can find a way in… In these two tales, the line between fiction and reality is blurred, and there is a striking resemblance between the old music teacher and the intrepid girl in her story.

ISBN 978-954-384-091-5

Read more Galician literature in English published by Small Stations Press!

*Fiction:*

Xurxo Borrazás, VICIOUS

Carlos Casares, HIS EXCELLENCY

Ledicia Costas, AN ANIMAL CALLED MIST

Álvaro Cunqueiro, FOLKS FROM HERE AND THERE

Xabier P. DoCampo, THE BOOK OF IMAGINARY JOURNEYS

Xabier P. DoCampo, WHEN THERE'S A KNOCK ON THE DOOR AT NIGHT

Miguel Anxo Fernández, A NICHE FOR MARILYN

Miguel Anxo Fernández, GREEDY FLAMES

Agustín Fernández Paz, NOTHING REALLY MATTERS IN LIFE MORE THAN LOVE

Teresa Moure, BLACK NIGHTSHADE

Miguel-Anxo Murado, ASH WEDNESDAY

Miguel-Anxo Murado, SOUNDCHECK: TALES FROM THE BALKAN CONFLICT

Xavier Queipo, KITE

Manuel Rivas, ONE MILLION COWS

Manuel Rivas, THE POTATO EATERS

Anxos Sumai, THAT'S HOW WHALES ARE BORN

Suso de Toro, POLAROID

Suso de Toro, TICK-TOCK

*Poetry:*

Rosalía de Castro, GALICIAN SONGS

Rosalía de Castro, NEW LEAVES

Xosé María Díaz Castro, HALOS

Celso Emilio Ferreiro, LONG NIGHT OF STONE

Pilar Pallarés, A LEOPARD AM I

Lois Pereiro, COLLECTED POEMS

Manuel Rivas, FROM UNKNOWN TO UNKNOWN

For an up-to-date list
of our publications, please visit
www.smallstations.com

For more information on Galician
literature in English, please visit
www.galicianliterature.gal